COLD CALL

A MYSTERY
INTRODUCING IRIS THORNE

DIANNE EMLEY

Originally published as *Cold Call* by Dianne G. Pugh in 1993 by Pocket Books, a division of Simon & Schuster, Inc.

Cover design by Kimberly King.

Arroyo Bridge
Books

Published by Arroyo Bridge Books, a division of Emley and Co., LLC.
First Arroyo Bridge Books trade paperback edition December 2011.
ISBN-10: 0984784659
ISBN-13: 978-0-9847846-5-3

:

For my husband,
Charles G. Emley, Jr.

ACKNOWLEDGMENTS

Special appreciation to Rowland Barber for the Saturday mornings of conversation and guidance on the art of novel writing. To Dana Isaacson, editor extraordinaire. To valued friends for commenting on the manuscript: Mardi Bettes, Greg Denton, Ann Escue, and Mary and Don Goss. To Katherine Johnson, for sharing her experiences on life in the securities industry. To my family for your support. To Charlie, for bringing bagels and having big shoulders to lean on

One

Alley Muñoz walked down the street, stepping heavily on his right foot, swinging the left in a semicircle behind, holding the aluminum briefcase close to his side in his good right hand, his left hand flapping from his bent-wing arm as if he were waving to no one in particular.

Two homeboys at the bus stop jabbed each other as he passed and it occurred to him that they'd been waiting for him. He tightened his grip on the briefcase and made an arc around them, writing off their staring to a stranger's fascination with his handicap, and continued walking down Lankershim past the clutter of shabby retail establishments like he did every day after work.

He reached the Café Zamboanga, the name "Studio Grill" still visible in faded paint on the brick sidewall. Paper-and-ink posters were taped in the café's big picture windows. *Carnitas. Menudo los Domingos.* An old man with his pants belted high around his waist sat at the chrome counter, his fedora at his fingertips, his cane hanging next to him, and watched Alley's lurching progress outside the café's windows through clouded blue eyes.

Alley put the briefcase in his bad hand, holding it high and close, and pulled on the heavy glass door with his good right. The door opened half a foot and he wedged his shoulder in, banging the briefcase against the frame before pulling it through. He took off his jacket, picked at invisible lint before he folded it over the back of a stool, and waved his good hand at the old man, who nodded back. He put the briefcase on the floor and slid his foot next to it.

A middle-aged Hispanic woman with thick black hair down the middle of her back and a pink waitress uniform came over to him from behind the counter.

"Hi, Alley. How are you today?" she asked, shouting.

He read her lips. "Fiii." He nodded, smiling with white, even teeth. A muscle spasm twisted his smile into a grimace, and a glistening drop of spittle fell on his chin. He smoothed his red-and-navy-striped tie with his good hand. "Haa ar ooh?"

"Not too bad. Coffee?" she said loudly, even though he couldn't hear her.

"Eesss."

She put a cup and saucer in front of him, the glaze shattered with spiderweb cracks, and filled it. Alley sipped and glanced at a Spanish-language newspaper that was on the counter.

"How's your mother?" the waitress asked.

Alley looked at her quizzically.

"Your mother? *Tu madre?*"

He nodded. "Eessss."

The waitress shrugged at the old man, who shook his head.

Alley saw and continued sipping his coffee. He rubbed the side of his polished loafer against the aluminum surface of the briefcase. He emptied the cup and pulled two dollar bills from a black leather wallet and put them on the counter.

"Thanks, Alley. *Hasta mañana.*"

He nodded and walked out onto the crowded sidewalk. Beads of perspiration formed on his forehead. It was still ninety degrees at 5:00 in the evening but he put his jacket on, setting the briefcase near him on the sidewalk.

Alley watched one of the homies from the bus stop walk toward him, his stride as precise as a march step, one arm swinging behind his back then in front, each shoulder lowered in time. His khaki pants came down low over his bright white Nike tennis shoes, and he wore a too-large, plaid, wool flannel shirt buttoned to the neck, in spite of the heat, the long tail trailing behind. His chin was cocked up and a cigarette was wedged behind his ear. He walked up to Alley and put his hand on his arm. "Hey, *ese*. You got a match?"

Alley smiled and a muscle spasm twisted his mouth. He pulled open his left jacket pocket with his good hand and looked inside.

Alley was shoved backward. He took his hand from his pocket and looked at the spreading red stain across the front of his shirt. He dropped the matches on the ground. He felt the pressure again, then looked up to see the ice pick come toward his chest a third time.

Alley screamed.

The boy watched him, his face serene and curious.

Alley screamed and screamed. He pawed the air and wailed the same note over and over. He staggered down the sidewalk, throwing his right foot forward, swinging the left behind.

The boy was already turning the corner onto a side street by then, running fast.

Some people ran after the boy and some watched Alley, not knowing what to do. There was so much blood.

Alley dropped to his knees, his breathing short. He fell back onto his good arm, then onto the sidewalk, his legs contorting under him. He screamed again and again, his tongue churning like a landed fish.

The waitress ran out of the Café Zamboanga and kneeled beside him. Alley tried to speak, but his tongue just flapped in his mouth. Then he died.

The waitress walked back to the doorway of the café, rubbing her bloody, trembling hands on her pink uniform. She shrugged her shoulders and moved her lips, telling herself there was nothing she could do, and then she saw the briefcase on the sidewalk. She pulled the handle. It didn't move. She got a better grip on it and picked it up, leaning to one side with the weight, and took it inside the café.

"Take it to his mother... *pobrecita*... that poor woman... *pobrecita, pobrecita.*

Two

Iris Thorne slapped the snooze button on the screaming clock radio with a thwack and fell asleep again. The synthesized, singsongy music on the New Age station wove through her subconscious and took her to a calm place. Seconds later, the radio screamed again.

Iris thwacked the snooze button two more times before she sat bolt upright in bed, turned off the damn thing, looked at the digital display that said 4:45a, and wondered what day it was.

"Workday," she said to no one, "and freaking late already."

She headed for the bathroom in the dark, tripping and cursing over a bundle of unfolded laundry she'd thrown on the floor the night before.

"...had to do the snooze five million times..."

She found her way to the kitchen in the dark and located the automatic coffee maker by its merrily shining red light and poured a cup into a squat-bottomed commuter mug.

"...Thursday..."

She took three sips and cranked into high gear.

"...meeting with the stupid Hollywood bankers..."

In the bathroom she wove through dangling tendrils of lingerie and yanked down a pair of panty hose.

"...and that weirdo from the morticians' association..."

She gathered handfuls of drying lingerie and threw them on the unmade bed.

"... oh God, Mr. Noone. The Nooner. Client From hell... Call him today..."

A champagne-colored teddy embroidered with little flowers was on top of the mound. Iris grabbed it.

"...better wear my bullet-proof vest..."

She plugged in the set of hot rollers, the curling iron, and the blow dryer, turned on the waterproof radio, and ran out of electrical plugs.

"...is this the one that rides up?"

She had showered, moisturized, and rolled her hair by 5:15, unshrouded a suit from the dry cleaner's plastic, dressed, and combed her hair out by 5:27, scooped her makeup into her purse, grabbed the handle of the pull-out stereo, looped her briefcase over her shoulder, and ran down the stairs by 5:29. At 5:30, she was in the garage, folding the cover back from the Triumph, rolling each side up, then rolling from front to back, her second cup of coffee in the commuter mug sitting on the concrete.

At 5:35, she shifted the TR into reverse, slid the stereo into its chassis, shifted to neutral, pulled out the choke, mashed on the accelerator twice, and cranked the ignition. The engine roared in the garage. She put her makeup on in the rearview mirror by flashlight while the engine warmed up, then backed the TR out five feet, put it in neutral, ran out with the flashlight and shined it on the drip pan, studied its nightly excretions as if they were runes, dabbed a finger into a new glob of something, and rubbed her fingers together to test the consistency.

"...need change oil..."

She got in and checked the gauges.

"...all A-OK."

She revved the engine. The vibration from the TR's baritone set off the car alarm on the Porsche in the next spot.

She tapped her fingers on the steering wheel as she waited for the automatic garage gate to crank open, hoping she could get out before the Porsche's owner came down, as attuned the sound of his own car alarm as a parent is to the cry of his own child.

At 5:55 she was at the mouth of the mighty Ten, near a sign that said CHRISTOPHER COLUMBUS TRANSCONTINENTAL HIGHWAY. She waited for the light to change and finished her mascara. She hooked her thumbs through her skirt into the leg openings of the teddy and jerked it down. This *was* the one that rode up.

At the green light, she orange-lined the TR and tore down the Ten going ninety with one eye in the rear-view mirror and one hand touching and punching the stereo's buttons like Braille and one-half a mind to drive on. Let's drive. Goddammit. Past Grand Avenue, past L.A. city, L.A. county, past the rest of it, flowing with the current of the mighty Ten, a straight shot to Jacksonville, Florida. Then north, goddammit, to Vermont or New Hampshire or someplace like that. Someplace with woods and ponds and stuff like that. She'd live off her credit cards and not think about tomorrow. She'd sell antiques and draw in pastels and maybe even buy a winter coat.

At Grand Avenue, Iris flipped on the signal indicator and the green "trafficator" light flashed on the TR's wooden dash.

The sun rose over the top of Bunker Hill, the heavy particles in the August smog diffusing the rays into a brilliant orange color wash.

The office was alive at 6:20.

"Good morning, good morning, hi, hi, howyadoin'?"

"Just superior, Iris, superior."

"Good morning. *Ça va?*"

Iris walked past her cubicle, down the corridor, straight to the last cubicle in the row. She reached in her briefcase, pulled out a large dildo, and slapped it on the desk. It made a wet noise like a blackjack on flesh.

"What?" Billy Drye said guilelessly.

There were stifled snickers from the fresh-shaved group within earshot. Guys craned their necks or half stood to see.

"Mr. Dick turned up in my briefcase during my meeting with the Armenian Merchants' Association," Iris said.

Hearty guffaws.

"I-ris… what makes you think…"

"Give it up, Drye," Iris said.

She was halfway down the corridor before they cut loose with ribald laughter behind her. The teddy crept up painfully, but she didn't dare touch it. She rapped twice on the metal door frame of the corner office.

Stan Raab was already on the phone to the East Coast, talking fast, pacing back and forth, spinning his phone cord into a tangled, tortured mess, laughing heartily now to what must have been a really good joke between really good friends. He glanced at Iris on a southward spin and shot his index finger up in greeting, then swung north, not missing a conversational beat.

She pivoted on her pump heel, ignoring the sound of her name behind her, and circled around the end of the suite on the way to her cubicle, passing the corner office opposite Stan Raab's where Joe Campbell lived. He looked up at her over a copy of *The Wall Street Journal* and smiled a little. She nodded back and the pit of her stomach tingled.

At her cubicle, she threw her purse inside a desk drawer and flipped on the computer terminal with a one-two snap and picked up a report that had appeared on her desk during the night.

Teddy watched her with his head perched like Kilroy on top of the cubicle wall dividing them. He was thirty-one but looked older with his thin hair brushed over the top of his balding head. He was grinning, his chubby cheeks round and pink, his tongue poking through the gap in his front teeth. He puckered his lips and blew at Iris's ear.

She unconsciously brushed at it.

Teddy's grin grew wider and his eyes narrowed to slits and sparkled gleefully behind thick lids. He blew again.

She reached her hand to her ear, then spun around.

"What are you doing?"

"Washing you, *ma cherie*," he crooned in pidgin French through pouting lips. He reached his big hand over the top of the cubicle and fluffed her hair. At six feet four inches, the top of the cubicle came to his waist. Red suspenders with little green dollar signs were pulled over his big belly. He wore a red silk tie with a small paisley pattern over a white cotton shirt with blue stripes. Sea Island cotton, he'd tell you if you mentioned you liked it.

"You're so smart to have gone lighter," he said, cupping Iris's hair. The index finger of his other hand dug deeply into his cheek. The irritated look in her eyes propelled him on. "You should as you get older."

"Teddy, I don't dye my hair."

"Of course you don't, dahling."

She reached over the cubicle and rubbed his bald spot. "Now I know it's going to be a good day."

"You have a run in your panty hose, dear."

"Shit!"

"Don't you just hate when that happens?"

Iris opened her top desk drawer and dug around the pencils, highlighter pens, paper pads, makeup, change for the vending machine, and crumpled memos, looking for the emergency panty hose.

"Damn, I need another cup of coffee."

"Ain't any."

"Why not?"

"Gimp's not here."

"Don't call him that. Why don't you make some?"

"Squaw work."

Iris found the package of panty hose behind an envelope that had traveled into a back corner. She uncrumpled the envelope and looked at the heavy-handed printing on the outside:

OPEN THIS. YOU WILL KNOW WHEN TO.

Joe Campbell walked by and glanced down at her. She quickly palmed the panty hose and the envelope and shoved them into her skirt pocket, her cheeks coloring.

"Go ask your girlfriend if she likes my gift," Teddy said.

Iris let out a long sigh. "What gift, Teddeee?"

"Just go ask her."

"Teddy, I told you about that."

"She's just playing hard to get."

In the lunch room, Iris held the refrigerator door open and spooned a cake leftover from somebody's birthday out of a pink box while waiting for the coffee to brew. The door to the lunchroom opened behind her and she heard a man's solid footsteps in heavy soled shoes. The footsteps were generic but she recognized the cologne. He left its oily resonance everywhere—on telephones, on papers, in rooms he had left. Iris liked the seductive fragrance. She had purchased it herself once for someone. She was sorry that now it would always remind her of Billy Drye.

He stood close behind her—too close for polite office chitchat. She didn't step away.

"Filling in for the beaner gimp today?"

"Don't call him that."

"'Don't call him that,'" he mocked.

Iris opened the cupboard, pulled out her BUDGETS ARE FOR WIMPS mug, and poured coffee.

"Do you do windows, too?"

"I type, make coffee, do windows, and screw," Iris said, turning around, "but not for money."

"What kind of a screw is Raab, just between us girls?"

"What's your point, Drye?"

"Why else would he have given Consolidated Industries to you?"

"You did it to yourself. You ran it into the ground."

"That's what he told you?"

"Why don't you ask Raab?"

"I just figured a freak show might be what Raab likes. You and the gimp…"

Iris picked up the spoon and turned back to the cake. "You're sick, Drye."

Drye put his hand on the full part of her hip and put his lips close to her ear. "I bet the Ice Princess can really heat up."

Iris swung her hip, throwing his hand off, and twisted around.

He was already at the door. "You've been to the gym. Good work." He grinned garishly and winked at her before closing the door.

She slammed down the lid of the cake box and stomped out the door, down the hall and into the last office on the left. She flopped in one of the two chairs facing the desk. "You know what just happened?"

"Good morning, Jaynie. How are you? I'm fine, Iris. And you?"

"Sorry. Good morning."

Jaynie looked up at her. "Drye?"

"He just put his hand on my ass."

"Document, Iris. It's all you can do."

"Raab thinks I'm being too sensitive. The Boys' Club is just high spirited... playing around to relieve stress... they're not picking on me personally... bullshit." She squirmed in the chair, yanking on the teddy. "I don't know why he dislikes me so much. I never did anything to him."

"You're sport for him. Plus you've outsold him four times in the past six months. But you're still behind Joe Campbell."

"G.Q. Joe with his Worldco account and those other offshore corporations, pumping money through here like crazy. Always sounded shady to me. Where's Alley today?"

"Late, I guess. Or sick. Odd he hasn't called. I'll call his house."

"So what did Teddy buy you this time?"

Jaynie's eyes rolled skyward as she took a small box from her desk drawer.

"Ohhh-la-la. *Très* expensive." Iris turned the box so the light reflected from the stones in the earrings.

"He just doesn't get it, Iris. What am I going to do?"

"Give him back the earrings, to start."

"I tried. You give them back to him."

"Me?"

"Please?"

"Awwwww…"

"Please?"

"All right. Okay. How did I get in the middle of this?"

"Thanks, I."

"Gotta go."

Iris walked back to her desk. The room hummed with voices.

"A mil of the two-five?"

"Cost of carry? Bullshit!"

"Sixteen bid, is that the best you can do? Try again, asshole!"

"A hundred thou of one and two hundred of the other and I need it like yesterday."

Iris put the earrings on Teddy's desk.

"I have to get back to you, Larry." He hung up and then rolled spaniel eyes at her.

"Don't look at me like that. I *told* you."

Teddy spun the box on his desk and sulked.

Iris threw up her hands and flipped through the cards in her Rolodex. She picked up the phone and punched in a number. Smile and dial. Her hot lead answered the phone himself. She had finally gotten through to Delarosa after two weeks. He had picked up the phone himself and said hello and she said to herself, *This is a good day indeed*, then she hung up on him. Delarosa had answered the phone himself and she'd hung up on him. She wouldn't have except someone had screamed that Alley was dead.

Jaynie walked out of her office with her hands covering her mouth. People stopped talking and hung up telephones. Everyone took dream steps to where Jaynie was standing.

"Murdered," Jaynie said, tears cutting rivers through her makeup.

Iris put her arm around Jaynie's shoulders and felt the refrigerated cake settle uneasily in her stomach.

Stan Raab walked quickly down the hallway. "What's going on? What happened?"

Jaynie hiccupped the story which caused tears and gasps and recollections of what had become people's last words with or sight of Alley.

Iris walked back to her desk and sat down. Teddy was talking but she didn't hear him.

Drye walked past her desk and said "Looks like lights out at the taco stand."

Iris yelled, "Shaddup! Just shaddup!"

"Ooohh, Ms. Thorne," Drye said. "Such emotion."

Iris got up and walked out of the suite. She punched the down arrow and rode the elevator to the eleventh floor, one floor below McKinney Alitzer. In the women's restroom, she went to the farthest stall, sat down and studied the back of the door. She sat there a long time. Finally, it became real, and she started to cry. She pulled off a long tail of toilet paper and sobbed, sobbing "Okay," when a stranger asked her how she was, sobbing, "Why" when she heard the door suction close and she was alone. When the sobs turned to hiccups, she wondered how long it would take for her face to be normal; it was still business as usual upstairs. She felt a bulge in her pocket and remembered the panty hose.

She took out the package and the envelope came out with it. Alley had given it to her, it must have been two, three weeks ago, and she'd put her hands on her hips and asked, "Now what are you up to you silly thing?"

"Take it, please," Alley signed, smiling brilliantly. "Remember, things aren't what you think. You have to be smart."

She didn't understand.
He spoke. "Ba smard, Iiiirssss."

OPEN THIS. YOU WILL KNOW WHEN TO.

She'd patted his head and thrown the envelope into her top drawer.

Three

Detective John Somers of the North Hollywood Division of the Los Angeles Police Department and his partner, Paul Lewin, sat like mismatched bookends in the McKinney Alitzer lobby, sunk back into the low mauve sofa, knees almost touching their chins, folded hands resting in the V's of their legs.

"I'll be the mouth," Lewin said. "You be the hand."

"No, I'll be the mouth."

"Remember, Professor, we don't got all day."

"Without context, you have facts in a void. Why is that a problem for you?" Somers asked.

"The problem is that you *forget* to get all the facts. The problem is that in your stream-of-consciousness dicking around"—his hands swam in the air— "you forget the point. The problem is that I have to get to parents' night at the school by six o'clock or have hell to pay."

"You'll be there."

"Don't wanna miss the banana sheet cake."

"Just remember the Saticoy Street murders," Somers said.

"Just remember the Burbank fuck-up."

"Memory like an elephant," Somers said. "You and my ex-wife."

"Just keeping you straight, Professor."

"This is detection for the New Age. We need to expand our boundaries."

"Don't fuck with me today."

"I'm just jerking your chain. Why are you so edgy?"

"I feel like I'm waiting outside the principal's office," Lewin said.

"I never waited outside the principal's office."

"Figures."

"What does that mean?"

"You were the quiet kid, right? Sat in the back, reading?"

"Daydreaming," Somers said.

"Me, I was just high-spirited."

"Sounds like something your mother told the principal."

"Fuck you."

"See."

"One, it was a loony"—Lewin grabbed his index finger—"or two, a gang initiation"—he grabbed his middle finger. "Three, a grudge... revenge. But given what we know about our victim, I don't think three."

"I have a feeling there's something more here," Somers said. "No robbery. Doesn't make sense. Something smells."

"You have a feeling. Maybe you should consult your whatchacallit... your whooooo"—Lewin wiggled his fingers at Somers—"type guy."

"Psychic advisor. Don't make me regret that I confided in you."

"Whooooo."

"Recalcitrant."

"I still don't know why you volunteered for this. I hate this corporate shit. I was going to have us canvass the neighborhood. I'd rather be outside in the smog."

"I did it to broaden your horizons. You look very handsome in your suit, by the way," Somers said.

"Hello." They both saw Jaynie's knees first, partially covered by a pink linen skirt, then glanced down to shapely legs, plain bone pumps, then tilted their heads to see her face. Blond. Straight WASP's nose. Pale features enhanced with light makeup.

Jaynie extended her hand. "I'm Jayne Perkins, Manager of Human Resources."

Lewin and Somers struggled out of the deep couch, the shorter Lewin using the taller Somers as a support. "John Somers. My partner, Paul Lewin."

They followed her into the suite, past cubicles humming with voices. No one looked up. It was 12:30 in the afternoon, one half hour before the market closed in New York.

Jaynie's office was at the end of the suite. The two walls that were not glass were painted pearl gray, one dressed with a torn-paper collage that looked like a selection by the interior decorating firm that had had its way with the rest of the suite.

She motioned for the men to sit in the twin chairs facing her desk.

Jaynie appraised Somers. He didn't fit her idea of a cop at all.

He stood over six feet, lanky and broad-shouldered with an adolescent looseness in his limbs. Late thirties. Freckles. Intelligent, pale eyes that had lost their luster. Short-cropped, wiry red hair and almost feminine Cupid's-bow lips that suggested vulnerability. He wore a tweed jacket with leather patches on the elbows and gold corduroy pants that looked as if he'd dropped them to the floor and stepped out of them the previous night just to step into them again this morning. Hot for August. Well-worn loafers. A tired knit tie dangled from his neck like a memory.

His partner, Detective Paul Lewin, was more in line with Jaynie's expectations. He was older than Somers, mid-forties, about five feet eight inches tall and bulldog compact, with biceps and quadriceps testing the seams of his inexpensive navy blue suit, that looked like it was brought out on special occasions. A self-indulgent belly sagged over his belt. His straight, dark hair was combed fifties-style straight back from his forehead, held by its own oil, as unadorned and uncomplex as his heavy features which were fixed in a no-nonsense expression. He continually shifted his position in the chair, looking as if he were ready to run from the room at any moment.

Lewin took a wire-bound notebook from inside his jacket, flipped it open with a snap, and clicked open a ballpoint pen. He looked at Somers. "You're the man."

Somers said, "Miss Perkins, tell me about Alejandro Muñoz."

"Jayne, please. 'Miss Perkins' makes me feel like the school-marm."

"Jayne." Somers smiled.

Jaynie smiled back. What a kind face he had. She noticed he wasn't wearing a wedding ring. Of course, that didn't mean anything.

"What do you want to know about Alley? We called him Alley."

"What kind of person he was, his work habits, what he liked to do, his friends. Whatever comes to mind."

"Alley started working here about a year ago. He was the office gofer. Did the mail, kept the vending machines and coffee pots full, things like that. Good worker. Punctual. Neat. Very particular about his appearance. Expensive clothes. One of those people who's always cheerful. He came from Mexico about ten years ago to go to a deaf school." She dabbed her eye with her middle finger. "Sorry."

"Take your time. I know this is upsetting," Somers said. "Can you describe his relationships with his coworkers?"

"He was popular, especially with the women. Very cavalier, bringing us little gifts, flowers, candy, whatnot." A tear broke loose and rolled down her cheek. She pulled a tissue from a box on her desk. "Standard equipment for the human resources manager. Everyone loved Alley. But some people used to tease him, take advantage. This can be a ruthless bunch. You knew he was handicapped?" She shook her chin-length blond hair that was permed, frosted, moussed, sprayed, and finger-crunched to look tousled and carefree. "Funny, I didn't mention it before.

Guess I got so used to it, I didn't notice it anymore. He had polio as a child."

"How did people take advantage of him?"

"Personal errands. Going to the cleaner's, making bank deposits, picking up flowers. I told Alley not to do it, that it wasn't part of his job."

Lewin looked up from his notebook, "Why did he?"

"Alley wanted to be liked. He was ambitious in his own way. Took classes at a junior college. Carried this expensive briefcase. Wore a jacket and tie even though he wasn't expected to. He was like the wimpy guy at school who hangs around with the jocks. A clique of our younger representatives that we call the Boys' Club made sport of him. Practical jokes, stuff like that. They kind of goad each other on, you know. Locker-room stuff. But I'm sorry to say that our department manager sent Alley to run around for him too. He never saw it as being out of line."

Lewin sighed and got up. He walked to the glass wall and looked out into the suite.

Somers ignored him. "How did you communicate with Alley?"

"He read lips. Of course he used to pretend he didn't understand when it was convenient for him. He had speech but it was hard to understand if you weren't used to it. He wrote messages if he had to."

She had been twisting the tissue as she spoke, rolling it into a thin thread. "I'm going to miss him." She laughed. "He was always underfoot. You'd turn around and he was there. I guess being deaf, he didn't think to knock or make some sort of noise when he entered a room."

Somers looked at Lewin who was watching a secretary in a short black leather skirt make photocopies. "You're up, Shamus."

Lewin raised his heavy eyebrows and turned the pad he was holding to face Somers. "Got it all down, Professor. Dry cleaner's, briefcase, gifts—everything."

Somers took a notebook and a pen from a jacket pocket.

Lewin sat on a corner of Jaynie's desk and leaned on his palm toward her. "When was the last time you saw Alley?"

Jaynie unconsciously slid her chair back a few inches and crossed her arms over her chest. "When he left to go home yesterday at three-thirty. Like every day."

"Was there anything unusual about yesterday?"

"No. Typical."

"Anything unusual happen during the past few days or so?"

"No. Everything's been very routine."

"How much did Alley earn here?"

"About sixteen, seventeen thousand a year."

"That's not much."

"No."

"But he wore expensive clothes."

"He was always nicely dressed."

"How did he afford them?"

"I don't know what his financial situation was."

"And an expensive briefcase, like you said."

"One of those aluminum ones."

"Did he leave it here?"

"No. He took it with him last night."

"You're positive?"

"I saw him."

"Somers, we didn't recover a briefcase, did we?"

"No, and witnesses said the suspect only had the weapon in his hands."

"There probably wasn't anything in it, anyway. It was sort of a joke around the office," Jaynie said.

"It was empty?" Lewin asked.

"No. He'd have his lunch, a couple of the self-improvement books he was always reading... those paperbacks... pencils and pens, notebooks. The rest was a bunch of junk, really."

"Junk?"

"He was sentimental. He kept cards, gifts the girls gave him, and carried some of it around in that briefcase. Blue Smurf figures, plaques with funny sayings, Cracker Jack prizes. Junk." She shrugged.

"Do you know anything about his family and friends?"

"He lived with his mother at his uncle's house in North Hollywood. He never mentioned any friends outside the office. Our relationship was pretty much just business."

Lewin stood.

Jaynie rolled her chair back to her desk. "Alley was friendly with one of our investment counselors, Iris. She's calling on a client, but she should be back soon."

Somers stopped writing. "Iris?"

"Yes. She taught the hearing impaired before she went back to school to get her MBA and change careers. She and Alley would converse in sign language."

"Iris Thorne taught the hearing impaired?" Somers said.

"You know her?"

"No, why?"

"You know her last name."

"Because you just said it."

"Did I?"

"No, you didn't." Lewin said, watching Somers.

"Oh, I must have read it in the employee roster McKinney Alitzer sent us," Somers said.

"Really? I handle requests like that," Jaynie said. "I didn't send the police department a list."

"It was… the main office. They sent it—rather, faxed it. This morning."

"That's impressive. They let my requests sit for weeks."

Lewin scrutinized Somers, his heavy eyebrows pulled together and eyes narrowed.

Somers stood and looked down at Lewin. "Got what you need?"

"Yep. Got what *you* need?"

"Yep."

"Detectives, if you need any more information, just give me a call." Jaynie smiled at Somers.

Lewin gave her his card. "Call if that briefcase turns up."

Jaynie looked at Somers. "Do you have a card?"

"Certainly." He fished out a card from his jacket and handed it to her. "Can we see Alley's work area and talk to some of his coworkers?"

"I'll give you a tour of the office."

Lewin turned to Somers. "Maybe Iris Thorne will show up."

Somers's red tone deepened slightly.

"She should be back any minute unless she got held up in traffic," Jaynie said. "You know how that goes."

Lewin and Somers stood back and let Jaynie through the door. Lewin stood close to Somers. "We didn't get an employee roster."

"You didn't see it?"

"Don't bullshit a bullshitter, Somers. Are you going to tell me now or am I going to have to find out?"

"Nothing to find out."

"I will find out, you know."

Somers stood back and swung his arm out, gesturing for Lewin to pass through the doorway. "Welcome to the world of high finance, Shamus, where criminals in handmade suits steal from widows and children…"

Lewin walked through the door, keeping his eyes on Somers.

"… and humble police detectives have their consciousness raised."

"Among other things?"

"Lewin, don't underestimate a good detective."

"I just might have to kill you, Professor."

Four

Iris could have walked the five blocks to the bank but it was hot and smoggy and she was wearing her good silk blouse that she had already cried on and her pumps pinched her feet because she'd bought them on sale even though they were too small and the TR was hot enough without walking. Besides, nobody walks in L.A..

She found a parking spot on the street right in front of the bank. She squeezed the TR in, pulling the steering wheel full right, then left, grunting against the manual steering.

Alley's envelope lay on the passenger's seat, the top jagged where Iris had torn it open. She took the key out and ran her thumb across the 137 embossed on the front, then slid it onto her key ring, pulling off the adhesive paper stuck to the back that said SAFE BOX 1ST FED. The sticky label and the envelope were the only notes Alley had left. Iris thought of saving the envelope, then balled it up. A memento should be from a happy time.

She walked up the steps to the bank and tossed the envelope toward a garbage bin a few feet away. She missed. She grumbled and picked up the envelope and walked it to the bin even though other pieces of trash lay on the ground around it. Her civic duty done, she watched as the driver of a beat-up station wagon parked in front of the TR started to pull out onto the street.

The woman was backing up much too fast.

Iris ran down the steps, her pump heels clicking sharply on the granite. "Hey, hey!"

Impact. Chrome against chrome.

"What the hell do you think you're doing?" She walked to the driver's window. "Don't you know that car's a classic?"

The woman driving the station wagon had stringy bleached hair with dark roots and raccoon circles under her eyes from mascara that had bled in the heat. This morning's lipstick had settled into the vertical lines in her lips. Her skin was thin and her face was lined, as if all of the youth had been sucked out of it even though she was about Iris's age. A toddler sat in a baby seat beside her and two older children sat in the back, fiddling with toys. The paint on the old station wagon had been faded by the sun, and the body was pocked with dents.

"Is that your car?" the woman asked. "I'm so sorry. Is it damaged?" She ran her hand through her hair. Beads of perspiration were on her upper lip. "Nothing's gone right, today. I'm a nervous wreck."

Iris inspected the TR's bumper. It wasn't dented. Steel was poured thick in '72.

"And then I hit your car."

Iris wanted to yell at her some more but couldn't. "Forget it. There's no damage."

Iris watched the woman drive off and felt conspicuously consuming in her Adolfo pumps and Anne Klein suit, her Louis Vuitton satchel over her shoulder. She felt materialistic and spoiled. Then she felt petulant and told herself she had earned it all and at no small personal sacrifice. Then she forgot about it.

In the bank, Iris stood near the gate to the safe-deposit boxes and caught Howard's eye. She smiled at him. He gestured that he'd be with her after he finished with his customer. He shot her a sidelong Lauren Bacall glance through his pale eyebrows then looked away when she caught him.

He walked over to her. Howard's chin receded so far that there was a straight drop from his mouth to his neck, the skin there peppered with old acne scars. Howard always looked at Iris with such longing that she felt like crawling into herself and pulling the door closed. She never let her uneasiness show, though, and was always friendly and pleasant. It was her job. She was in sales. Now she'd have to use whatever she had to get into that box.

"Iris, you don't have a safe-deposit box with us, do you?"

She flashed him a bright smile. She reached out and touched his hand for good measure. *Of course I don't, you silly guy.*

"I'm doing a favor for a friend. You know Alley?"

"That weird-looking deaf guy? He comes in here a lot."

She gave Howard the key. "Alley's holding some stock he needs to unload pronto. He's not in today, so he asked me to get his certificates for him." She was sure "liar" was forming in welts on her forehead. *Keep smiling.*

Howard gave Iris the sidelong glance again. "Well, this is irregular, Iris." He flipped through a box of cards on the desk. "It flies in the face of bank policy."

"I know it's a big favor, Howard. I guess I'll just have to wait until Alley gets back." She sighed, shook her head sadly, and gave a shrug of resignation. "I just wanted to do this deal before Alley lost even more money. Well, it's money he won't be sending home to Mexico." She hoped Howard didn't know that certificates didn't have to be presented to be traded.

"Well…" He turned the sidelong glance the other direction. "You do have the key." An illicit spark of deviousness flashed in his flat gray eyes. "But on one condition."

"What's that?" *Smile. Don't say it. Please, don't say it.*

"Well… there's something I've been wanting to know…"

"Sure." *Don't ask. Don't ask me out. I'm sure you're a nice guy, Howard, but…*

"There's something I've been wanting to ask you…"

I am not a snob. I am not a snob.

The hand that was holding the card was trembling. "Oh," he said, his voice pitching higher. "It's nothing."

"You're sure?" The tension left Iris's shoulders.

"Yeah." He reached beneath the counter and buzzed the gate open. He took Iris's key and returned with box number 137.

Iris reached to shake Howard's hand. It was soft and moist and limp-fish. "Thank you, Howard. Thank you so much. Alley will be so glad."

"Don't stay too long. My boss is coming back soon."

Iris went into a small room and locked the door behind her. She set the box on a shelf, flipped open the metal lid, and smiled a small smile. She took out a miniature pair of leather cowboy boots attached to a key ring. She rubbed her thumb against the leather.

"You little jerk. You were supposed to use this for the keys you kept carrying around loose. From my trip to Santa Fe. You said you'd lost it."

She stood the boots on the shelf, reached into the box, and took out a graying white chocolate rose on a long wire.

"From Jaynie for Valentine's Day."

She laid the rose on the shelf.

"What's all this junk?"

She took out a tin of lemon drops, a brass angel, and a dried carnation and lined them up on the shelf, wiping away the tears that streamed down her face.

"Oh, man. I'm really pissed off at you, Alley."

She took out a silver-and-abalone ring and slipped it on her finger.

"You bastard. The ring from Mexico. My gifts. You were supposed to enjoy them, Alley. Live and enjoy them."

She sniffed and took a deep breath, then another and another until the tears stopped. She drew her fingers across the top of what was left.

"This must be what I'm here for."

She started taking out the cash. There were mostly hundreds. She piled the bundles in front of her, twenty in all. She thumbed a bundle and did some multiplication. About two hundred thousand dollars.

She chewed her thumbnail and looked at the ceiling, then at the floor, deciding what to do next. She dug her hand into her purse and pulled out a plastic bag from a Rodeo Drive boutique. She rolled her hand inside the bag and found the bracelet she was going to return. She put the bracelet in her pocket, pulled the drawstring on the bag wide, and scooped in the cash. Then she reached in the safe-deposit box for what was left, some paper folded to lie flat in the narrow box. She opened it. It was a bunch of stock certificates for a company called EquiMex.

"EquiMex... EquiMex?"

She counted. Fifty thousand shares. They went into the bag with the cash. Then the trinkets followed.

She waved good-bye to Howard and walked back to the TR. It was stifling inside. She rolled down the windows and unzipped the back window panel. The air was still. She started the engine. The plastic bag was on the passenger seat. She touched it.

"Alley, what the hell am I supposed to do with this? What the hell is this?"

Her voice rose and she flailed her hands.

Passerby ignored her. Happened all the time, people raving to themselves. You're better off not seeing anything.

"Look at my face." She opened the glove compartment. The only thing she could find was the paper towel she had used to check the oil. She found a corner without oil and blew her nose.

"I won't let you down, Alley. I won't sell you out."

Five

Two hours had passed. Four secretaries and two sales assistants had said that Alley was polite, friendly, punctual, always ready to lend a hand and very particular about his appearance. They wanted to know who could have done such a terrible thing and why would somebody want to hurt such a nice man. Lewin kept saying, "There's a lot of evil in this world, ma'am," until Somers made him stop.

Alley's work area was a desk wedged into a closet-sized supply room. Rubber bands, paper clips, bottles of Liquid Paper, and yellow sticky notepads were organized in separate compartments in a plastic tray on top of the desk. A figurine made out of glued shells holding a small plastic guitar with MEXICO painted on the base stood in a corner next to a blue Smurf figure wearing glasses and holding a silver briefcase. A miniature sombrero with MEXICO on the brim was on the Smurf's head. A silk rose was stuck in a pencil box. A DON'T WORRY, BE HAPPY bumper sticker was taped to the wall.

The drawers were neat and unrevealing. Two well-thumbed paperback books, *Be The Best You!* and *Yes, You Can!* were inside, along with pads of paper, envelopes, a box of tissues, a knife and fork, and several cans of cola.

A blotter with a big calendar pad was in the middle of the desk. A partially completed supply order form, written in ball-point pen with a heavy hand, was tucked in the corner. Notes were written on the calendar days in the same heavy, angular handwriting. An algebra class met Tuesdays and Thursdays and an English class met on Wednesday nights. *Tío* Tito's birthday was in two weeks. OAXCATIL was written over three of the weekends, once at the beginning of the month, once two weeks after that and again over the upcoming weekend. Somers wrote OAXCATIL in his notebook and debated with Lewin over whether it was a person, place, or thing.

Somers now sat in a straight-backed chair outside Stan Raab's office. Raab had made three phone calls and taken one since his secretary had said he'd be right with them. He was still on the phone. The secretary had left ten minutes ago.

Most of the brokers' cubicles were empty. Cigarette smoke drifted out of Raab's office along with loud and jovial laughter as if a lot of backslapping would be going on if there had been any other backs to slap in the room.

Lewin paced the floor and looked at his watch.

"You'll be home on time," Somers said.

Lewin paced back toward Somers and leaned toward him. "This is exactly the kind of wait-on-me crap I hate."

Somers couldn't disagree. He stood up and started to pace in the opposite direction. He stopped at one of the cubicles and picked up a snapshot in a Lucite frame off a desk.

"A girl and her car," Teddy Kraus said, sitting in the adjoining cubicle.

Lewin stood next to Somers. "Great car. Cute chick."

"That's about the only thing the Ice Princess warms up to," Billy Drye said from across the room.

"The Ice Princess?" Lewin said.

"Mizzzz Iris Thorne."

"Oh, Miss Thooorne," Lewin said, appraising.

"Mizzzz Thorne," Drye corrected. "The TR. The red car. That and a looong stock portfolio, throbbing with blue chips." He giggled a hybrid of Vincent Price and Beaver Cleaver.

"Now, Billy, leave Missy Thorne alone, hear?" Teddy said, affecting a Southern tinkle. He sniffed and pulled at his nose. "Jus' wanna tear the girl righ' down. Da-dada-duhn-da-da baby!

Got me on my knees!" His fingers twitched over the neck of his air guitar. "Slow hand."

Lewin wondered how much coke he had done. "What's your name?"

"Who are you? Joe Friday?" Teddy asked.

Billy Drye laughed.

"I asked you what your name is."

"T. K. Three," Billy Drye said.

"I asked him."

"Theodore Albert Kraus the third, sir!" Teddy saluted and sniffed. "Talk straight for the man." Teddy stood and adjusted his suspenders. He towered over Lewin. His fingers twitched on the air guitar. "You need a high school diploma for this job or what?"

Lewin stood with his legs apart and looked up at Teddy, his hands rolled into tight fists in his pockets, putting more stress on the seams of his suit pants. "You get high every day?"

"Yeah, man. High on life. You get high? Probably come across the primo shit, huh?"

"Must be hard to make a good dollar in this business these days," Somers said, diverting attention.

"There's always money to be made for a clear-headed, quick-thinking guy," Drye said. "So who killed the gimp?"

"Who do you think?" Somers asked.

"I did! Slow hand!" Teddy roared laughter.

"You're a smartass," Lewin said.

"Smartass? Now you've hurt my feelings, man."

"He was pathetic," Drye said.

"Seems like he was handy to have around," Somers said.

"You've been talking to Jayne Perkins. What did she say about me? Billy Drye?"

"Why should she mention you?" Somers said.

"I'm notorious around here. My unique worldview. She didn't mention me?"

"Your unique worldview," Somers said.

"Yeah. Take Alley. Everyone crying, 'Poor Alley, poor Alley,' doesn't mean diddly squat to me." Drye leaned toward

Somers. Confidential. "You never know what someone like Alley can get himself into."

"Meaning?"

"Mexicans," Drye whispered, loud. "Third-world types."

"Go on," Somers said.

"Gangs, drugs, theft… it's a way of life. And this handicapped business? He used it, let me tell you. You should have seen the way the women sucked up to him. Made me want to get an eye patch and gimp around myself. Know what I mean?"

"Can't say I do."

"So you're on the gimp's side."

"I didn't know we were picking sides."

"You always pick sides in life, Detective," Drye said.

"I have to agree with you, Mr. Drye. You do have a different way of looking at things."

Drye smiled, self-satisfied. "See?"

"Hey, man. Don't be pissed," Teddy said. "I just can't help myself sometimes." Teddy extended his palm. "Friends?"

Lewin didn't move, his hands still in his pockets.

"C'mon man. Some of my best friends are cops."

Lewin stared at Teddy. "This isn't a joke, pal."

"Suit yourself, Joe Friday," Teddy put on his jacket.

"Where you going?" Lewin asked.

"Quittin' time. Places to go, people to see." Teddy clicked off his computer terminal. "Things to do. A budding executive's day never ends."

"Don't leave town, Mr. Kraus."

"What?"

"You're a murder suspect."

Teddy sputtered through his full lips. "Com'oooonnnn!"

"Teddy!" Drye said, "What shit you been talkin'? Can't turn my back on you for a minute."

Teddy grinned ear to ear. "I'm outta here." He formed his hands into pistols and leveled them at Lewin. "The man, Joe."

He turned to Somers. "And the big man, the red man, the quiet man"—Teddy fired six-shooters at Somers—"and the thin man, the real man, the one and only"—Teddy threw a series of fast balls down the corridor— "Billy Drye."

"Hey! Ted-ster!" Billy Drye made one-two punches with his fists, finishing by snapping his fingers and pointing at Teddy.

"See ya!" Teddy thundered down the corridor. "*Hasta la vista*, baby!"

"I'm gonna end up punching that clown out," Lewin said out the side of his mouth to Somers. "I'd rather be on the street with Paco and Flaco. At least you know where they're coming from."

"Hey, I gotta go," Raab's voice went from a close murmur to loud enough to be clearly heard outside his office. "I got two cops waiting to talk to me. Our mailboy was murdered last night. Terrible, terrible thing. I've kept these good men waiting long enough."

"You guys are up," Drye said.

Stan Raab put out his cigarette and ran his fingers through his short, receding, sandy blond hair, touched each corner of his mouth to remove any goo, put on his suit jacket, and pulled his shirt cuffs down beneath his jacket sleeves, one quarter inch all around. He walked out to the detectives, extended his palm, and smiled the smile that had closed a thousand deals.

"Gentlemen. Stan Raab."

"I'm John Somers and this is my partner, Paul Lewin."

Lewin gave Raab a look that would sour milk.

"Forgive me for making you wait." Raab distributed a firm, dry-palmed handshake, not releasing first.

"We've been talking with your junior associates here," Somers said. "Very enlightening."

"I've got quite a group. Some great guys and girls... ah, women. Be lost without 'em." He pointed at Drye and winked.

"Come in and sit down."

Raab's corner office had two glass walls that overlooked the city, facing west. On a clear day, he could see the ocean. He'd probably have to wait until March. His office was cluttered with toys—a basketball hoop and Nerf ball, a dart board with brass darts, a brass Slinky, and a Lucite frame with chrome pins that held the impression of any object pressed against it. Framed pictures of a pretty wife and kids and a pretty boat and airplane were on the desk. Larger pictures of the boat and the airplane were on a wall along with degrees and certificates. The office was crowded with heavy antique furniture.

Somers walked to look at the documents. There were resin-sealed diplomas—a bachelor's degree in 1972 from Dartmouth, a Stanford master's in business administration in 1974, a high school diploma and attendance award from a chi-chi San Fernando Valley prep school—certificates from seminars and speaking engagements, and a plaque from the Rotary Club proclaiming Raab as one of the Fine Young Men of 1971. It looked as if every official-looking document that passed through Raab's hands made it to the framers.

Lewin sat stiffly on a tapestry-upholstered chair facing the desk and stared at Raab.

Somers studied the airplane and boat pictures.

"Beauties, aren't they?" Raab asked.

"Nice," Somers said.

"Just flew the plane back from Tahoe last weekend. Building a house up there."

"Hmmm," Somers said. He looked at a picture of a young Raab in the middle of a group of young men who were all wearing the same tie and all looked pretty much like Raab. A fraternity picture.

"North side of the lake, one of the new developments there."

"They're overbuilding in that area," Somers said, "It's polluting the lake."

"I'm very concerned about that. There's a no-growth movement up there and I'm all for it."

"As long as your house goes in, of course," Lewin said.

Raab opened his mouth to speak, then closed it.

"Mr. Raab," Lewin said.

"Call me Stan."

"Let's get on with our business. My partner and I have spent enough time here already."

"Detective, you're angry with me."

"We have a murder to solve, sir," Lewin said.

"I made you wait. I'd be angry, too. Unfortunately, I had a previous obligation. Know that I have tremendous respect for the job you do and I'm as eager to find Alley's murderer as you are." Raab stood, walked around his desk, and extended his hand to Lewin. "Partners?"

Lewin begrudgingly stood and took Raab's hand.

Raab put his other hand on top of Lewin's, kept it there for several long seconds, and met Lewin's eyes. "Partners, Detective?"

With effort, Lewin cracked a smile. "Let's do it."

Raab circled back to his desk, patting Somers on the back. "So what's your background, Detective Lewin?"

"I started with the force after the Navy, fifteen years ago. Been detective for seven and with Somers for six."

"Working with a partner for so long must be like a marriage, huh?"

"You finish each other's sentences." Lewin looked at Somers. "And I can tell the Professor is anxious to get on with this. I have to be someplace, too."

"Just cut me off. I'll gab all night. I'm fascinated by police science and criminology. I've done some study in the field. A person's work habits and associations, all the small facts can be very telling, right?"

"Absolutely," Lewin said.

"Stan, when did you last see Alley?" Somers asked.

"Right. Let's move forward. Yesterday, about eleven o'clock. Had him run papers down to the escrow office for me. I tell you, this house thing is something else. Escrow was supposed to close three different times now, but there's been construction delays, then they poured the driveway wrong and—"

"Stan," Somers said, "did you notice anything different about Alley during the past few days, anything unusual?"

"No. He was around, or underfoot," Stan laughed. "Poor Alley. I had him run fabric swatches to the furniture manufacturer the other day. My wife wanted to order from the same guys that did our house down here. She doesn't know anyone in Tahoe—"

"Did Alley frequently handle your personal business?" Somers asked.

"You know, fellas, some folks around here didn't care for that, but Alley loved it. I gave him a little extra, you know, and I really needed the help. This house business is taking too much time as it is. My wife likes the sun. We have the house in Palm Springs, but I like the snow. Tahoe's good for both of us. We'll get a ski boat and the kids—"

"Thank you for your time, Stan," Somers said.

"You guys done? That's it? Listen to me go on. Can I get you some coffee? My girl's gone home, but I can get it."

"We'll call you if we need anything else," Somers said.

Lewin was quickly out of the chair and in the doorway.

"Hey, any time." Raab pulled a leather briefcase onto the desk and started gathering papers into it. "Have any leads yet?"

"There were a lot of witnesses, but thousands of men in Los Angeles fit the killer's description," Lewin said.

"And there's no statute of limitations on murder, right?"

"That's right," Lewin said. "But the trail can get pretty cold after a few weeks."

"Excuse me, Stan." A tall man with dark hair and a face that could get away with murder stood in the doorway. His expensive gabardine suit draped his athletic frame without a fold or pucker. "I'm going to meet my dad. I'll see you tomorrow."

Stan introduced Joe Campbell. "We were just talking about the odds of solving Alley's murder."

"Does it look good?" Joe asked.

"We'll get the bad guy," Lewin said.

Somers thought Joe Campbell looked familiar. He glanced at the fraternity picture again and saw Joe standing to the left of Stan Raab.

"But Alley's murder, someone walking up to a guy on the street, killing him, disappearing—the odds of solving something like that must be pretty slim," Raab said. "That's scary."

"I haven't seen the perfect crime yet," Somers said.

"The perfect crime must be a real challenge for a criminal mind," Campbell said.

"Cases break with dogged, routine work," Lewin said. "Criminals aren't usually tidy… or smart."

"Let's hope so, for Alley's sake. See you tomorrow, Stan."

"Give your dad my best."

After Campbell had left, Somers said, "You and Mr. Campbell went to college together."

Raab walked to the door. His head reached Somers's shoulder. He was a man who gave the impression of being much taller. "Very observant, Detective. Joe and I have been friends since our fraternity days. So, what's our next step?"

"The case isn't twenty-four hours old yet," Lewin said. "We continue the investigation."

"Of course. My salesman's need for closure. Sunshine, go home," Raab said to someone outside the door. "My star. Can't keep her away from the office even though her friend was killed. That's who you should talk to, gentlemen. Iris Thorne, friend of birds with broken wings and disabled mailroom boys. Iris, Detective Lewin and Detective Somers."

Iris met Somers's eyes and stared openmouthed for a second before remembering herself. She extended her palm to Lewin and shook his hand firmly in the Raab style. "Detective Lewin. Pleased to meet you. Detective Somers." She took Somers's hand and quickly let it go. She smiled tightly and looked at Raab and did not look at Somers.

Lewin looked from Iris to Somers.

"Iris has an interesting background," Raab said. "She got her MBA from UCLA after teaching Special Ed. She was a risk for me, no business experience"—Raab put his arm around Iris's shoulders—"but she's been just a little blond stick of dynamite"— and squeezed—"even though she *is* a public school MBA" He gave her shoulder a shake and laughed.

Iris laughed too, even though it was clear to Somers that she didn't think it was funny. Raab didn't seem to notice.

"I have to leave you gentlemen." Raab gave them the two-handed politician's handshake, the left hand clasping the elbow.

"If you need my help in any way, don't hesitate to call." He started walking. "Promise to let me know about any developments right away. Let's catch this creep." He winked at the detectives. "Good night, Iris."

"'Night, Stan."

"So you're Ms. Thorne," Lewin said. "We've heard a lot about you."

"Have you?" she asked.

Somers looked at his shoes.

"My partner's talked about you nonstop."

Iris turned cool blue eyes on Somers. "Really?"

Somers blushed wildly.

"I'd love to stay, but… banana sheet cake time," Lewin said. I'll leave you with my partner, Ms. Thorne. You're in good hands. I guess you know that."

The red flush crept up Somers's neck again.

"I'll expect your report tomorrow, Professor. Ma'am." He gave Iris a half-bow then left.

The heavy glass door of the suite swung closed with a sucking noise.

Somers let loose the grin he'd been wrestling with.

Iris kept her arms folded and turned up one corner of her pursed lips. "You shaved your beard."

"About nine years ago."

"Isn't this rich?" Billy Drye said. He appeared at the top of a nearby partition, his head propped up on his palms. "The cold-call cowgirl and the cop."

Six

"Duhda dudah DUNGH DAAAH...ba baba ba ba BAAAH..."

Teddy Kraus smacked the strings of his air guitar, the fingers of his left hand trembling on the cords. His back arched toward heaven. His head writhed against the guitar neck. Rock out! Get up! Everyone was out of their seats.

The elevator arrived.

Teddy got in. He faced the back and blotted his huge forehead and dome with a folded handkerchief. Everyone shuffled around to avoid touching each other. They uncomfortably avoided making eye contact with Teddy.

Two young women in cotton summer blouses, work skirts, and white pumps giggled.

"You're looking lovely today, ladies," Teddy boomed.

More giggles.

"Why is that funny?"

There wasn't a good answer.

The doors opened on parking level two and Teddy got out. "Remember, folks. Today is the first day of the rest of my life." He hummed as he walked through the garage. He put his hand in his pocket and a shiny, candy-apple-red BMW with vanity plates that said MAKE ME chirruped electronically and flashed its lights twice.

"Lassie waits for her master outside the school gates."

He gave a thumbs-up to a parking lot attendant who sat in a glass kiosk reading the *Star*. Teddy stopped at the garage exit and slid the sunroof open. He jutted clenched fists skyward and screamed.

"Arrgghhh!"

He listened to the noise then screamed again.

"Arrgghhh!"

The parking lot attendant laughed.

Teddy circled his fist around his right ear in a cranking motion and barked, "Rwoof rwoof rwoof rwoof rwoof."

The parking lot attendant did the same thing back. The energy level in the garage escalated.

Teddy floored the Beemer and was out of there.

"Bell! Here I come!"

He drummed his hands on the steering wheel.

"Bell babell babell bell bell rwoof rwoof rwoof rwoof."

Teddy turned left on Third Street, entered the One Eleven south, then circled around the interchange to the Five. He cut a diagonal across four lanes to cruise in lane one, the fast lane.

He punched in the heavy metal station on the radio and raked his fingers through his sparse hair, which danced in the wind.

"Daddy's coming, baby!"

He twisted the volume up and the bass down and turned on all four speakers.

"Arrgghhh!"

Teddy rode up the tailpipe of the car ahead of him. The driver held his position for two minutes then violently pulled into lane two. Take, it buddy. Teddy did. Then he rode up the tailpipe of the next car. In your face, man. Make me. Just make me. The car pulled over. This was too easy. Then the car in front of that and the car in front of that and then the next one and the next one and the one after that and the one after that. Make meeeeee!

The next car wouldn't move.

Make me.

The other driver covertly glanced in his rearview mirror without turning his head. He held the lane.

Teddy got closer.

The other driver didn't care. Teddy didn't exist. He was a hallucination, a specter, a commuter's nightmare. The other driver wasn't moving. He'd take a stand for decency and fair driving habits. Go away, ghost of bad driving. I am not afraid.

"You shit-head-dick-head-sphincter-sucking-dog-fucking-asshole!" Teddy waved his fists menacingly through the sunroof.

The other driver smiled slowly. His adversary was displaying his crucial weakness. I am not afraid.

Teddy pulled right, fast. Across lane two, lane three, touching down in lane four, then back, pedal to the metal, across three lanes. The other driver sped up too, losing his Zen in the adrenaline rush. Teddy came anyway, fast, faster, fastest, cutting in front of the other driver's front bumper with a hair to spare.

"Arrgghhh!" Teddy held the steering wheel with his knees and raised both arms with clenched fists.

He was king. King of Lane One.

Teddy pulled a glass vial from his jacket pocket, flipped the stopper off with his thumb, and took a victory snort.

At Florence Avenue, he got off the freeway. Teddy had arrived in the city of Bell.

"Made it in half an hour. Gawdalmighty. Where the hell are the cops in this town?"

He drove down Florence Avenue past fast-food restaurants, car dealerships, and corner strip malls.

"Bell! You're beautiful!" Teddy crowed to the brown air. "I'll take Jaynie here. Jaynie! Jaynie! Jaynie! She loves me! She just doesn't know it. Women are like that. Misguided."

The Four Queens card palace juts from Bell's stucco L.A. suburban landscape like a piece of Las Vegas sent flying across the desert, over the Sierra Nevadas, landing on Florence Avenue. One by one, the neon queens in the giant fan of four cards glowed red, white, and green. White lights circling the roof blinked crazily off and on, an effect that was lost in the flat, smoggy late-summer sunshine.

Teddy pulled the Beemer into a spot near the door. He took another snort, wiped the residue from around his nose with his index finger and rubbed his finger against his gums. His elastic face stretched into a dreamy smile. He pocketed the vial and chirruped on the car alarm.

He pushed open the swinging doors of the Four Queens and sauntered through the red-and-gold lobby dangling a lit cigarette from his right hand. He paused in front of a large gold-framed photograph that he especially liked of several blond models dressed in period saloon-girl costumes with cleavages squeezed into tight bustiers, standing with their arms around a gambler in a shiny brocade vest, cards held close to his chest, a cigarette on his lower lip. Teddy took a drag on his cigarette, exhaled a long stream of smoke, and imagined his face in the models' cleavage. Tits galore.

"Non-smoking, one holder, one game, seat open." The reservation hostess's amplified voice carried across the room.

"M.S. for the one-three stud."

The card room was as brightly lit and shadowless as a supermarket. Rows of oval tables made parallel lines across the floor, each dealer's blue ruffled shirt a dot against the center edge. Voices were subdued with concentration. Poker chips clattered like a field of insects.

The hostess, a heavy-hipped woman in a blue ruffled shirt and tight black pants, stood on a raised platform in front of a large, white board, marking reservations and announcing tables through a microphone suspended from her neck. "Three-six low-ball blind for G.R.. Again, one-three stud for the person with initials M.S. Listen up, folks."

Teddy made his reservation—"T.K. for five-ten stud, smoking"—then leaned against a brass rail that circled the platform. He drummed the rail with the palms of his hands in time with the band in the lounge and the band in his head, his class ring tapping against the brass. His fingers twitched in an air guitar riff.

"*Ted*-dy!"

"Ma'am, follow Frankie to your seat," the hostess said.

Teddy kept tapping.

"*Bud*-dy!"

Teddy looked out then down into Bobby's acne-pitted face. "*Bob*-by! The man!"

Teddy enveloped Bobby's chubby fingers with his paw.

Bobby clenched the sleeve of Teddy's jacket and laughed through his nose. He ran his hand up and down Teddy's arm. "Sheeet. Buddy, where you been?"

Teddy drummed on the rail. "Gardena. Change of scenery."

Bobby pulled down on Teddy's sleeve and stretched toward his ear. "Eddie looking for you."

"M.S. for the one-three stud. Last call."

Teddy stopped drumming and took a drag from his cigarette. He put the butt out on the brass rail and looked around for a place to throw it, then cupped it in his palm.

"Eddie who?"

Bobby stared at Teddy. Then he laughed through his nose and rubbed Teddy's sleeve. "Sheeet. Funny guy." He pulled on Teddy's sleeve and stretched toward his ear. "You know Eddie who." Bobby looked across the card room and jerked his head toward a door with a window mirrored in two-way glass.

"Oh, *that* Eddie." Teddy flicked the cigarette butt toward the mirrored glass. "Place is quiet since they closed down the Pai Gow games. Sent the Vietnamese boys home. Better lock up Fido. Rwoof, rwoof!"

Bobby snorted. "Vietnamese. Cambodians. No class." He wore a silk sport coat with an open-necked shirt and a thick gold chain with a shiny flat link around a chubby neck that grew out of his shoulders like a tree stump. The rings of flesh were moist even in the air-conditioned room. He opened his angled eyes wide. "You want Pai Gow? We go Westminster." He stretched toward Teddy's ear, looked around the room, and whispered, "Private game."

"Little Saigon? I'd be the only round-eye there."

"You think I'm like them? I'm pillipino." He jammed a finger at his chest. "I look behind me in Little Saigon." He twisted his stubby body at the waist to demonstrate. "Not smart trust them. Little Seoul, too." He nodded sagely.

"One seat one-three twenty-one, no-smoking. Follow Frankie to your seat."

"So, whaddid Eddie say?" Teddy drummed and strummed.

"Ask me if I see you." Bobby leaned close to Teddy. "Told me tell him if I see you."

"Frankie will show you to your seat."

"Eddie Schmeddie."

"I won't tell I see you." Bobby winked theatrically.

"Awwww." Teddy waved at the air. "He just wants to talk to me about a deal I'm putting together for him. You know, finance."

Bobby pursed his lips and nodded.

"I should have gotten back to him sooner, but I've been busy."

Bobby nodded again.

"Shoot, you know the way the market's been."

"Very busy."

"T.K. for five-ten stud, smoking, T.K. for five-ten stud, smoking. Follow Frankie to your seat."

"That's me, buddy. See ya."

"Buddy, remember what I tell you." Bobby pretended he was locking his lips closed with a key.

Teddy pointed his index finger at Bobby.

Frankie stood on the casino floor, holding a two-way radio like a bat and not smiling. He gave Teddy a once-over, then turned without speaking and started to walk.

"Good to see you, too, Frankie."

"Asshole."

"Unsweet, Frankie."

Teddy followed Frankie across the casino, walking with his body tipped back from the shoulders, a cigarette dangling from one hand, the other hooked by the thumb in his pant pocket. He winked at a red-eyed woman at the bar.

"C'mon, talk to me Frank-eee."

"Eddie's seen you here."

"So?"

"You just forgot about Sally Lamb?"

"I don't keep company with people like that, Frank-eee."

"Asshole."

Frankie pointed the walkie-talkie at the one empty chair at a full table.

"Sit."

Frankie turned on his heel and left.

Teddy rolled back the chair with a flourish and sat with a plop. "Good afternoon, men. Men, men, men, men," he sang. "Hey, there's my friend, Sammy." He leaned over the table to shake hands with a muscular black man in a tight T-shirt. And ladies! Good afternoon." He bowed toward a matron in a mint green polyester pantsuit.

Her diamond-and-platinum wedding rings cut into her plump fingers. She giggled. The other woman was in her late thirties and was extravagantly dressed in a lavender jumpsuit with a lavender fedora angled over her eyes. Teddy bowed toward her and she nodded like the Queen of England.

Three Asian men in sport coats and open-necked shirts sipped beer. The last man was middle-aged and cowboy handsome, wearing a flat-brimmed hat with a string of silver medals circling the brim. He leaned heavily on tanned, muscular arms that protruded from the sleeves of a white polo shirt.

Teddy pointed at him. "You on TV?"

The man gave a slow smile. "Sometimes." His skin was flushed and covered with a web of broken veins.

"I've seen you."

The man failed at concealing his delight.

Teddy pulled out a silver money clip engraved TAK III, peeled off ten hundred-dollar bills, and handed it to a passing chip attendant, who wore a red shirt with the Four Queens logo embroidered across the back. Teddy got back several piles of multicolored chips.

The dealer was a Hispanic woman with thick, shag-cut hair and long silver fingernails. She solemnly shuffled the cards, cut, pulled the first card off the top, and moved it underneath the deck. She dealt, sliding the cards off the top with the flat part of her fingers. Her silver nail polish reflected the light.

Teddy reached for his cards.

Frankie and another man took long strides across the room and stood on either side of Teddy. Frankie leaned over and spread his hand across Teddy's cards, holding them down.

"What?"

"Get up."

"Why?"

"Eddie wants to see you."

"Oh man," Teddy whined, "I just sat down. I can't get a decent game at this place anymore."

The dealer gathered the cards, sliding her fingers underneath, her nails scratching the felt table surface. The woman in the mint green pantsuit looked disappointed.

Frankie called the chip attendant over. "Cash him out."

Teddy folded the cash into his money clip. He straightened his tie and his expression. "Sorry to interrupt the game, ladies and gentlemen. Eddie wants to talk to me about a deal we've been working on. Gonna write me a check." He winked.

Teddy got up from the table and pulled his arm away when Frankie tried to put his hand on it. Teddy made a beeline toward the door with the two-way glass on the other side of the casino. Frankie almost jogged to keep up with him.

Teddy rapped furiously on the door, bouncing on his toes and smoothing his sparse hair in the mirrored glass. The door opened and Teddy pushed his way in, slamming it in Frankie's face.

The room was vulgarly lush, with a polished black lacquer desk and padded silk on the walls. Eddie sat behind the desk in a white leather chair. He was fortyish and getting even handsomer. He was wearing a big gold watch and big diamond ring and his clothes shouted European. His salt-and-pepper hair was swept back from his Roman face.

"Teddy," Eddie cooed. "So nice to see you again. Please sit down."

Teddy nodded feverishly. "Right, Eddie. What do I have to do to get a decent game in this place?"

"Teddy, my apologies for interfering with your evening. Won't you greet my other guests?"

"You mean the two garlic cloves?"

"Tsk," Sally Lamb clucked. "These words from such a well-bred boy." He was fortyish with olive skin and flat, too-black hair combed straight back from his forehead, colored with the comb-through men's dye that promises subtle changes that no one will notice. A greasy concoction froze the comb's tracks on the surface. He was a collision of textures and seasons, wearing a wool brown-on-brown houndstooth jacket over a tight, European-cut brown shirt tucked into white, beltless polyester pants. He wore a five o'clock shadow on a bloodhound face. A gold crucifix meshed with the sparse black-and-gray chest hair that showed through the V of his unbuttoned shirt. He was leaning against a wall with his head against the padded silk.

Eddie stood. "I'm going to do my rounds. Make yourselves comfortable." He shot a glance at Sally Lamb's head on the silk wall before he walked out and closed the door.

Teddy dropped onto a leather chair facing the desk, his legs sprawled out. "Hey, Sally. The seventies are over."

Jimmy Easter snickered. He was in his late twenties with olive complexion and black hair cut short and preppie-neat. He was pretty-boy handsome and would mash anyone who said it. He was wearing an expensive raw silk jacket over a plain black T-shirt over a free-weight-big chest and black Levi's 501s pulled down over black boots with silver tips. The sparkling diamond in his earlobe matched the sparkle in his cobra smile. He was cleaning his nails with a red-handled pocket knife and had not looked up once.

"You're one real smart-ass, aren't you, Teddy?" Sally said.

"Sally, the Grecian Formula needs a touch-up," Teddy said.

Jimmy snickered louder.

Sally gave Jimmy a hurt look.

"Who else would tell you these things, Sally?" Teddy said.

"That just goes to show you what a dumb fuck you are, Teddy. And you"—he shot a look at Jimmy—"had better shut the fuck up."

"Yeah, Black Bart," Teddy said.

Jimmy snuffed his smile, glowered at Teddy, and continued to clean his nails.

"What do you two bongos want?" Teddy said. "I've got things to do."

Sally folded his hands in front of him and nodded his head slowly up and down. "You think you know everything, don't you? Got it all tied up."

Teddy raised his eyebrows and opened his mouth in mock confusion.

"Here you are. College education. Smart boy. Bright boy. And look at you. A disgrace to your mother."

"Get real. My mother's a lush. She's too busy trottin' around Greece with her boyfriend to care what I do."

"Shame on you, Teddy."

"Get a life." Teddy started to get up. Jimmy snapped out of his chair, caught Teddy by the shoulders, and pushed him back down. Teddy's complexion reddened with indignation.

Sally put his face close to Teddy's. "Sit there until I'm done with you."

Teddy touched Sally's spray on his cheek.

"Let's not forget the order here. You're the one who got yourself into this mess. I'm the one you came to for help." Sally leaned over and jabbed a finger against Teddy's chest. "And I helped you. We made a deal. Then what do you do? You don't follow through. Now, I don't call that very smart for a smart boy like you. Do you, Teddy?"

Teddy stared a hole through the desk.

"I said, do you, Teddy?"

"No."

"No, that's right. Very good, Teddy. Mr. College Educated from Big University and he still don't know how things work." Sally flicked his hand against the back of Teddy's head.

Teddy mumbled, "MIT and Harvard."

"What?"

"I got my B.S. from MIT and my MBA from Harvard."

"That's swell. Were you were a Boy Scout too and helped old ladies cross the street?"

"Those are top schools. You don't realize…"

"I said it's just swell, Teddy. Just swell. Now, give me my money."

"I don't have it right now."

Silence.

"You don't have it right now."

"I don't have it right now.

"Hear that, Jimmy? He says he don't have it right now."

Jimmy Easter balled his hand into a fist, admired it, then looked at Teddy, and raised a dark eyebrow.

"I gave you everything I had last week. But I get my commission check next Friday. I'll give you that. That'll be a start. I'm trying, Sally," Teddy whined.

"There's no merit badge for trying. And now you owe me five grand more. For interest and for being an asshole."

Teddy rubbed one big palm inside the other. "I had the money, Sally. More than enough. But it got away from me."

"You mean you put it up your nose and gave it to the tables out there."

Teddy looked at Sally dolefully. "You'll get it all on Friday. I promise."

"You promise. What kind of a candy-ass are you, anyway? You promise, you promise. You promised me last week."

Teddy's voice went up. "I said I'll get it for you next Friday."

"You know, guys like you turn up all the time whacked out and left to rot in the canyon. Faces half-eaten by rats by the time anyone finds 'em."

Jimmy spoke. "Ever wonder what it would be like to have your balls in your mouth while you were bleeding to death?"

Teddy's Sea Island cotton shirt grew deep circles under the armpits beneath his handmade suit jacket. He slumped further down in the chair.

"What am I going to do with you, Teddy?" Sally paced the room with his hands behind his back. "You got a girlfriend, Teddy?"

"No," Teddy breathed.

"What's that?"

"No," Teddy said, louder. "I had a girlfriend. We broke up."

"Dumped ya, huh?"

Teddy pulled the corners of his broad mouth down. His full cheeks were blotched red. His bottom lip rolled out. Perspiration shined through his sparse hair.

"Girls don't like losers." Sally shook his head. "You need to clean yourself up, Teddy. Find a nice girl. Get a nice life. Stop being a jerk."

Sally paced and stroked his jaw. "Damn shame." He sucked air between his teeth. He stopped pacing in front of Teddy. "Teddy, I don't know why I feel sorry for you. I do business with a lot of scumbags. Everyone's got a story. But you really tear me up." He sighed. "But business is business, Teddy. You're a businessman. You understand that."

He put his face close to Teddy's. "I got *my* reputation to think about. I got a boss to report to, too." He took Teddy's chin in his hand and squeezed. "Next Friday. I don't care what you do or how you get it. And don't make me come lookin' for you."

Jimmy Easter ran his tongue over his teeth.

Seven

John Somers wanted to gush, to tell Iris how great she looked, that it was wonderful to see her, that she hadn't changed a bit even though she had somehow. That she'd never left his thoughts. Maybe during the early years of his marriage, but not after that, and even then not really. He marveled at the twist of fate that had made their paths cross, even though he could have found her if he had wanted to. If he thought she might have wanted to see him.

How should he start? He showed her his shield. "I'm investigating the Alejandro Muñoz murder."

Iris took the shield and looked at it up close, running her thumb over the bas-relief insignia. She looked at him. She laughed. "The family legacy caught up with you, huh?"

"Yep." Somers laughed even though he felt stripped bare, as people out of the past can make you feel. "And you—what happened to that PhD?"

"*Touché.*" She laughed again.

Somers remembered that laughing had always made her face light up.

"Life's weird, isn't it?" she gave him his shield back.

"It has a way of creeping into your dreams," he said.

"This is really cute." Billy Drye laughed sardonically.

"Drye. Go home," Iris said.

"Not on your life."

"You're investigating Alley's murder," Iris said. "Small world."

"Yeah. Small world."

"You didn't know I worked here?"

"No. Well... I mean... I sorta knew. Those notices in the alumni magazine?"

"My own PR. How ungracious of me."

"I was glad to see you're doing well."

"Things are good... Things are okay. So, you want to talk to me about Alley?"

"Everyone says you're the one I should talk to."

"You want to talk here? We can go into an office for some *privacy*." She looked at Drye, who was staring at them with a bemused grin.

"How about dinner?"

"Dinner?" Iris said.

"Dinner?" Drye said.

Somers shrugged. "It's dinnertime. Aren't you hungry?"

"I don't know if you can afford her on a cop's salary, buddy," Drye said.

"Shaddup, Drye," Iris said. "I had some work to do, but... okay. There's a place around the corner."

"You going to Julie's?" Drye said. "I'll call the guys."

"Dream about it tonight, Drye. Don't forget the handcuffs and *The Wall Street Journal*." She gathered her stuff and walked in front of Somers out of the suite.

"Interesting people you work with," Somers said.

"It's the boy's locker room wardrobed by Brooks Brothers."

On the elevator down, she watched the floor numbers. Somers watched her.

"You're staring at me."

"You look different."

"I was twenty the last time you saw me."

"You're different, but you're the same too."

"Is this police business or something else?"

"I'm investigating the murder of Alejandro Muñoz." Somers smiled at the elevator floor.

"No problem. I just want to know what the score is."

They crossed a street logjammed with solo drivers fleeing downtown for the San Fernando Valley, Orange County, the San Gabriel Valley, the beach cities, or some other suburban safe harbor with clean people. Anywhere but here. Carpooling's inconvenient and no one wants a subway stop on their street and only sad people without cars ride the bus and the bus would take just as long anyway so everyone commutes—two to five hours every weekday.

The restaurant had high ceilings and marble floors that elevated the noise level to a tinny whine. Happy-hour revelers waiting out drive time were wing tip to wing tip to pump, crowded around an oval bar in the center of the room, having garlicky focaccia and cocktails and virgin drinks. The place reeked of gabardine.

The host wore the uniform of the bored chic—a black suit with an oversized jacket over a black T-shirt. His hair was long, blunt-cut and bleached blond on top, and dark and shaved short on the bottom. A diamond stud sparkled in his earlobe. He took a long minute before he looked up from his table grid, then kind of looked past Somers and Iris and asked his obviously tiresome questions: "Have a reservation? Smoking or non?" Then he gave a look that said he expected they would answer a certain way. He raked his hand through his hair and stared off as he decided at which far corner and noisy table by a waiter's station to seat them.

He wove through the crowd to a row of small gray marble tables with a padded bench on one side and a hard-backed chair on the other. Iris turned sideways to squeeze between the tables, dragged her skirt across the table top, and sat on the bench, her elbows inches from the people on either side of her. The host dropped menus in front of them.

A waitress with a wild mane of long, twisted hair dyed the red of the moment, wearing a leather mini and a tight, off-the-shoulder midriff top, recited a memorized list of specials, stumbling on the French sauces. Iris ordered a glass of chardonnay, the duck ravioli with pink caviar sauce, and an endive salad with raspberry-walnut vinaigrette. Somers ordered a beer and a burger, well done.

"Iris, remember the Hip Bagel Café? Sprouts, sunflower seeds, and cream cheese on a bagel. Washed down with a protein banana smoothie."

"It's a Fatburger now."

"And the rock station is New Age."

"I listen to that station," Iris said. "It wakes me up every morning."

"Music to find our lost souls by."

"Lost souls?"

"I feel that way sometimes."

The waitress brought their drinks.

Iris took the opportunity to drop the bait and move on. "So, do you have any leads about the murder?"

Somers shrugged. "Probably some cracked-out punk who didn't like the way Alley walked. I found out today that you taught the deaf. When?"

"For a couple of years after I got my bachelor's."

"How did you land at McKinney Alitzer?"

"Restless. Wanted to see the world, or at least what was west of East L.A., make a lot of dough, live at the beach, lead the glamorous life I thought everyone else was having." She lifted a shoulder and flicked a wrist. The subject was dismissed. "It's been good… been great."

Somers sipped his beer. "Ever get married?"

"Nope."

"I'm surprised."

"I thought we were here to talk about Alley."

"C'mon Iris. I haven't seen you in fifteen years. I'm curious. Didn't you ever think about me?"

"Sure. From time to time. How's Penny?"

"Fine, I guess. We're divorced." He shrugged.

"You dumped me for her and it didn't even last?"

"You're kidding. You know that's not true."

"Sure, I'm kidding," she said. "How long ago?"

"Three years."

"What happened?"

"Whatever happens. Things."

"Sure."

"You dating anyone?" he asked.

"I thought we were here to talk about Alley."

"We are... I..."

"You're just curious."

"C'mon, Iris. We were friends once. It was pretty nice, wasn't it?"

"Yeah, it was." She took a sip of wine and looked at the crowd.

"Careful, hot plates." The waitress turned the plates to achieve the ultimate presentation.

Somers piled lettuce, tomato, pickle slices, and Bermuda onion on his burger. He wiped a knife full of mustard on the patty, then smacked on a glob of ketchup, trailing it over his fries. He took a big bite, sending a red-and-yellow stream out the back of the bun. He dabbed at his mouth with a napkin and smiled sheepishly.

Iris picked a walnut off the salad with her fingers. "Most people think the deaf are mentally deficient. You know, 'deaf and dumb'?" She dragged her fork across the skin of the ravioli and brought the pink speckled red caviar sauce to her lips. She lifted the top off one and scraped out the duck filling. "The deaf don't like the word 'mute.' There's usually nothing wrong with their vocal cords. Please stop staring at me like that."

"Like what? I'm listening."

"You're not interested in hearing about Alley."

"I'm listening to you. Go on."

"Alley was so sweet. He'd do anything for you." She looked at nothing across the restaurant. Her eyes glassed. "Sometimes people were mean, mostly unintentionally. Could be just a look.

Or a look away." She looked back at Somers and touched her eye. "He used to put flowers from his yard on my desk."

"Think he had a crush on you?"

"A crush? No. He was just that way. Very sweet."

"And you were nice to him. And you're... you."

"Yeah... and... ?"

"I can see how someone could have a crush on you."

"What's your point?"

"I never got over my crush on you, Iris."

Iris winced in disbelief. "You son of a bitch. This isn't about Alley. You could care less about Alley."

"Of course I care about Alley, but I'll be frank with you. My partner and have a couple of leads and the murder is looking like a gang initiation. It's cookbook. It's sad, but it happens all the time."

"Poor Alley. People are still using him for their own ends."

"What do you mean?"

"What good fortune for you that a guy in my office was murdered. What an opportunity for you to come down here and drag up our ancient history. Damn, you're jaded."

"I've been a homicide detective for eight years, Iris. My investigative instincts are good."

"Some instincts. Alley knew. He knew no one would dig beneath the surface."

"What did he know?"

Iris threw her napkin onto her plate. "Nothing. What's to know? It's cookbook, right?" She fished her briefcase and purse from between the chair legs and squeezed between the tables, gathering her skirt in her hands to keep it out of the food.

"If it's about Alley, call me at the office. Otherwise, any unresolved issues between you and me are strictly yours." She spun on her heel and walked away, her pumps clacking against the marble floor.

Somers finished his beer while he watched the pink lobster caviar sauce seep into Iris's napkin and studied the cold space in his stomach. He'd screwed up with her again.

Eight

Joe Campbell brushed his hair in the rearview mirror and saw the gray coming in and decided it was good. He touched his finger to his tongue and touched each eyebrow, smoothing the natural arch. He checked his look one last time and it was correct, appropriate, maybe even a little bit handsome, like everyone kept telling him he was but that he couldn't really see, himself. He could see it a little bit now, but then the light was flattering.

He traded his fawn Jaguar for a disclaimer: "Cars left with the valet service are done so at the owner's sole risk."

Small white lights woven through the branches of Popsicle-shaped trees bordering the facade of Sonny's twinkled off and on in the pink dusk. Joe walked down a red carpet underneath a white- and forest-green striped canopy and pulled on the edges of his summer-weight suit jacket so that it fell smoothly.

"Good evening, Mr. Campbell," the doorman said as he held the door open and waited while Joe made sure the dimple was still folded into the knot of his tie.

"Good evening, Rocky."

Sonny himself was leaning against a podium inside the door, his half-glasses on the end of his nose, scanning the reservation list with a Mont Blanc pen, and shaking his head. Carmine, the maître d', stood stiffly nearby and smiled with ersatz sympathy at two couples in pastel poplins who looked as if they'd driven in from the outskirts of some dry, distant suburb where housing was still affordable, probably drawn by the blurb describing Sonny's as a "Dining Experience" that consistently appeared in a local restaurant reviewer's annual survey.

Sonny looked up accusingly from the page at the suburbanites over the top of his half-glasses, "Are you *sure* you have a reservation?"

"Three weeks ago," one of the men said, irritated.

When Sonny saw Joe Campbell walk in, he made a brushing gesture with the back of his hand to Carmine, "Seat them at table nineteen." Sonny walked up to Joe with arms open and kissed him on both cheeks. The violinist swung by and nodded. A waiter changed directions to shake Joe's hand.

"Joey, so good to see you. What a beautiful suit," Sonny said as he rubbed the fabric of the cuff between his thumb and forefinger. Sonny walked Joe into the restaurant with his hand on his back between his shoulder blades. "How are things? Good?" He pointed across the room. "Your party's already seated at your table."

The room was a large, high-ceilinged oval, circled with Ionic columns. The bar was on a second floor loft and a catwalk with an arcade extended from the bar around the perimeter of the room, the arches backlit with a soft pink light. A brass-and-beveled glass art deco chandelier etched with lotus blossoms was suspended in the middle of the room. Fired-glazed tile covered the ceiling and pink marble and oriental rugs covered the floor. Mahogany chairs with lotus blossoms carved into each back were upholstered in the same peach color as the tablecloths and napkins that were arranged on the mahogany tables. Tall and wide fresh floral displays were everywhere.

It was still early and most of the tables were empty. A group of men with short haircuts and their suit jackets off, sleeves rolled up, and ties loosened sat at a table, listening, nodding, and periodically laughing. A business meeting.

Industry People, people in The Business, people working for The Company Town's company were scattered at other tables wearing expensive, rumpled clothing with everything on top up—sleeves pushed up on summer crew-neck sweaters, collars standing up on polo shirts, loose-cuffed sleeves pushed up on linen jackets—and wrinkled linen or carefully faded denim below. The women wore short and tight if they had youth and tone or wore loose and long if they didn't.

A man and a woman sat at a center table nuzzling each other. The woman toed his calf and thigh under the table with a lizard pump. He held her hand with one of his, a gold Rolex screaming bright on his wrist, and talked on a cellular phone held in the other. She chewed his unoccupied ear, eyes lidded, apparently not caring whether anyone was watching, then looked around the room to make sure everyone was.

"Check that out," Sally Lamb said from his seat at the mahogany-and-brass upstairs bar. "He ought to do her right there on the table." He took a sip of his Campari and soda, relaxing after a hard day of shaking down deadbeats at the Four Queens, but not relaxing too much. He was still on the job.

"Bad lay," Jimmy Easter said.

The woman below made eye contact with Jimmy while her friend nuzzled her neck. Jimmy puckered his lips at her.

"Why bad lay?" Sally Lamb asked.

"All show and no go. Know what that broad needs?"

"What you got, right?"

"Well...yeah...," Jimmy ran his hand through his thick hair. "Know what else? An attitude adjustment. She's comin' on to every guy in the room. And that guy puts up with it. What a wuss. But what can you expect from someone who dresses like that?"

"Hey," Sally nudged Jimmy and pointed with his chin toward Joe Campbell crossing the room.

"Daddy's pride and joy," Jimmy said. "Wonder where he gets his clothes."

* * *

Joe Campbell walked to the usual table, unconsciously smoothing his tie and looking at his watch again without seeing the time. He stood at the table and extended his palm.

"Hi, Pop."

Joe's father, Vito, set his cigar in the ashtray, a martini in a still-frosted glass in front of him, and took Joe's hand, pulling him down and kissing him wetly on both cheeks.

Joe lightly caressed his father's shoulders. "How are you, Pop?"

"You act like you're gonna jump outta your skin. Say hello to Wendell. Sit down."

"Hello, Wendell." He shook the other man's hand and sat. "How are you?"

They were at a large table with five chairs, even though there were just three of them.

"Just great, Joey," Wendell Ellis said. "How about…"

"Why are you sitting there?" Joe's father asked.

"For chrissakes." Joe pulled out the chair to his father's right so he wasn't sitting with his back to the door.

"My son. He knows everything. How come you know so much? What are you drinking?"

"Mineral water," Joe said.

"They have the new Beaujolais. Try that."

"I'm good with water right now, Pop."

"How are you doing, Joey?" Wendell Ellis asked. He was light and dark. His silver hair and bonded teeth contrasted with the tan he carried all year from golf and tennis in Palm Desert during the winter and boating off Balboa Island during the summer. His navy blue suit was brushed lint free and his crisp button-down shirt looked frosty white against it. Blue eyes bright like marbles, Wendell Ellis had a warm and friendly face. Easy and confident, his manner was understated, as that of the powerful can be.

* * *

"Who's the nerd?" Jimmy Easter asked, filing his fingernails with a Swiss army knife attachment.

"Lawyer," Sally Lamb said.

"Let's order," Vito said. "I'm starved."

He called to a passing waiter who quickly came over.

"Wendell," Vito said to the attorney, "lombatino di vitello again? With a carpaccio appetizer. And gnocchi with the garlic and butter as secondi. All around."

"Nothing for me," Joe said. "I had a late lunch."

"Bring him that spaghetti with the pepperoni—what is it?"

"Pop, I said I had a late lunch."

"You can't come to a place like this and not eat. What's that dish?"

"Spaghettini con pancetta, cipolle, e pepperoni."

Joe exhaled and spun a cut crystal rose bowl filled with sweet William that sat in the center of the table.

"Bring him that. And we'll have the zabaglione for dessert. And bring that wine we had last time."

"Sir?"

"That Italian red wine. You know. Ask Sonny."

The waiter left, walking with quick, purposeful steps.

"What's wrong with you?" Vito asked. "You had a late lunch… We're supposed to be having dinner."

Joe spun the bowl one last time. "I'm meeting some friends later for a bite."

Vito raised his eyebrows. "Friends? What friends? A girlfriend?"

Joe shrugged. "Friends."

Vito said to Wendell. "He's so mysterious. So, you're meeting friends. Why the big secret?"

"Pop, did you have a reason for calling this meeting other than to give me a hard time?"

Vito leaned forward on his elbows. He pointed toward the center of the table then pulled his hand back and began stroking the bulb of his long nose. The shadows in his face deepened.

Joe looked as if he was about say something, then settled back into his chair.

No one spoke.

"Joey," Wendell finally said, "There's an issue we need to discuss, an irregularity…"

Vito pulled his hand away from his nose and twitched it at the table. Wendell stopped talking.

"Joey, look. We need to talk about Worldco."

"It's doing well," Joe said.

Vito twitched his hand at the table again. "I know, I know."

"Joey, you've done remarkably well managing the Worldco portfolio," Wendell said. "Especially considering the volatility in the market lately."

Vito's eyes went glassy. "I sent him to Dartmouth and Harvard. Ivy League, like the Kennedy boys."

"That performance is completely on the up-and-up, Wendell." Joe said. "No manipulated funds or insider information… and I don't intend to start."

"Not this again," Vito said.

Joe sat stiffly in the lotus blossom chair. "The SEC would have my license if they knew how Worldco's funded."

"Nobody asked you to do anything," Vito said.

A different waiter displayed a wine bottle in front of Vito.

"That's it. That's the red. Robert, where you been? We had to give our order to that other guy."

"I apologize," Robert said. "We're busy tonight."

"You're busy. Busy is good. Have some wine, Joey. Why are you so tense?"

"I told you I'm not drinking tonight, Pop."

"Pour him a glass. You're tense."

The waiter filled the glass half full. Joe raised it and toasted his father.

"Look, Joey… Wendell was in St. Martin last week, in the Caribbean, where Worldco is set up."

"Incorporated offshore, for the tax benefits and confidentiality about corporate ownership," Wendell said.

Vito put up his hand. "Joey, I'll show you how it works." He took packets of sugar from a silver basket and placed them in a semicircle on the table. "Say these sugars are the Caribbean islands." He took out a pen, picked up a packet, and marked it with an X. "And this one is St. Martin."

"I know how it works, Pop," Joe said.

"Listen because you might learn something." On the back of St. Martin, Vito wrote WORLDCO and drew a little stick figure of a man. "This is me." He placed St. Martin at the edge of the semicircle. "Okay, this basket"—he pulled the silver basket in front of the Worldco packet—"is the corporate veil. All everyone outside sees is—" he picked up a saltshaker and plopped it on top of the Worldco packet, the silver top visible behind the basket—"the local man in charge."

"Local administrator," Wendell said. "Countries friendly to offshore corporations have local administrators to handle the corporations' routine transactions. Only one director of the corporation must be on record and this person is usually a local agent-nominee, shielding the true identity of the owners from federal investigators from the States."

"Point is," Vito said, "me, I'm protected by the corporate veil." He took a handful of blue-packaged sugar substitute out of the basket. "Money comes in"—he dropped some behind the basket—"some call it 'dirty,' and money goes out, clean"—he took blue packets from behind the basket—"to buy real estate and securities." He nodded at his son. "Through the laundry. And no one knows who the money belongs to except this guy." He tapped the top of the saltshaker. "The local administrator, who knows how to keep his mouth shut."

Joe refilled his wineglass.

"And over here"—Vito picked up a sugar packet at the other end of the semicircle—"is Curaçao." He palmed the sugar packet and wrote something on it, showed it to Joey, then put it back in its place in the archipelago.

"EquiMex?" Joe said.

Vito looked at Joe mischievously. He dropped his peach napkin on top of the EquiMex packet, "corporate veil," grabbed the pepper shaker, danced it across the tablecloth on its base, then put it on top of the EquiMex packet, wrapping the napkin so that just the silver top of the shaker was visible. He tapped the top sharply with the nail of his index finger. "Local administrator for EquiMex."

Vito took four blue packets of sugar substitute. He wrote $100,000 on one, $500,000 on another, and $4.7 million on each of the last two. He stacked them behind Worldco's corporate veil. "Our dough. From business operations." He slid the $100,000 packet across the Caribbean and underneath the corporate veil of EquiMex. Then came the $500,000 packet, then the first $4.7 million packet, then the second one.

He held his palms open over the table, then leaned back in his chair, picked up his cigar from the ashtray, took a puff, and exhaled a long stream of white smoke. He was finished.

Joe pointed at the display. "You're saying that ten million dollars was transferred from Worldco to this Curaçao corporation called EquiMex?"

His father puffed on the cigar and nodded slowly.

"Why?"

"For management services rendered," Wendell said.

"Who authorized it?"

Wendell flipped open the lock on a broad-bottomed leather briefcase on the floor by his feet. He pulled out a manila file folder that had WORLDCO typed on the tab, took out four slick-surfaced faxes, and displayed them on the table.

Joe picked up the faxes and gaped at them. The moisture from his hands dimpled the paper. "I never signed these. This isn't my signature."

His father made a brushing motion. "Joey, I know."

Joe dropped the faxes. "Who are these EquiMex people?"

"We don't know," Wendell said. "We can only know the name of the local administrator and one director of record, who's usually also a local citizen. That's the nature of a Caribbean corporation. It's precisely what we've used to our advantage with Worldco. But this EquiMex situation is very curious. The director of record is an employee of McKinney Alitzer, a man by the name of Alejandro Muñoz."

"Alley? He's the mailroom boy." Joe looked at his father. "Or was. He was murdered last night."

"Murdered?" Vito said. "Humph." He turned the pepper shaker onto its side.

"Joey, do you think this Muñoz could have acted on his own?" Wendell asked.

"He was the mailboy. He was handicapped. Deaf. Even if he had schemed this, why list himself as director? That defeats the point of an offshore corporation."

Vito threw EquiMex's peach corporate veil aside with a flourish. He picked up the sugar packet beneath it and showed it to Joe. A stick figure and question mark were drawn there. He tapped the stick figure with his index finger.

"This guy ripped us off. Set up this Muñoz and ripped us off. Found out about Worldco and took advantage of you, Joey."

He leveled a gaze at his son. Everything dark about Vito got darker. "No one rips us off."

Joe rubbed his jaw. "I told you it would get screwed up, that it would catch up with us, but you couldn't leave it alone."

"We're not talking about this now," his father said.

"Yes, we are talking about it now. You're always looking for angle, even when it comes to *my* career, *my* life." Joe looked accusingly at his father.

"Now, Joey—" Wendell began.

"This is between me and my father, Wendell. My father, whose motto is: 'What's mine is mine and what's yours is mine, too.'"

Vito tamped his cigar. "A man asks his son, the high finance expert, to manage his dough. Something wrong with that? I put you through school. I made you who you are."

"To do your bidding," Joe said under his breath.

"Excuse me?" Vito asked.

"I said, what do you want me to do?"

"I want you to figure out how we're going to get ten million back and from who. This is your world, not mine."

"Could have fooled me."

"I'll pretend I didn't hear that."

The waiter brought the food.

"Let's eat," Vito said. "Looks great, huh?"

Joe stabbed the spaghetti with his fork and began eating to please his father.

After Vito and Wendell had savored a few bites, Vito said, "Joey, the birthday party for Stan's son is on Sunday, right?"

"Yes, Pop."

"Your mother'll like that. She loves Disneyland." He rolled a paper-thin slice of carpaccio on his fork, held it in front of his mouth, then leaned toward his son. "I love it, too. Especially that ride with the singing dolls."

Joe twirled his fork in the spaghetti and shoved some in his mouth. It was delicious, but it was ruining his appetite for his dinner later. He sat through the meal quietly, listening to Wendell and his father talk about people whose names he mostly didn't recognize. They wouldn't talk serious business in front of him. His father sheltered him from that.

After the zabaglione and espresso, after an interminable period of time, they rose to leave.

As they walked across the marble floor, two men entered the restaurant and stood at the podium while Carmine checked their reservation. One was tall and black and the other was tall and white. Both wore their hair in long, matted dreadlocks.

"Check out the hair on those guys," Sally Lamb said.

"I wonder what it would look like on fire," Jimmy Easter said.

Sally nudged Jimmy and jerked his head toward the lower level where Vito Camelletti and his party were walking out. They threw money on the bar and left.

Nine

Alley was standing on the crest of a yellow hillside. It was the hill next to the house where Iris grew up. Slender, dry weeds undulated in the wind. Alley waved his arms and gestured for Iris to climb. It took a long time, but she finally stood next to him. Alley's face was shiny caramel, his eyes were chocolate, and his hair was coal. He laughed at her, a gurgling sound, and handed her a knife. She swallowed it. She was supposed to. Then she saw the knife lying on the dirt. She grabbed her middle but there was no wound. The knife had passed through her. She was whole. She was safe. She turned to looked at Alley and share her amazement but they were standing on a city street and Alley was on the ground, bleeding through big holes in his chest. He handed her a bloody key. "Ba smard, Iiiirssss."

Iris started awake ten minutes before the New Age music clicked on, her heart pounding hard against her ribs. She wrestled with the damp sheet that shrouded her legs and sat up through dense layers. The clock read 4:25a.

"What day is it?" She had to think about it. "Work day. School day. Friday. Thank God."

She pawed through her closet, throwing discards onto the bed in a heap. Everything was either wrinkled or spotted. Nothing to wear. She had nothing to wear. She'd paced the floor last night until it was almost time to get up, mourning Alley, reviling Billy Drye, lecturing Teddy, and cursing John Somers for his hidden agenda. Seduced and betrayed. Screw him. Screw all of 'em. Every last one.

She pulled a pair of panty hose from the dirty clothes hamper, unballed them, and held them to her nose. They'd do. She rifled through her lingerie drawer and settled on a stretched-out, fraying bra. It was her statement. To hell with everyone.

Shower, coffee, lotion, deodorant, fragrance, clothes, hair, jewelry, shoes, jacket, purse, briefcase, pull-out stereo.

She grabbed the rest of her makeup, filled her commuter mug again, and grabbed the Rodeo Drive shopping bag with the cash and stock certificates. It was coming with her. It was like leaving Alley behind.

At 5:30, she pulled out the choke on the TR, stepped on the accelerator twice and turned the ignition key. The engine roared in the garage. She finished her makeup in the rearview mirror by flashlight, pulled the TR out five feet, and examined the pattern of its nightly excretions. There was a new plop of undetermined origin. Great. Just freaking great.

The radio announcer said there had been a 3.9 temblor during the night.

"Alley's dead, I have a pile of cash in a plastic bag, John Somers appears from never-never land, Los Angeles is falling into the ocean, and I'm going to work," she said to the TR.

At the mouth of the Ten, she floored the TR like there was no tomorrow. "Chris Columbus. It's you and me, babe."

At the office, individual concerns had been gray color-washed by quotidian routine. Jaynie showed a temp how to sort the mail. Joe Campbell read The Wall Street Journal in his office. Iris met his eye and her stomach did an adolescent somersault. The Boys' Club was clustered around Billy Drye, looking over his shoulder and snickering. Their voices dropped when they saw Iris.

"Morning boys," she said.

They nodded and pointed. A simple "good morning" didn't carry quite the right cachet.

Stan Raab pushed past Iris in the narrow corridor, putting his hand on her lower back as he walked by. "Hi, sweetheart."

"Morning, doll," she retorted.

Stan half turned, wondering if he'd heard correctly, then kept walking.

Teddy read a pink newspaper at his desk and didn't look up when Iris sat down. She threw her purse and the Rodeo Drive shopping bag in her lower left drawer and slammed the drawer hard.

Teddy's jaw tightened in his focused denial of her existence.

Iris persisted, her bad mood finding an outlet in a mean kid's taunt. She circled her palm on his shiny, bald pate. "Now I know it's going to be a good day."

"Knock it off."

"Teddy, sweetheart, baby cakes... so glum on a Friday morning?"

Teddy finally looked up at her.

"Cripes! What happened to you?"

Teddy's right eye and cheek were flowering in shades of red, black, and blue. "I ran into a door."

"It must have been wearing brass knuckles."

Teddy looked as if he might cry. "Iris, everything's out of control."

"Get the monkey off your back."

"Monkey? Shit. That's what I get for asking Ms. Straight Arrow. You don't understand. Forget it."

"Right."

Teddy ran a pen down the columns of the pink newspaper.

"Gonna buy some penny stocks from the pink sheets?"

"Yeah, so?" He sniffed and pulled at his nostrils.

"Okay. I guess we're not talking about pink sheets. Want to ride together to Alley's funeral tomorrow?"

"I'm not going."

"Why not?"

"Unsweet. I don't need to see a dead man."

"C'mon, Teddy. It's Alley's funeral."

"You don't give up, do you?"

"I'm in sales. I don't know how to take no for an answer."

"Isn't the man poison going?"

"I assume you're mean Jaynie? She's going to a wedding."

"Why? To tell them they're making a mistake?"

"Teddy, come with me."

"Iris, you're a pain in the ass."

"Yeah... What's your point?"

"All right. Fine. You win. I'll go."

"I'll pick you up tomorrow at ten."

Billy Drye walked past Iris's desk and dropped a Polaroid snapshot on it. It was Billy standing with his suit pants around his ankles, being given a blow job by a woman with long, dark hair. The woman was holding her hair away from her face to give the camera a clear view. A tense silence fell over The Boys' Club clustered in the cubicles behind her. There was money on this one.

Iris's face flushed red with anger and humiliation. She resisted the urge to grab scissors and cut the photo into a thousand pieces and then do the same thing to Drye's flesh. But she would not let him win.

She counted slowly to ten and regained a skittish control. She turned around and smiled big and disarmingly, then held her hand in front of her face with her thumb and forefinger measuring a two-inch length.

The group whooped and hooted. That Iris.

Billy Drye laughed too, an insincere good sport, and paid off those who had bet on Iris's moxie. He stopped laughing when Iris took a pair of scissors from her desk and snipped the photo in two, turning him into a eunuch with one clip. She dropped the pieces into her wastebasket.

"Hey!" Drye yelled, walking fast down the corridor and retrieving the two pieces. "That's mine."

"I thought it was a gift."

He fit the pieces together and glared at her.

She snipped the scissors together sharply three or four times. "Come into my parlor?"

The market opened.

"Albuquerque munis at ten and five points."

"Do a call at seventeen. It's going up."

"Make me a price on six month T-Bills. C'mon, you can do better than that. Look, shit for brains, get me a better deal. This is bullshit. How the hell do you expect me to sell this crap?"

"Dickhead, you wrote this order wrong, I said thirty-four and a half, not thirty-four and two points. Yeah, well, fuck you. You just cost the firm ten grand."

Iris scanned the names on the prospect list that she had prepared earlier in the week and flexed her dialing fingers.

"The cold call cowgirl rides again." She dialed the first number. "Hello. Is Jerry there?"

"Who's calling?"

"Iris."

"What does it concern?"

"It's personal."

She counted on the secretary figuring the guy was fooling around on his wife and putting her through without asking questions. Maybe the guy was single. Better yet.

"Hi, Jerry. You don't know me and I'm probably an intrusion right now but you're obviously a person with substantial net worth and business acumen and a person like you is busier making money than investing it. My business acumen is in turning money into more money."

"I don't have time for this."

"We're all busy, Jerry, but invest just a small amount of time with me. It'll be worth your while. I'm Iris Thorne from McKinney Alitzer and I have high-caliber credentials just like you. I also have an MBA from a top school and I've made a lot of money for busy business people like yourself."

"I have another call on hold."

"So do I, Jerry. That's why I'm only going to take five minutes of your time. Our time is valuable and so is the money we work so hard for. Jerry, you know that it's not what you earn but what you keep. My return averages about one hundred twenty-five percent. My firm has been involved in venture capital deals where the return was two hundred percent."

"I'm sure you're a nice lady, but I already have another broker."

"No doubt someone with your credentials does, but I bet your broker doesn't have the research department that McKinney Alitzer has. I can save you money on your taxes. Just let me know what your needs are and I'm sure I can satisfy them with McKinney Alitzer's diversity of products."

"Well, taxes are eating me alive."

Hooked him.

Teddy opened his fountain pen and ran it down the stock listings in the pink sheets.

"Aaron Enterprises, closing at two and a half cents. Accfnds, what's that, Accurate Funds? AcmeInc. They're kidding. The CEO is the Roadrunner, right? Closing at two. What a racket. Hello. Advanced Products, closed yesterday at a penny a share."

Teddy wrote a buy for five hundred thousand shares of Advanced Products for Salvatore Lambertini. Then he wrote a buy order for himself for five hundred thousand shares.

"Advanced Products. Nice name. Good name. What do you guys do for a living? With a name like that, I'd say you make something high-tech. Computer components. That's it."

Teddy spun his Rolodex and punched a telephone number into the phone dial. He ran his hand through his sparse hair as he waited for someone to answer.

"Sammy? Hi, it's Ted with McKinney Alitzer. So, how did the tables at the Four Queens treat you? No, I talked to Eddie for a couple hours. We're putting a deal together.

"Listen. I have something really hot. Advanced Products. It's a little firm that makes some sort of electrical components for personal computers. Yeah, right, electronic, not electric. What the fuck do I know about computers? I just know a good deal when I see one. They've just got a contract with IBM and they're going to be hot. The stock's undervalued at a penny a share. Of course it's legit. Sammy! This is Teddy! I can put you in one hundred thousand shares for a thousand bucks. You can paper your bedroom with the certificates. See, penny stocks only have to go up a penny in price to make some nice walking around money. No, you can't track it on Nasdaq. It's listed in something called the pink sheets. Let's write an order for two hundred thousand. That's my boy."

Teddy spun the Rolodex again.

"Bill? I've got something really hot but a little out of the ordinary for your personal account, but I know you're a risk-taker and know a bargain when you see one. Listen, consider a penny stock called Advanced Products. Yeah, I know there's been a lot of press on penny stocks. Here's the deal. Some sleazebag firms trade on stocks priced at a few cents a share, artificially creating a market and pushing up the price. With penny stocks, they can mark up the price one hundred percent, say from a penny to two cents, without the investor flinching.

"Then they hire this hungry sales force to sell the stuff to widows and orphans. Problem is, the widows and orphans buy product at a high price that they can't resell because the stock is worthless. In the meantime, the firm makes out and the sales turkeys make a commission on every transaction, buy or sell.

"But you know me. This isn't a boiler room. This is legit. If I hear about something, I naturally want to pass it on to my better clients. Could you handle two hundred thousand shares? One hundred thousand? Great." He hung up.

"Billyboy, don't worry. I won't stiff a friend."

Teddy drew a grid on a yellow pad and labeled the columns: Customer, Original Price, Trading Price, Customer Profit, and Commission.

In the Customer column, he listed: Salvatore Lambertini (Sally Lamb),Teddy Kraus, III, Sam Allen, Bill Zajack.

Next to their names, he listed the number of shares they bought and the price.

"Now, resell at a higher price. Create a market for this crap."

Teddy went to a back storeroom and opened a cabinet door. Telephone books for the greater part of the United States were piled on top of each other with the spines facing out. He pulled one out of the stack. "Let's see how this plays in Fresno." Back at his desk, he dialed one of the Fresno numbers.

"This is Teddy. Is Carl there please? Carl, I'm Teddy Kraus from McKinney Alitzer and I—"

Carl of Fresno hung up in Teddy's ear.

Teddy went to the next name. "Is this Mrs. Abel? This is Teddy Kraus from McKinney Alitzer. You don't know me and I'm sure you're very busy but my firm comes up with investment opportunities from time to time that are tailor made for people like you—"

Mrs. Abel said, "No, thank you," and hung up.

Teddy went to the next name. "... who want to get into the stock market but just don't know how and don't have a lot of money to risk. You are of course familiar with McKinney...

"... Alitzer? We're a full-line investment firm with seventy-five years of experience and an excellent track record. My personal credentials speak for themselves. You've seen the firm's ads? Good. Then you know who you're dealing with."

The A's weren't panning out. Teddy turned to the B's.

"I have a customer who just canceled a buy order for a stock called Advanced Products. It's already gone up in price and I can offer you part of the trade the other investor canceled but only if you act right away. Could you handle a hundred thousand shares? How about fifty thousand at two cents a share?

"Sammy. Hi. Teddy. I have a buy order for the two hundred thousand shares of Advanced Products you just bought at a penny for two cents. You just made two grand, buddy, sitting on your butt watching T.V. Isn't America great? Let's roll that over into another penny stock.

"Mr. Lystrum, just think, you could own a hundred thousand shares of stock for just two thousand dollars at four cents a share."

It was 12:00. "Bill, I can sell your hundred thousand for two cents."

Teddy filled in the grid on his yellow pad. Salvatore Lambertini. Buy five hundred thousand at one cent. Sell two hundred thousand at two cents. Two-thousand-dollar customer profit. Sell three hundred thousand at four cents. Nine-thousand-dollar customer profit. Same profit for Teddy plus the commission on the sales. Sammy's two-thousand-dollar profit rolls over into another stock. Bill takes out his thousand profit. Teddy tracked the buys and sells down the page.

The customers who bought early at a low price made money on the trades that Teddy made with others at a higher price. After he found buyers at four cents, Teddy stopped cold calling.

"Mr. Lystrum," Teddy said to himself, "lotsa luck finding a buyer for your hundred thousand shares of Advanced Products at four cents. Maybe you can find out what they do for a living."

Iris returned to her desk with a salad. "Lunch wagon's here. Aren't you eating?"

"Not hungry."

"What the hell have you been doing all morning?"

"Making the American dream real for a few at the expense of many."

"What?"

Teddy took the grid and put it into the top drawer of his desk. "Never mind." He put his jacket on and patted his inside pocket, feeling for the vial. "I'm going out for a few minutes. See ya, cowgirl."

Ten

Iris peeked over the short wall separating her cubicle from Teddy's and scanned his desk to see if she could figure out what he'd been doing. The marked-up pink sheets were folded in a corner. Other than that, his desk was clean. Teddy was exceptionally tidy for an excessive man.

She speared lettuce and tomato on her fork and dipped it in the ranch dressing she'd ordered on the side, putting a miserly coating on a small corner. She crunched on the salad and glanced around the office to see who was nearby.

Most of the sales reps were working through lunch. Billy Drye had his ear to a phone, a sycophant's grin on his face. Smile, they were taught, and you'll have a smile in your voice.

Iris opened the bottom drawer of her desk, pulled open the drawstring on the Rodeo Drive shopping bag, dug her hand around, and dragged out one of the EquiMex stock certificates. She glanced behind her again and put the certificate on her desk.

She tapped EquiMex into her terminal.

No response.

She tried EqiMx, EqMx, EqM, and EM.

Nothing.

She typed EquiM and jumped when her phone rang.

It was Stan Raab. "Iris, can I see you, please?"

She moved her salad on top of the stock certificate and walked to the corner office.

When she stood in the doorway, Stan got up from behind his desk and moved to one of the two matching antique chairs facing it. He gestured for her to take the other chair. This meant he either had something great to tell her or she was going to get blasted. Come from behind your desk, the textbook says. It removes the barrier between you and your employee. Use his or her name frequently, make eye contact, and periodically touch him or her on the arm or hand to convey sincerity.

Iris braced herself. She casually rested her hands in her lap without clasping them—too girlish—crossed her legs at the ankles, not at the knees—too floozyish—tucked her legs under the chair, sat straight, smiled benignly, and assumed the recommended posture and attitude of the executive woman, somewhere between shrinking violet and castrating bitch.

"Iris." Raab dropped his clasped hands between his knees, and leaned toward her on his elbows. "I had a complaint about you from Joe Murphy over at Birmingham Brothers."

"Oh?" She was going to get blasted.

"He thought you were unsympathetic the other day when you refused to cancel that deal."

"I'm a little confused Stan. I told Murphy what you told me to tell him."

"Iris, clearly there's a misunderstanding."

"You said the company doesn't make refunds."

"Iris, I said we have to evaluate each incident on a case-by-case basis. If we've made a mistake, it's our duty to right it. I said that refunds are not our policy but we have to consider this situation on its own merits. It's the only responsible way to run a business."

Iris's skin felt hot. She was blushing from anger but knew he would think she was embarrassed. A little voice told her to sit quietly. A more insistent voice egged her on.

"Stan, you said I wanted to give away the store. You said Murphy was a hothead and that everything would blow over in a few days." She crossed her arms over her chest and immediately uncrossed them. Too defensive.

The corner of Stan's left eye started to pulse.

Iris wished she'd listened to the little voice. Too late. She kept forgetting—honesty is not always the best policy.

"I should have been clearer in my communication." He touched her on the forearm. "I'll accept that as my mistake."

His eyes didn't leave hers. "Iris, you're an asset to the firm, but you need fine-tuning in handling difficult client situations. It's your Achilles' heel. You put your ego in front."

"All due respects, Stan, but I don't think that's true."

The eye pulsed. "With your ego out in front, you only hear what you want to hear. Like the guy who's putting in the Jacuzzi at my Tahoe house. I wanted the dark gray bottom but he insisted the white was better.

"So what does he do? Pours the white! He thought I said white. It was what he wanted to hear. He had to redo it in gray... at his expense, of course." Stan looked out the window. "Had to be at his expense. I've already spent a fortune." He turned back to her. "I see this as a growth opportunity, Iris, not as a problem."

She nodded. She'd try to redeem herself for the mistake she hadn't made by being cooperative. "What's our next step?"

"Well, we've canceled the deal, like we should have done in the first place. And"—he paused—"Murphy's asked for another sales rep. I'm giving him Billy Drye."

Iris nodded, her jaw tight. "Murphy's satisfied?"

"Yes. He's fine now."

"Whatever's best for the firm."

"I knew I could count on you to be a team player, to see the big picture." He stood. It was his signal the conversation was over.

She stood.

He rested his hand against her back and guided her to the door. "Everyone makes mistakes, Iris. The tragedy is not learning from them."

"I learn something new every day, Stan."

"That's the spirit."

Outside, she saw Billy Drye standing over her desk, browsing. He casually nudged the salad aside and looked at the EquiMex stock certificate underneath.

Iris turned back to Stan even though she wanted to run out and wring Drye's neck.

"You've come a long way since you came aboard, Iris. I'm proud of you." He gave her a sincere-looking smile and extended his hand.

She shook it firmly. "Thanks Stan."

"Say… Drye says you know one of the detectives who were here yesterday."

"Did he?"

"The tall one. John Somers?"

"We went to college together. Small world."

"Sure is. Did you have a chance to catch up on old times?"

"We chatted for a while."

"Did you?" He looked at her meaningfully and said nothing.

This was her cue to spill her guts. She knew the technique. He had taught her. Simply stop talking. People can't stand silence in a conversation and will chatter to fill the uncomfortable void. Stan loved gossip. He was always trying to pry into her personal affairs and dish the office dirt with her. She'd throw him a bone every once in a while, but she wouldn't give him that satisfaction today. Information is power. She was holding hers. Three long seconds passed. She met his stare, smiled sweetly, and batted her baby blues.

He broke the silence. "Let's hope they find out who did that hideous thing to Alley."

She left Stan's office in time to see Drye casually slide the salad back where she had left it and cruise into the lunchroom. She passed her desk, scooped up the salad, slid the certificate into a drawer, and walked in after him. Drye, Joe Campbell, and a few other sales reps were looking at a newspaper that was spread on a table.

"Iris, seems like I was right about your boy," Drye said. "Listen to this: 'Local Man Murdered on Street in Broad Daylight. North Hollywood resident Alejandro Muñoz, twenty-two, was stabbed yesterday in view of dozens of witnesses on Lankershim Boulevard near Burbank Boulevard as he walked home from work at about five o'clock Wednesday evening.' They describe the murder, blah, blah, blah, 'Mr. Muñoz was an employee of McKinney Alitzer, the investment services firm, at their downtown Los Angeles offices...' blah, blah... here we go... 'The police currently do not have any suspects. One of the investigators on the case, Detective John Somers'"—Drye looked up at Iris meaningfully—"'would not discount the possibility that the murder was gang- or drug-related.'"

"Bastard," Iris said. "One Mexican kills another and the police assume it's gangs or drugs."

"Sounds like a clear-thinking individual," Drye said, "your buddy the cop."

Iris blushed.

Drye opened the door to leave.

"Drye? Let me know if I can help you find anything."

"What are you talking about?"

"You know what I'm talking about."

"I wasn't looking at anything on your desk. I was just walking by."

"Then how do you know what I'm talking about?"

Drye's face reddened. The group laughed and started to file out, pushing Drye in front of them. He stuck his head back in the doorway.

"Iris. Sorry about Joe Murphy. Raab says he's confident I'll be able to turn your mess around."

"Screw you."

"Promises, promises." He closed the door.

Joe Campbell was still in the room, pouring coffee into a mug.

Iris met his eyes, then looked down at the newspaper.

"Those guys really give you a hard time, don't they?"

She looked up at him. "Yeah. It's mostly Drye, but the others don't discourage him. It's a herding instinct."

"You handle it well. It's a tough situation."

"Thanks. I have to be on my game all the time." She sighed at the newspaper. "All everyone's done since Alley's murder is Alley bashing. Stupid cops. Gangs and drugs weren't Alley." She dropped the newspaper. "At least it's Friday."

"It's been a tough week."

"Tell me about it. On top of everything else, Stan just read me the riot act and took away one of my accounts and gave it to Drye. I don't get Stan. Sometimes I think we're communicating and other times I feel like we're on different planets. I think I'm doing what he wants me to do, then he changes the rules."

"I'm sure he hated to take your account away."

"I just did what he told me to do."

"Maybe a difference in interpretation?"

"That's what he says. Why am I telling you this?"

"It won't leave the room. I've known Stan a long time and I know he comes off wrong sometimes, so I feel an obligation to put in my two cents about him whenever I can. He's really a great guy. He's always spoken highly of you."

"You knew him before McKinney?"

"We met at Dartmouth. Two L.A. boys in New Hampshire. We kept contact through the years and when Stan moved to McKinney, he recruited me from my other firm."

"Nice."

There was an awkward moment of silence when they just looked at each other. She thought he looked tired.

"Don't worry." He gave her a big smile that she thought was forced. "Everything's going to turn out fine. Have a good day." He left the lunchroom.

"Who was that masked man?" she said to no one.

She left the lunchroom and spun through the doorway of Jaynie's office, the plastic salad container still in her hand, and sat on one of the chairs facing Jaynie's desk.

"Hi, I. How's your day going?" Jaynie asked.

Iris moved some of the papers scattered across Jaynie's desk to clear a space for the salad.

"You know what? Bucks-up probably told the Jacuzzi guy to pour white and forgot about it. Either that or he's believing his own bullshit."

"What are you talking about?" Jaynie rearranged the papers that Iris had moved. "Put this back. If something isn't sitting right in front of me, I forget about it. You mean Stan?"

"Yep. He hung me out to dry for carrying out a decision of his that backfired."

"Does it involve Joe Murphy from Birmingham Brothers?"

"Yeah, why?"

"Murphy called here wanting to know the phone number of the head of the division."

"I knew it. Stan's boss came down on him and he offered me as the sacrificial lamb. No wonder that eye was twitching. If I were Stan, I would have admitted I made a mistake."

Jaynie shrugged. "Put yourself in his shoes. Maybe it's more important for him to save face. He is the boss."

"You and Joe Campbell. He was in the lunchroom telling me what a great guy Stan is. I don't know. I might have done the same thing in Stan's position."

"Did you put your makeup on in the car again? C'mere."

Iris leaned across the desk and Jaynie thumbed a peach-colored gash on Iris's cheek. "You actually had a conversation with G.Q. Joe?"

"He's nice. After you get past that aloofness and"—Iris sighed—"that face and that body and those eyes and... You mean I stood there and talked to him with screwed-up makeup?"

"Is the office rumor mill going to start churning?"

"It's already whirling like a dervish. Drye saw me talking with that cop, John Somers, last night—"

"The tall one? He's cute."

"Yeah... well... he doesn't seem too cute to me today. He and I had this... thing... in college and he wasn't exactly discreet in front of Drye. Even Stan asked me about it today. I guess it's all over the office by now."

"Why am I always the last to know? So what happened?"

"We were pretty involved. Then he dumped me, and I didn't even know it. In college, I spent a year studying in Europe. He couldn't go because his grades weren't good enough. So, I didn't hear from him for a while. Then my girlfriend writes me... he'd dropped out of school, moved away, and *married* someone else."

"Wow."

"I'd figured he just wasn't a letter writer." Iris laughed without amusement. "So, he shows up here last night. I hadn't seen him for years. Told me he knew I worked here... been keeping tabs on me."

"I knew no one had sent him an employee roster," Jaynie said.

"He used Alley's murder as an excuse to reopen a dialogue with me. My friend's dead, right? Then I read in the paper that he said Alley was involved in gangs or drugs."

"That doesn't sound like Alley."

"That's what I would have told him last night if he wasn't so busy putting the make on me that he forgot about Alley. We went out to eat and I walked out on him, I was so pissed off."

"You sound kinda hostile."

"Hostile? I'm not hostile."

"Not much. He seemed like a nice guy."

"My ass."

"There are two sides to every story. Maybe he thought you weren't coming back from Europe. Maybe he felt he wasn't smart enough for you."

"There's only one side to this story. He's a jerk. And I don't want him in my life."

"Is he still married?"

"No. It was all for nothing."

"That's how he might feel. It's shattering when a marriage breaks up. It was for me. He was probably embarrassed to tell you about it. He might feel he made the wrong decision about you. C'mon, Iris. You were kids then."

"Don't make me feel sympathetic toward him."

"Eat yourself up. I don't care. He seemed like a nice, genuine person. Throw him my way if you don't want him."

"I had some information about Alley, too. Then when he acted like such a jerk, I changed my mind about telling him. After that thing in the paper today, I can't risk trusting him. He'd just use it to crucify Alley."

"What information?"

"Probably nothing. I haven't figured it out yet."

"You should tell the police, whatever it is."

"Not now. Not after what they said in the paper."

"I guess you know what you're doing."

"Not really, but I'm doing it, anyway. So, what's going on this weekend? Going out with that guy again?"

"Michael… third date."

"Uh-oh. The Third Date. Fuck him or forget him," Iris taunted.

"Cynic."

"Realist. So… ?"

"So, what?"

"Are you?"

"I don't know. I'm gun-shy after Teddy. He called again last night. Late. I think he was high."

"Probably."

"He starts out slow. Tells me how much he loves me, maybe we can get together again, and so on. Then he escalates. Calls me a bitch and a whore. Tells me I'll be sorry."

"He threatened you? He's basically a nice guy but it's getting harder to care about him."

"I hate looking over my shoulder. I feel like I make one error in judgment and it's going to haunt me my whole life. So, what are you doing this weekend?"

"Going to a party with Steve tonight."

"That's still going on?"

"It's still going on. Why?"

"He's a noncommittal womanizer."

"He's cute and laughs at my jokes and listens to me and isn't judgmental and we have great sex."

"You sound like you're trying to convince yourself."

"You sound like my mother."

"You deserve more."

"Probably. He's like junk food, I guess. I gotta get back. See ya." Iris chucked the half-eaten salad in Jaynie's trash and walked back toward the sales department. The administrative area was quiet at lunchtime. She walked past the empty photocopy and fax room, then wheeled around and started walking toward the other end of the suite, toward the supply room, toward Alley's desk. It seemed natural to visit Alley. It seemed odd that he wouldn't be there, filling out his supply orders, keeping everything neat and straight, chastising people who pulled out a ream of paper or legal pads and left the neat stacks unaligned, or took too many pens, rationing them, taking them out of folks' hands, taking his job very seriously, sitting at his desk, eating the burrito his mother had made for him and that he'd warmed in the microwave, watching the numbers count down on the dial, since he couldn't hear the buzzer, reading one of his self-help books while he ate, turning and smiling up at Iris when she walked in and put her hands on his shoulders to announce herself, swatting at his mouth with a napkin held in his bad hand and smoothing his tie with the other.

Alley wasn't going to be in the supply room. Iris wanted to look at his empty desk and know what it was like for him to be dead.

The supply room lights were on. She walked closer and stopped dead when she heard her name from inside. A chill went down her back. She remembered the dream and considered with dread that Alley might haunt her, that he might be a ghost and she got angry. He'd already given her too much to think about. On the other hand, ever practical, maybe she could ask him what he expected her to do with the safe-deposit box.

She heard her name again. She stopped outside the door and flattened her back against the wall. It wasn't a ghost. It was Stan Raab, speaking quietly.

"... relationship with Drye and I hated to do it, but Drye's my other top person."

"I just saw Iris in the lunchroom. I told her I'd keep our conversation confidential, but…"

Thanks, Joe, Iris said to herself.

"… she'd just left her meeting with you and was pretty upset. Drye had made some crack about it."

"I'd hoped I could avoid that," Stan said. "That Drye… if his numbers weren't so good."

"Anyway, I told her that you'd always spoken highly of her and that you were doing what you had to do to please the client."

"Was she better?"

"She understands. She has a lot of savvy. We're lucky to have her."

You're back to being a good guy, Joe.

"Joe, you know I value your input. I couldn't run this place if you weren't here with me, if I didn't have one person I could trust implicitly."

"A lot of water under the bridge, Stan."

"Sure is. I don't see anything here."

"What do you think he meant by this on his calendar, this wacatil… O-A-X… ?"

"Who knows? Joe, I've been thinking. Maybe we should let the police in on Worldco."

"C'mon, Stan. We'd both go to jail."

"They wouldn't have to know the details. We could just say that Alley manipulated a client's funds. It would make their job easier."

"Can't do it, Stan. It can't go any further than you."

"It never has. It's just that I feel responsible about Worldco, Joe. My mailroom clerk embezzled ten million dollars from my best friend's father, who's also one of the firm's best clients. On my fax machine! Let's get out of here."

Iris walked as fast as she could back to her desk, her heart pounding. She picked up the phone, punched in the number of the next person on her prospect list, and turned to watch Teddy hard-sell penny stocks to strangers.

Eleven

Madonna or whore? Whore. Definitely. It had been the kind of week that cried out for something saucy, something different, something to help her drop the work week like a dead skin. Something to let her forget herself. Steve would like it.

The freeway condition sign reported heavy traffic. Iris knew this. She drove with one eye on the TR's temperature gauge. The needle had passed the midpoint and was two-thirds to "H." One more tick and she'd take the surface streets. It wouldn't be any faster, but she'd get some speed up and pull air through the radiator, cooling the engine down. The TR hated traffic.

"There's T.M.C. on the freeways today, folks," the radio announcer said. "Too Many Cars. It's a parking lot on the One-thirty-four near Figueroa. A brush fire on the hillside has jumped the center divider…"

An older Buick splashed with gray primer was in the lane next to Iris. Its windows were tinted black and rolled all the way up. It casually drifted across the dashed white line into her lane. She held her ground but the small hairs on the back of her neck stood up. She was in the line of fire. A target.

Relax, she told herself. *They couldn't escape in this traffic without a helicopter.* Then she thought, *What if they don't want to escape? What if the driver has a suicide note in his pocket?*

"A trailer hauling barbecue sauce dumped its load on the Five past Slauson. Traffic's tied up for ten miles in both directions. A load of chickens was lost on the Six-oh-five between Rosecrans and Alondra. Now, all we need are some briquettes."

A Mercedes convertible with the top down, its tanned, balding driver talking on a cellular phone, his big gold watch reflecting the sun, moved out from behind the TR and sped up to slide in front, a breath away from the TR's bumper, making the Los Angeles drive-right-or-fuck-you statement in response to Iris's not tailgating. He gained one car length.

She yelled, "What's your hurry, asshole? Reservations aren't until eight-thirty," but he didn't hear her.

A pick-up truck that was behind the Mercedes, sitting high above the asphalt on balloon tires three feet in diameter, a decorative roll-bar behind the cab, rushed to close the gap the Mercedes had left. Its polished chrome bumper obliterated the TR's rear window. The bass from the truck's stereo moved the earth.

"Cocky bastard," Iris muttered. "I'll slam on my brakes. Explain *that* to your insurance company, if you have insurance."

She punched the button for the New Age station, watched the temperature gauge, and tried to rise above.

A man on a motorcycle wove through the stagnant traffic. White letters were stenciled on the back of his leather jacket: DO U KNOW JESUS?

No. What kind of car does he drive?

At the mall, Iris wandered slowly, window-shopping and eating a frozen yogurt. A woman behind her walked close enough to brush Iris's skirt with her packages. Iris abruptly stopped walking and the woman crashed into her with a crumple of shopping bags. She skirted around Iris without looking at her or apologizing. Iris smiled. It was a small amount of control, but she'd take it.

She bought a black leather bomber jacket with silver zippers and grommets and a matching thigh-high miniskirt after gasping at the price then deciding she had to have it, couldn't live without it. She bought a black merry widow and G-string set and black stockings with dots and a jogging bra in the lingerie department, squirming when she handed her selections to the sales clerk, who was about her mother's age.

At home, Iris threw the bags onto the raw silk couch and opened the sliding glass door. The sea air blew in. There were two messages on her phone machine. One from Steve, confirming that he'd meet her at Josh's house. One from her mother, checking in.

Iris poured a glass of white wine and finished half of it before she felt up to returning her mother's call. She took the cordless phone onto the terrace.

"Hi, Mom. Nothing's wrong. You called me, remember? Guess who I ran into? Remember John Somers? On the street."

She didn't tell her mother about the murder. Even though it had happened to someone else somewhere else and had nothing to do with her, her mother would worry about Iris's brush with violence, would worry that Iris was next, would worry every time Iris went to work. Would worry.

"He's a cop. Isn't that a scream? He was not a hippie, Mom. He's divorced. That's ancient history. People don't change that much. To a party with Steve at his friend's house. Steve *has* a job. Nothing's wrong. How can I sound worried? Everything's fine. I just had a long week, okay? I gotta go. Okay? Me too."

She refilled her glass and paced the living room. The taste of the wine hardly mattered anymore. She drank expensive chardonnays and jug Chablis with the same mindlessness. All she tasted was the cool bite on her tongue while she waited for the tension to be released.

She walked out onto the terrace and looked at the sun sparkling on the ocean. She dug her finger around in a clay pot on the terrace wall where an anemic philodendron lived, its leaves coated with small, black particles that fell out from the smog. She splashed some wine into the pot and told herself to water it later. Then she forgot about it.

She went inside, opened the shopping bags, and displayed her purchases on the Oriental rug that covered the hardwood floor. She plopped into the leather recliner, sat for two seconds, then got up and started to pace the room again.

She ran water in the bathtub and squirted liquid bubble bath where the water hit the porcelain. She covered herself with bubbles, sipped wine, read her horoscope in *Cosmo*, and finally started to relax. She read the column where people write in for help with their problems. She was better off than those people, she told herself. Most of them just lack the gumption to get what they want in life, to ask for what they need, to raise their hand. Not Iris. She had set her goals and worked hard to achieve them. She had got just what she wanted. She was just where she wanted to be.

She pulled into the driveway of Josh's Pacific Palisades home at about 9:45, shooting for fashionably late but still too early, judging by the availability of street parking. She pulled down her leather mini and bomber jacket and fluffed her workday hair that she had moussed and pulled into a wild mane. She opened the door and walked confidently into the house, copping the distant, jaded attitude of Los Angeles's night-crawling hipsters and trendzoids. The other people there casually looked at her, but not too long, not wanting to seem too interested. She looked for a familiar face and didn't find one.

She walked into a bedroom where everyone was throwing jackets and purses and stashed her slim shoulder bag between the mattress and box springs. She located the bar and poured a glass of white wine and finally saw Steve through the French doors, standing on a flagstone terrace that overlooked the undeveloped Santa Monica Mountains and the ocean.

A petite brunette was talking to him. She was wearing flowing harem pants that were wrapped around her legs somehow so that the wind that always blew off the ocean through the canyon lifted the fabric, revealing leg almost to her waist. The wind pressed the thin fabric of her blouse against her braless breasts, which Iris could tell at a distance of thirty feet were bigger than hers. The girl caressed Steve's cheek with her palm.

Iris stood in the doorway, wondering whether she should approach him or disappear, wondering whether Steve had said, "Come to the party with me" or "Come to the party," wondering whether she was his date or just another guest.

"Well, *Ms.* Thorne," Steve smiled at her, his hazel eyes sparkling.

He was leaning against the wooden terrace railing, wearing faded Levi's, a faded polo shirt, and weathered deck shoes with no socks. The thinned fabric of the worn clothing lay close against his body, which was tan-on-tan and muscular from outdoor work. His sun-bleached hair was freshly brushed, the front cut short and the back falling to his shoulders. A dangling silver-and-turquoise earring sparkled against his tan skin.

She walked toward him, like an arrow, just like she had done the first time she had seen him at another party six months before, forgetting the other femme, forgetting all. He circled his arm around her waist and kissed her on the lips. The brunette mumbled something and excused herself.

"*Ms.* Thorne, you look delicious." He nuzzled her neck, tickling her. She twisted in his arms, giggling wildly. He wrapped his arms around her ribs and squeezed tighter and tighter while she gritted her teeth and tried not to make a sound but ended up forcing out a mouse squeak. He laughed and rhythmically squeezed her again and again. She squeaked and he laughed. Their game. It was silly and made her feel giddy, as if she was thirteen and holding hands with her first beau. She laughed until tears popped into her eyes. It felt good.

"How was your week?" he asked.

She shook her head and shrugged and waved her hand toward the railing, pushing it out to sea.

"Look at these stockings." He crouched beside her and picked at the dots with his fingers. "Very nice." He ran his hands up and down her legs then stood up again and pulled her close.

His skin smelled of lemon-scented soap. The fibers of his clothes were puffy and soft and smelled freshly laundered.

She put her nose against his neck and guzzled his scent. She ran her fingers through his soft, fine hair and down and across his neck and shoulders, squeezing the lean muscles. She wished she were alone with him. She wanted him to tickle her and make her laugh and look at her the way that he did, both knowing and appreciative, the look that she couldn't get enough of, that made her stomach spin around.

A dry Santa Ana breeze blew. Iris felt it suck the moisture out of her face. She stood in the crook of Steve's shoulder and they faced the canyon and listened to the darkness. A coyote yipped somewhere on the hillside. Steve yipped back at it. The coyote answered. He laughed.

"I should greet the other guests," he said. "I'm supposed to be the co-host."

He didn't ask so she didn't ask to go with him. She leaned against the railing and watched him walk up to a group of people who put their arms around him. Everyone wanted to touch him.

Crickets chirped. The wind rustled dry weeds on the hillside and Iris felt unconnected. She gathered herself. She looked great. She would have a good time.

The bass on the stereo was turned up and the down beat pounded through the house. Iris refilled her glass. She was drunk enough to feel reckless enough to talk to strangers face-to-face, without a telephone in between. She roamed through the house, bouncing her shoulders with the music.

"I was, like, I'm so sure. He had, like, a new Beemer, you know? But he was, like, a major geek. Totally DD," a girl said to her friend. She wore a black bra top studded with silver grommets and a black nylon net skirt over black lace leggings. Her crimped hair was wrapped with a floppy bow on the side of her head.

Her girlfriend wore a black bra with black fringe dangling from the middle and tight black toreador pants laced together at the sides that let tanning-salon skin peek through all the way up and a Spanish-style broad-brimmed black hat with little balls dangling from the brim. "Ohmygod, DD—doesn't dress, doesn't dance," she said. "I'm so sure. Tell him to get real. Get, like, a life."

Iris wandered into the kitchen and stood near four men wearing earth-toned Levi's Dockers, open-necked cotton shirts with the sleeves rolled up, short haircuts with sideburns clipped even with their ears, and spreading hips.

"The One-eighteen was beautiful today. Took me twenty-five minutes."

"Yeah? The One-oh-one was easy too. Only took half an hour instead of an hour and a half."

"Well, the Four-oh-five was, you know, the Four-oh-five. A couch fell off a truck. Two hours to get from the Valley to Manhattan Beach."

Everyone grimaced.

One guy said, "Yeah, Four-oh-five means it'll take you four or five hours to get there."

They all cracked up.

"I go the back road, the Four-oh-five to the One-oh-one to the One-thirty-four to the Two-ten to the Six-oh-five to the Ninety-one. I used to go the Four-oh-five to the One-oh-one to the One-eleven to the Ninety-one…"

"Right through downtown. Brother."

"Really. I save half an hour this way."

"The Ten's open every day for me," Iris said brightly.

They turned to look at her dispassionately although she'd been standing on the edge of their circle for several minutes.

"I take it at five-thirty in the morning," she said, picking up her own bait.

"Five-thirty?" Four-oh-five said. "Wait, you're in the financial markets, right?"

"With McKinney Alitzer."

He smiled and nodded, punctuating his insight. "So, you're there when the market opens."

"Yeah. It's a bear getting up, but the traffic's great."

"Anyway," Four-oh-five continued, "what amazes me about this town is how everyone has to stop to look at a ladder that fell off a truck."

"Where are you from?" One-eighteen asked.

"Chicago. You?" "New York."

"I'm from New Orleans."

"I'm from L.A.," Iris said.

They looked at her as if she'd said she was from Mars.

"New Orleans?" One-eighteen said. "Great town…"

Iris drifted into the dining room where she picked at a plate of cubed cheese and raw vegetables on the table and wondered if the men had noticed she'd left.

"My agent told me to get the gray out, that it made me look old," said a guy wearing a black T-shirt, a rumpled black linen jacket, stone-washed black jeans with too-long legs crumpled on top of heavy black cowboy boots, and a black belt studded with silver grommets. "So I dye it, right? And I get called in on an audition for a commercial and they say, 'Your hair's different.' They'd looked at the old head shots and wanted a graying executive type. I lost the gig."

A statuesque woman, wearing a black off-the-shoulder cocktail dress, dramatic eye makeup, and fuchsia lipstick on voluptuous lips, her hair auburn and cut in a smooth Dutch-boy bob, said, "One told me to go darker. One even told me to go blond. Like, I'm really the blond type, right? They don't even know what's selling." She munched on an undressed carrot stick. "So… you been working?"

The master bedroom was crowded with women in line for the bathroom. Two women and a man pushed their way out of the bathroom together, giggling. "Have any left?" someone in the crowd asked.

Three girls jockeyed for position in front of a mirror hanging over a chest of drawers, passing around a can of hairspray, bending their heads over their knees, back brushing their hair and ratting it with combs until it was matted and pasted into halos two feet in diameter.

Iris looked at herself in the mirror. She noticed how much older she looked than these girls. Like Blanche DuBois, she was grateful for the dim light.

"So, he's putting me in a music video he's doing next week." She was buxom, wearing a loose-necked gold lamé top that teased open when she leaned forward and a skintight mini that barely covered her cheeks.

"For real? How cool." She was wearing a sixties retro op art go-go dress with an open midriff that was attached to the dress's bottom half with big gold rings all around. She wore hot pink thigh-high vinyl boots, neon blue stockings, and double rows of false eyelashes with little ones painted on with eye liner underneath. A Twiggy homage.

Iris pulled up her skirt to adjust her stockings and the girl in the gold lamé crept her skirt up to her waist with hot pink porcelain-tipped nails, revealing the merry widow underneath. She wasn't wearing the G-string that came with the set.

"Look, I have the same one," she said. "Isn't it cool?"

In the living room, Iris leaned next to the fireplace where a fire was crackling against the August chill that blew off the ocean. It was probably down to a chilly sixty-eight degrees outside. People were dancing in a glass-walled room off the living room. She thought she saw Steve's shirt bouncing in there. A man wearing baggy khaki pants and a loose white shirt, his hair cut short, was also standing by the fireplace. He was friendly.

"Know anyone here?" he asked her.

"Just Josh and the co-host, Steve."

"I just know Josh. Great house, huh?"

"He bought it after he got a part as a regular on that sitcom," Iris said.

"Who's Steve?"

"He's around here somewhere. I think he's dancing."

"Is he an actor too?"

"Yeah, but he mostly gives sailing lessons and does maintenance for a sailing school in Marina del Rey."

"Seems like everyone here is an actor or a writer but they do something else in real life."

"Really." Iris was relieved to have found someone to talk to. "Do you have a real job?"

"I'm Josh's stockbroker."

"Who do you work for?"

"Burns Fenner Smith."

"I have the high net value accounts for McKinney Alitzer."

"McKinney Alitzer. I know some people there. Warren Gray?"

"Sure."

"Billy Drye?"

"Oh, yeah."

"Billy makes himself known, doesn't he?"

They both laughed.

"Say, didn't I hear that some guy who works in your office got murdered last week?"

"Yeah."

"Did you know him?"

"Slightly."

"Wow. That's pretty weird. What happened?"

"I'm sorry, I see someone I know. Excuse me. Nice chatting with you."

"Have some pie," John Somers said. A wedge of hot apple pie sat in a puddle of vanilla ice cream on a plate in front of him.

"I'll just have coffee," Paul Lewin said. "My wife has me on a diet. Oatmeal and nonfat milk and crap. My cholesterol's two fifty-three. What's yours?"

"I don't know."

"Unwedded bliss."

"Did you read the coroner's report?"

"Yeah."

"Changes things, don't you think?" Somers ate forkful of pie.

"It's weird, but I'm not sure it changes things."

"The weapon made small, round entrance wounds and punctures five inches deep. Like an ice pick. Not a homeboy's weapon of choice."

"I'm still holding to a gang initiation. I want to question Flaco and the Cirrus Street boys."

"It wasn't a local," Somers said. "Witnesses are afraid to come forward, but my longtime informant in that neighborhood told me that word is, everybody got a good look at the killer and no one recognized him."

"How do you see it?"

"A hit."

"Mafia-style? That's not their M.O.," Lewin said. "Alley Muñoz? What for?"

"Maybe he saw something or knew something."

"Stop complicating my life," Lewin said.

"Then why did our guy use an ice pick?"

"It was handy."

"If it was a homeboy, why didn't he use a gun?"

"He hocked it."

"Or a knife?" Somers said.

"I don't know, Professor. You're giving these guys too much credit. They don't think this stuff through."

"Think about it. A handgun leaves bullets behind. You might as well leave fingerprints. But you can stab him and be halfway down the street before anyone realizes he's been stuck. You gotta be precise with a knife, but our boy made sure he got close enough. But what if the knife blade bends? Or breaks on a rib? An ice pick is sturdy. Innocuous. Just clean it off and put it back in your neighbor's garage. The guy is smart. A disguised murder-for-hire, in full day. A street gang doesn't disguise a murder. It's public relations."

"You're thinking too hard. A *vato* wants in the gang. The boys give him a job. Done."

"But he didn't make any mistakes."

"He got lucky."

"But he wasn't from the neighborhood," Somers said.

"Maybe the witnesses know your informant talks to the cops. The witnesses are covering up. They think it'll happen to them next."

"I don't think so," Somers said.

"Why not?"

"Just doesn't feel right."

"You and your feelings again. Just follow the evidence, Professor."

Somers finished his pie and ice cream. "The wake's going on right now. Should we go over there?"

"The funeral will be enough. They'll be a better turn out. The wake's family and close friends. Give them their privacy."

"I'm gonna re-canvass the neighborhood."

"It's been done. Rodriguez and me. We got it all when you were busy with your daughter."

"I want to have a look myself."

"Go ahead," Lewin said. "Say it was a hit. Who'd want this guy dead?"

"I don't know. Maybe he had a secret. We don't know enough about him. Change of heart?"

"I'm not dropping the gang angle, but I think the hit idea's worth a pass-through. Alley was a fly on the wall. Maybe he saw something he wasn't supposed to. What did that Iris Thorne chick have to say?"

"Not much."

"What did you ask her?"

"The usual."

"Like what?"

Somers bristled. "When was the last time she saw him, what did she say, what did he say, how did he act, did he have any enemies, was anything different the past few days. The usual. Okay?"

"And what did she say?"

"Nothing"—he shrugged—"nothing significant."

"You didn't question her."

"I did."

"So?"

"So? So nothing. Oh, hell. We caught up on old times and it got late."

"You caught up on old times? What kind of old times did we have?"

"It was a long time ago, all right? Ancient history."

"But you dug it up."

"What's your point?"

"You gonna interview her for real or dick around?"

"Why the focus on her? Eighty people work in that office."

"She was Alley's buddy in that office. I'll talk to her," Lewin said. "Since your personal relationship with her is interfering with your ability to do your job."

"I'll talk to her."

"When?"

"Tomorrow."

"At the funeral?"

"Ease up. I'll talk to her, all right?"

"All right."

"I can keep my professional distance."

"No problema, Shamus."

"I'll talk to her."

"That's what you said. I'll be waiting for your report."

Iris wandered back into the kitchen, where the four men were now beating up sports. She leaned in the doorway with her back to them, facing a mirror hung on the wall of a entryway. She admired the carved wood frame and was speculating about how much an actor on a sitcom could pull down when she caught her reflection in the dim light. Slender, patrician, expensively dressed and coiffed. Apparently confident. It was definitely her.

She met her eyes and they teared up. Can count friends on one hand. The through-thick-and-thin type. Now, there's one less. She felt she hadn't been a good enough friend to Alley and spun a swirl of remorse. Like that envelope. She'd figured it was nothing and had forgotten about it. She'd discounted Alley, too. Little Alley. Even though he'd helped her in the past. Gave her information that kept her from making a stupid mistake.

Iris watched the party goings on behind her in the mirror. She could still do right by Alley. He'd told her that things weren't what they seemed. The best thing she could do for him was to believe that. No one else did. She could repay Alley's favor. Make it square. She wouldn't be able to live with herself otherwise. She looked away from the mirror and counted to ten and found the familiar, practiced control. She decided to get another glass of wine.

A woman wearing a floppy hat, a flowing Indian-print silk dress, and two chiffon scarves draped around her neck breezed through the front door, trailed patchouli past Iris, and swooshed into the living room. People turned to look at her. She held her head high and smiled. She was lush-figured and pretty. The woman lasciviously looked around the room, taking everything in.

"Bernice!" Josh suddenly appeared, TV handsome and polished, and gave her a wet smack on the lips, which Bernice returned along with a firm hug.

Steve was next. Bernice kissed him on the lips while cupping his rear end. Everyone laughed. She was the type of gal who could get away with it.

Steve laughed too, and pulled on her scarves. Bernice cooed something in his ear.

Iris shook her head as she considered Steve's extensive tastes in women. Definitely a man for all seasons. She slipped through the kitchen and down the hall and found an empty back bedroom. She closed the door and sat on the bed. She found issues of *Golf* magazine and thumbed through them. She decided to go home.

"There you are!" Steve walked toward her in the hallway. "Where have you been?"

"Around. Where have *you* been?"

"I've been neglecting you. I'm sorry. There's a lot of people here I know."

"Seems like you know Bernice well."

"Oh… That's just Bernice. I've known her forever." He tickled her stomach with his forefinger. "I've been thinking about you all week."

"No, you haven't."

"I have too. I missed you."

"You missed having sex with me."

"I missed *you*." He tickled her harder.

She grabbed his hand and moved it out of her space. "I'm going. Then you can talk to your friends without worrying about me."

"Iris. Stay. We'll leave soon. What's wrong? You've been really quiet."

"You and my mother. Nothing's wrong. I'm just tired."

"Tired?" Steve flipped the bedroom door closed and backed Iris against it. "I know just the thing."

He kissed her, pressing his pelvis against her. He slid his hands up her thighs, beneath her skirt, feeling the garters of the corset.

"Ms. Thorne, what have we here?"

He dropped to his knees and slid her skirt up over her thighs.

"Ooohh. I like it."

He pulled at the G-string with his teeth, moving the fabric from between her legs. She slid down so that her legs fell open.

He probed with his tongue, slid his hands behind her, and grabbed her butt. She grabbed two handfuls of his hair and went with it. She was water. She was earth. She was heading toward the carpet.

Someone turned the doorknob.

Iris caught her breath.

There was knocking. "Is someone in there?"

"Yes," Steve said.

"We have to get our stuff to go home."

"Okay."

Panting, Iris pulled down her skirt. Steve gave her a long kiss, smearing her lipstick on his face and hers. They opened the door and a man and woman came in, sensing the charged atmosphere, and went straight to the closet with eyes averted.

Steve gave Iris a wicked smile.

She walked in front of him down the hallway. She knew he was watching her hips move in the snug leather mini. He walked close behind her and let his hand rest against her hip, his hand riding with the motion of her walk.

"One more hour," he said. "Then we'll go."

"Okay," Iris said, wondering why she was such a fool. *Addicted to junk food.*

When they got to the living room, Josh handed Steve a guitar. Bernice was going to sing. Josh sat on the floor behind an electronic keyboard on the coffee table, facing the fireplace. Steve sat on the couch with the guitar. The big-boobed brunette with the harem pants rushed to squeeze beside him.

Iris leaned against the wall and thought about her own scent now on Steve.

The electronic keyboard rang shallowly through the house and Bernice started to sing a campfire song in a large, cabaret voice, giving the old ditty a racy interpretation. She got everyone to join in on the lively refrain. Iris sang too, not wanting to, but not wanting to look like a stiff. At the end of the song, someone requested the theme song from a current movie and Bernice faked most of the lyrics, making the group laugh. She knew how to work the crowd. Then came something soulful that made chills run up and down Iris's spine and Iris hated her for it, hated Bernice for her voracious appetite for life and her seductive manner.

Iris considered that she herself had been seduced too often by the quick, the obvious, the easy. By things that ended up different than what they seemed at first. She felt empty and used up. Bernice begged off from singing another song and the crowd scattered.

Steve walked up to Iris. "Just let me make the rounds and say good-bye to some people, then we'll go."

Forty-five minutes passed. Iris kicked her butt for thirty of them, but still didn't take action. She felt lonely and vulnerable. She was trading self-esteem for hugs. She should know better. She of all people should spot a bad trade. She got her purse and had found Josh to say good-bye when Steve walked up behind her.

"Ready to go?" he asked.

Bernice sauntered up to Steve, swaying her ample hips. "Leaving before I've had a chance to say good-bye?" She grabbed Steve in a bear hug and kissed him on the lips.

Steve slid from her grasp, making a joke, and looked apologetically at Iris. Bernice gave Iris a bold up-and-down look and sashayed away.

Somebody's car alarm barked one high then one low tone.

Iris was awake, lying on her back, staring up through the porthole in the bow cabin of Steve's boat. The boat rocked in the Santa Ana winds, the dock lines creaking noisily. Steve was asleep on his stomach with his arm limp and heavy across her waist. One patterned stocking clung to the goose down comforter and trailed off the edge of the bed, the other one was crumpled in a ball on the floor. Her leather miniskirt was doing a handstand against the door to the head.

She was still wearing the merry widow, which had painfully crept up around her ribs. She pulled it over her head and threw it at the miniskirt. Steve turned on his side, tightened his grip on her, and pulled her close. She put her nose in the soft hair in his armpit. It smelled faintly of deodorant. She rubbed her forehead on his biceps and circled her hand around his neck, squeezing the lean muscles.

"Steve?"

"Hhh?"

"What am I to you?"

He opened his eyes a slit. "Wha…?"

"What am I to you?"

Eyelids heavy, he rolled onto his side and pulled her close, draping a leg over her torso. "What do you mean?"

"Are we something or nothing?"

"What brought this up?"

"What am I to you?"

"You mean a lot to me."

"I'm not the only woman in your life."

"You're the most important woman in my life."

"The most important woman in your life. I guess that's about what it is, isn't it? Between you and me."

"You said you were happy with the way things are."

"I was."

"What's going on?"

"I don't know. I just... I don't know."

She put her nose in the hair above his ear. A sob welled up inside and she tried to catch it. Too late.

Steve leaned back his head to see her better. "Iris, what's wrong?"

"Alley was murdered last week."

"Your deaf friend at the office? How?"

"Somebody stabbed him on his way home from work."

She put her head on his chest and sobbed. He wrapped his arms around her and held her close. The tears ran down her face and onto his chest. He didn't reach for a tissue or tell her it was going to be all right so she could stop crying now. He just held her without saying anything.

Twelve

"Lighten up. Brighten up. Alley's in a better place. He's standing tall and walking straight, talking lies and chasing ass. He spits no more. He wouldn't have wanted you to be blue."

"It really fries me when people talk about what dead people would have wanted. If it were me, I'd be totally pissed and I wouldn't want any platitudes about how I'm in a better place. Who the hell knows, anyway?"

"Whoa! What happened? Didn't your swordsman come through last night?"

"Fuck off."

"I know just what you need. A little pick-me-up." Teddy pulled a glass vial from his jacket pocket, dipped in a tiny spoon, and held it up to her. "Have a toot."

"No thanks."

"C'mon, Iris. I thought you were cool. Aren't you cool?"

"I just see the clothes I could have bought instead. Besides, I'm hung over."

"Just the thing."

"You should ease up on that stuff."

Teddy held the spoon to one nostril and snorted wetly. He tipped the spoon in again and did the other side. Then he gently ran his finger around the edge of each nostril, gathered the stray particles on his fingertip, and rubbed his finger against his gums.

"Ahhh, breakfast of champions."

"I care about you, Teddy."

"That's special, Iris. Thank you for sharing that with me."

"Why do I care about people who don't care about themselves? Maybe I don't care enough about myself."

"We can pick up a book on codependency. There's about twenty-five of them out."

"I don't care if you fry your own brain, Teddy. But if you're ripping off investors and harassing a friend of mine, I have an obligation to speak up."

"Hey! Don't ruin my day by mentioning the man poison. She's history, all right?"

"It's over?"

"Yeah, it's over. I don't need someone who gives my gifts back."

"And the penny stocks?"

"That's all on the up-and-up. Just... you know, Iris... don't take care of the world."

"Nobody gives a damn about anybody anymore. No one has any time."

"Can you see the black eye behind my shades?"

"Yeah, your cheekbone's all bruised."

"Shit. Where the hell are we, anyway? Mexican heaven?"

"Pacoima."

"Watch out for stray bullets."

"Watch for Louise Street," she said.

"Seaview, Seashell, Seamist and Seabreeze. A developer's wishful thinking. Mary Ellen, Donna and... Betty Street. Fifties ladies. Why are those men doing the third world squat on the sidewalk?"

"They're looking for work."

"On the street?"

"People drive by and pick them up for day work. Construction and gardening and stuff."

"All we need are a few chickens and a couple of stray dogs…"

"At least the streets have life. In Beverly Hills, all you see is a gardener clipping a hedge or a maid walking to the bus stop."

"Streets are for driving. You'd think it'd kill them to throw a little paint on these houses. There's Louise. There's the church. Big turnout."

"There are the cops. Crap."

Teddy swung his head around. "What cops?"

"The cops that were at the office."

"What the hell?"

"Check it out," Lewin said. "Chuy from the Cirrus Street gang and his girlfriend, Blanca, helping Alley's mom out of the car. Touching. They related?"

Alley's mother was a small woman dressed in head-to-toe black. Her veil was pulled back over the top of her hat and draped down both sides of her face. She was somber and composed. Nothing left but dry grief. She held the arm of a younger man dressed in a short-sleeved, loose shirt, buttoned to the neck, the tail dropping almost to his knees, his hair slicked back, and his expression set in don't-fuck-with-me stone.

A rotund, fortyish man with pomaded hair and a suit with western-style detailing took the arm of a tiny woman with gray hair wrapped and pinned into a bun, who was the next one to step out of the big, older car.

"Must be the grandmother," Somers said.

The two detectives were standing on the sidewalk in the shade of a huge elm tree growing in the parkway.

They watched as a woman with a thick braid, doubled in half and pinned base-to-end at the back of her head, anxiously stared at Alley's mother, leaning forward on the balls of her feet, a large manila envelope in her hands. She took a tentative step toward Alley's mother, then stopped.

"That's Carmen," Lewin said. "The waitress from Café Zamboanga. A lot of people here we haven't talked to. Check it out."

Lewin jerked his head in the direction of two young men wearing wraparound sunglasses and long, loose shirts buttoned to the neck over pressed khakis and white Nike tennis shoes.

"Flaco and Tiny, from Cirrus Street."

"Means Cirrus Street didn't do Alley. They wouldn't come to bury the guy," Somers said.

"Why was Alley so popular with the homies?"

"Chuy's blood?"

"Makes Alley a good target for a rival gang."

"Gentlemen, good morning."

Lewin and Somers turned to face a smiling Stan Raab and a sedate Joe Campbell.

"Stan," Lewin said, extending his palm. "And Joe."

"I was just telling Joe that I was surprised to see you here, Detectives," Stan said. "Then I remembered reading that attending the funeral of a murder victim is standard police procedure, correct?"

"Absolutely," Lewin said, amused.

"People will reveal things about the deceased that they wouldn't if the person was alive," Stan said.

"People talk"—Lewin opened and closed three fingers against his thumb several times—"in their grief. Money trouble, love trouble, habits—anything. You're absolutely correct."

"And the perp might even show," Stan said.

"The perp?" Joe Campbell said.

"The perpetrator," Lewin said.

"Why do you think so?" Joe asked.

"He might feel remorse or disbelief about the crime," Stan said. "The funeral validates the crime. So, keep your eyes open, Joe."

"You're quite a Renaissance man, Stan," Lewin said. "Building houses, flying planes, sailing boats, studying criminology…"

"Life's not a dress rehearsal. That's what I always say. How's the investigation going?"

"Only a matter of time," Somers said.

"That's good news. This must be a tough one with so many men in L.A. who fit the description of the perpetrator."

"It's the kind of case that usually gets solved sooner or later by careful, routine police work," Lewin said.

Joe slipped his hand into a pocket of his slacks. "That's not always true, is it, that the perpetrator feels remorse?"

"What do you have in mind, Joe?" Somers asked.

"Like, a professional. There's no remorse... wouldn't seem."

"Generally, no. That's like a business transaction. Why?" Somers said.

"Just thinking."

"The paper said you're holding to the theory that it's gang- or drug-related," Stan said.

Lewin became distracted. He leaned toward Somers's ear and said, "Look at baby in black, traveling with my favorite asshole."

Somers turned to see Iris and Teddy walking down the street.

When Teddy reached the edge of the church grounds, he cut across the lawn, and headed toward the back of the building. Iris called after him but he waved her off and kept walking.

Somers watched Iris's legs in black stockings and Lewin watched Somers watch Iris's legs.

"Morning, Detectives, Stan. Hi, Joe," Iris looked at Somers a second less than cordial.

Somers half-turned away with the frost. He became interested in a ramshackle tree house built in a giant elm that was growing further down the grassy sidewalk parkway. The elm's old roots had raised the sidewalk in slabs.

"Iris," Stan said, "we were talking about the detectives' theory that Alley's murder might be gang- or drug-related."

"That theory stinks," Iris said. "With all due respect for your professional opinion, Detectives."

Stan laughed. "You have to admire Iris's frankness. You always know where you stand."

"No doubt," Somers said.

"Iris can probably put a unique spin on the situation," Stan said. "She and Alley were quite the office buddies, as you know, Detectives."

"Yes," Lewin said, turning to Somers, who was still looking down the street, "we know."

"It's textbook, Stan," Iris said, facing Raab but speaking loudly, "One Mexican kills another, and the cops blame gangs or drugs instead of doing a thorough investigation. Or is 'cookbook' the appropriate jargon?"

"You think we're off track, Ms. Thorne," Lewin said.

"I think you're very busy. So you do your job as best you can and you're off to the next thing. It's reality. Alley wasn't very important in the scheme of things."

"Iris, you have to give the police credit for expressing an opinion based upon experience," Stan said.

"I'll give credit when it's due. The drug theory stinks. Alley had been ill so much of his life that he was very careful about his health."

"He didn't have to do them to be involved with the trade," Somers said, turning back, pushing his suit jacket aside and putting his hands on his hips.

"He was very caring about others," Iris said, her hands now on her hips. "And the idea of gang involvement is ludicrous. Anyone who knew Alley would tell you that."

"Seems like all we gotta do is ask you, ma'am," Lewin said.

"I'd be happy to give you any information about Alley if anyone *cared* enough to ask, *sir.*"

"It's a lovely, old street, isn't it, Iris?" Joe asked her.

"Excuse me?" Iris was biting her lower lip.

"It's a lovely, old street."

"Yes," Iris said, "it is."

"It's too bad the houses are so run-down," Joe added. "But the church is beautiful. Big and open. It's fitting for Alley." He smiled at Iris.

Iris sucked her lower lip and bit back a tear. "There are a lot of people of here. Where's Alley's mother? I want to make sure I greet her."

"I think she went inside," Somers said.

Lewin caught the eye of Carmen, the waitress, standing hesitantly underneath one of the parkway elms. He gave her a short nod. "Ma'am."

Carmen nodded back, clutching the envelope to her chest. She looked at Iris, looked as if she were about to speak, then turned and walked quickly up the church steps.

"Who is that woman?" Iris asked.

"She's the waitress who works at the café where Alley had coffee every day after work," Lewin said.

"Why is she watching me?"

"She's probably admiring your taste in clothes," Joe said.

Iris cocked her head and smiled at the broad complement.

"Everything's going to be okay, pal."

"Thanks, Joe," Iris said.

Somers looked at Joe, the only man in the group who stood even with him, then took interest in a group of people getting out of a car.

"What a surprise," Stan said. "Here comes Bill Drye."

"Good morning, everyone," Drye said brightly.

"Pleasant surprise, Drye," Iris said.

"I wanted to pay my respects to my coworker, Alley."

"Ms. Thorne, didn't I see you drive in with Teddy Kraus?" Lewin asked.

"The Tedster's here?" Drye said. "All right."

"He had to use the restroom."

"I didn't see him come up the steps," Lewin said. "Why didn't he come in the front door?"

"You'll have to ask him, Detective Lewin."

"I'll do that, ma'am."

"A lot of people here to see Alley off," Drye said. "I didn't know he was that popular. Probably all that drug money he spread around." He winked at Iris.

"Well, let's let these men do their work," Stan said. "They have it cut out for them. Let's go inside."

"Teddy," Iris whispered. "Where have you been?"

"In the head, like I told you." He was still wearing his sunglasses.

"All this time?"

"I'm not feeling well, okay?" He was breathless.

"Did you eat anything today?"

"Cool it, Mom."

"I got you a program. Here."

"Keep it. Why are those cops at the front of the church?"

"To see what they can see. The murderer might show up." She raised her eyebrows. "Or perpetrator, to use Stan's word."

"They know that?"

"Criminology. Stan was just bending my ear about it. I begged off to come sit back here. This is a McKinney circus. I can't deal with it."

"What's Drye doing here?"

"Brown-nosing Stan, as usual. Joe Campbell's here."

"Is it true his shit don't stink?"

"Lay off. He's good people. Shhh. They're starting."

Teddy drummed his palms on the back of the pew in front of them.

"Stop it," Iris hissed.

He sat on his hands and bounced his feet on his toes. "That short cop is staring at me."

"The tall one is staring at me. I'm getting tired of pretending I don't notice him. The short one wanted to know where you went."

"What did you say?"

"That you had to use the restroom. He wanted to know why you didn't come in the front and I said he'd have to ask you and he said he would."

"Why is he so fucking interested in me?"

"He's a jerk. His stupid ma'ams and *Ms.*Thornes."

"Fucking do-gooder." Teddy mopped his dome with a handkerchief and dug his fingers under his shirt collar. "This whole thing's in Spanish? Oh, man. And what's that? Sign language?"

"Will you relax? I'll translate the sign language. What's wrong with you? It's not hot in here."

Teddy put the handkerchief up to his mouth. "I can't catch my breath." He belched.

"You're pale."

"I told you I don't like funerals. I've got to go. I'm going."

"How are you going to get home?"

"I've got to go. Let me through."

He stood, banging his knee against the pew in front of them. She pulled her legs underneath her, but he still kicked her ankle with his big wing tip as he stumbled out, holding his handkerchief over his mouth. People turned to see what was going on.

The congregation started a hymn. Iris fumbled through the hymnbook and rubbed her ankle. She silently mouthed the words.

They kneeled. They stood. They kneeled. Iris leaned her forehead against the back of the pew in front of her and picked at graffiti carved there. She cocked her head and thought she heard Teddy retching on the church steps. She said the Lord's Prayer, drawing the words out of her memory, like the Pledge of Allegiance.

A priest delivered the eulogy. Iris looked away from the woman signing at the front of the church and studied the stained-glass windows, lined on the street side with protective wire mesh. Bright colors. Yellow, green, red, blue. The sunlight behind them threw colored spots on the stone floor. Jesus as a shepherd leading a flock of sheep. Jesus speaking to a crowd kneeling at his feet. The priest's musical Spanish circled around her. *Alley is dead.* She looked front again and saw John Somers watching her. His face seemed schoolboy smooth and sorry. She was sorry too. Let's do it over, from the top. Life is too short. Too short.

It was time to pay her last respects. She was afraid. She slid out of the pew and stood behind Stan Raab and Joe Campbell.

Drye hovered among them, not wanting to miss a scrap of conversation. They looked down at Alley in the open casket.

"He looks peaceful," Raab said.

"Yes," Drye said, breaking a red carnation off of one of the floral displays and putting it in his lapel.

Raab frowned at him.

"I want to keep it as a memento."

"I guess you can never really know a person," Campbell said. "There's always something inscrutable."

Iris stood quietly, her hands clasped in front of her.

Somers stood a few feet away, watching.

"His face," Raab said. "His death wasn't a struggle. It was easy. A relief, really. Look."

"They did a good job," Drye said. "Looks like he's just asleep."

"The makeup's not right," Iris said. "It's too dark."

"Leave it to Iris," Drye said.

She twisted the silver-and-abalone ring on her finger, then impulsively pulled it off. She reached in the casket and slipped it on one of Alley's fingers.

"She's touching him!" Drye said in a loud stage whisper.

Campbell put his hand on Drye's sleeve to quiet him.

Iris put her hand on Alley's black hair and rubbed a few strands between her thumb and fingers. She gave it a final pat and turned, almost walking into John Somers. She saw sympathy in his eyes. She quickly walked away, blinking back tears. She started the ten count to control. At ten, the tears had been shoved back.

She found Alley's mother. In her, Iris saw Alley's high cheekbones, sculptured jaw, arched eyebrows, and caramel color. Iris couldn't remember her high-school Spanish. She tried signing. "Alley was my friend. He was dear and generous and loved."

Alley's mother reached her arm around Iris's neck and pulled her close, laying a black-gloved hand against Iris's cheek.

Lewin whispered to Somers, "When are we going to talk to her?" nodding toward Iris.

"Not now. She's too upset."

"That's the best time."

"I'll call her on Monday."

"And our killer will be in Guatemala by then. We're talking to her today. I'll haul her into the station."

"I told you that I'll take care of it."

Iris walked toward the rear of the church, which seemed a million miles away. She heard Drye's eager whispers to Raab behind her. She ignored them. It meant nothing.

Carmen, the waitress, turned to watch Iris pass.

Iris was unlocking the door to the TR when Somers walked up to her.

He held his big, square hands open. "Iris?"

"Yes."

"Iris…"

"Yes, again."

"I want to apologize for being out of line."

She sighed and drew the back of her hand against her forehead.

Somers continued. "You're right. I haven't been upfront with you. But here's the deal. I'm conducting this investigation and you're part of it. That's half the loaf. I want to get to know you again and I don't know what that means exactly. That's the other half. I'll try to keep the two halves separate. I don't know if I can, but I'm too stubborn not to try. So, have dinner with me tonight, at my house."

She opened her mouth to speak.

"Wait. Before you jump to conclusions… It'll be very low key, casual, with my daughter and my dog and we can talk without surly waiters and pink food or you can have pink food if that's what you want. I'm—"

"Okay."

"—a good cook and I know it's short notice and you probably already have plans, but if you don't, you might not want to be alone tonight and—"

"Okay."

"Okay?"

"Yeah. Okay. I don't have plans and I don't want to be alone tonight. Thank you for the invitation."

"Sure. Ahhh, well, are you going to the grave site?"

"No. I've already said good-bye to Alley. I'm sick of this circus."

"I'll give you directions to my house."

She looked in her purse for something to write on and pulled out a funeral program. She wrote down the directions, folded the program, and put it in a suit jacket pocket.

"Say, six o'clock?"

"Fine."

Somers walked over to Lewin who was leaning against an elm tree watching them.

"So. Did you make arrangements to interview her?" Lewin asked.

"Yeah, done."

Thirteen

"It's not that they don't care." "I won't do it. I won't sell Alley out!"

"That's right, keep talking to yourself."

"What?" Iris said.

"Just go ahead. Happening more and more."

"Who's that?" Iris looked around.

"Down here. Couldn't spare a quarter?"

The bag lady was sitting under the portico of the McKinney Alitzer building. Her face was tanned and weathered, her hair was combed but dirty and unevenly hacked short. She wore a baggy T-shirt, too-large baggy khakis rolled up at the waist, and a tailored women's suit jacket, probably lifted from the chair back of a careless downtown executive. The effect was a sort of soiled fashion statement.

Iris opened her purse, angry for being hit up but caught by a slender fish hook of guilt.

"'Course, a quarter hardly gets you anything anymore," the bag lady said.

Iris had to respect the trade-up. She pulled out five dollars.

"Thanks. Great suit. Not many people can wear black and not look like they're going to a funeral."

"You're in the wrong line of business."

"Maybe you are."

Iris's stomach pinged at the incidental truth. She stepped past the woman, opened the glass door, and walked across the marble lobby to the security guard's desk.

"Hi, Nicky."

"Iris. Here on Saturday again. Work, work, work."

"Gotta stay a step ahead."

"It's too nice to be inside today."

"We're having a stage-three smog alert."

"It's sunny and beautiful out."

"The burden of another sunny day. The curse of Southern California. Who's the bag lady?"

"Lucille? She bothering you?"

"No. Do I have to sign in, Nicky?"

"You don't want to?"

"My boss has been on my case about all the overtime I've been putting in and if he shows up and sees I've been here, it won't look good."

"Gotcha."

"In fact, if he shows up, can you call me upstairs? You know who he is, right? Stan Raab? Short guy, blond hair? Just call the office number, then I'll know he's on his way up. That'll give me enough time to leave. Okay?"

"Sure, baby doll."

"Now that I'm thinking about it, why don't you call me if anyone comes up to McKinney, okay?"

"Your wish is my command. How about I stay home and keep house while you bring home the bacon? A executive woman. Would suit me just fine."

"You wouldn't like it."

"Oh, I would."

"You'd have to ask me for spending money."

"I'd love it. House husband to an executive woman."

"It gets complicated. Trust me. 'Bye, Nicky. Don't forget to call upstairs."

The glass doors to the McKinney Alitzer suite had already been unlocked by the cleaning crew. Two big yellow trash bins on wheels with rags, sprays, and plastic bags stuck into leather thongs belted around their perimeters were on the mauve carpet in the lobby. Iris heard doors being unlocked and a man and a woman shouting down the corridor to each other in Spanish.

The office was illuminated by feeble light coming through the tinted windows. Iris went in the lunchroom. The vending machine buttons glowed in the semi-darkness. She put in twenty cents and punched the buttons for black coffee. She grabbed the flesh on her belly between her thumb and index finger, testing its thickness to gauge whether she should or shouldn't. She shouldn't, but she would anyway. She fed in forty-five cents for a package of Oreos that dangled from a metal clip in the snack machine. The cookies slid out on a track, then dropped two feet, smack, into a steel bin.

She opened the package, twisted apart the halves of a cookie, and scraped the cream filling off with her bottom teeth. She opened a drawer near the sink and dug through packages of artificial sweetener, single servings of ketchup and salt from a local fast-food restaurant, plastic utensils, chopsticks in paper wrappers, and rumpled paper napkins before she finally found the butcher knife. She took the knife and went back into the suite.

She set her purse on her desk, sat down, and ate another cookie. The cleaning crew had turned the lights on and were dumping wastebaskets on the other side of the suite. Iris reached over the divider separating her desk from Teddy's and tipped his wastebasket toward her with the knife blade. She churned wrappers from strawberry Zingers, chocolate mini-donuts, peanut M & M's, and CornNuts. The penny stock pink sheets were at the bottom, folded like a fan. She speared them and pulled them out. Teddy had torn the edges into a tight fringe all the way around. The first five stocks that closed at a penny a share were circled.

She walked around the divider and sat at Teddy's desk. She tried the center drawer. It was unlocked. Pens and pencils were neatly lined up next to erasers next to pads of yellow lined paper next to a box of business cards with the lid inverted and filled with change for the vending machine. A stack of ATM receipts were piled on one side, all of them for credit card withdrawals.

She flipped through the yellow pads. The penny stock grid was underneath the last one.

On the up-and-up my eye. You can't do this nonsense, Teddy.

She pulled out the stack of yellow pads to put the grid back and saw a photograph in a corner. She expected a Billy Drye hard-core special but the photo was of Iris and Teddy and Jaynie at the company picnic. Teddy was in the middle and the women were on either side with their arms around him. Iris had a copy of the same snapshot, but hers wasn't like this one. In her copy, Jaynie had a head. In her copy, Jaynie wasn't bleeding red ink from a wound drawn on her chest.

A chill tickled Iris's spine and she put the photo back where she'd found it, peeking in the back of the drawer for the missing head. She looked through the other drawers and found everything to be ordinary and neat.

It was time to get down to business. Iris took the knife. She walked down the corridor and into Raab's office. She sat at his desk. The top drawer was locked. She ran her hands up and down the desk's inside edges but there was no latch. She wasn't getting in today. That was okay. He usually kept client information in the tall oak filing cabinet in the corner. That's what she needed to get into.

The filing cabinet was locked, the button lock pushed in. She grabbed the handle of the top drawer with her left hand and held the latch with her thumb. With her right hand, she shoved the knife blade into the gap between the drawer and the frame. She probed with the blade and jiggled the drawer at the same time. Something released and the drawer slid open on oiled rollers.

She set the knife on top of the filing cabinet, took off her black linen jacket, and tossed it over one of Raab's chairs. The air conditioner was off and it was hot in the suite. She walked her fingertips across the tops of the manila file folders, closed that drawer, then opened the next one. Midway through, she found a folder labeled WORLDCO. She grabbed it and pulled hard. The drawer was crammed full. The file popped free. It felt light. She opened it. It was empty.

She looked on the floor on the chance that something had fallen out. Nothing had. She opened the file again. Even the pink phone message slips and business cards that she knew Raab stapled to the inside cover of the client files had been pulled off, leaving little perforations one-half inch apart.

She lay the Worldco file on top of the cabinet and pulled a few other client files. There were copies of buy and sell orders and an overview of the account inside each one. Phone messages and business cards were stapled to the inside front covers.

She re-filed the folders. She started from the top drawer again, deciding to look for something on EquiMex, when she realized the phone was ringing. She held her breath and listened harder. It was the phone in the reception area. She ran toward it. When she was halfway down the corridor, it fell silent. She ran back to Raab's office and opened the second drawer.

If it's Nicky, someone's on their way up. She opened the third drawer. Her fingers walked across the manila tabs. *Could be a wrong number. Say it's worst case… Raab. I have a key… I have a right to be here. But why leave the funeral to come to here?* She opened the forth drawer and knelt on the ground. *I was upset…* She flipped through the tight folders. *I thought work would distract me. It's goosey but I can pull it off.* She got up. There was no EquiMex file. *No. The best thing is to disappear.*

She heard Raab's voice at the door of the suite. Then she heard another voice. She grabbed her suit jacket from the chair, sprinted to her desk, snatched her purse, and looked for a hiding place. She could make the lunchroom, but he might go in there. She didn't have enough time to reach the other end of the suite and duck into the supply room. Now she didn't have enough time to duck anywhere. She crawled underneath her desk and rolled her desk chair over the opening.

"Is he sure? I mean, how credible is this guy?" Raab was talking.

"Wendell Ellis has worked for my father since before I was born. He's credible."

Joe Campbell and Stan Raab moved to stand in the corridor next to Iris's desk. She clutched her purse and jacket to her chest and held her breath.

"Why would someone pull off a scheme like this EquiMex thing, then blow their cover by listing their own name as director?" Raab asked.

"That's why Pop thinks someone's behind it."

"I'm afraid it's someone from the office."

The strap of Iris's shoulder bag looped out from beneath the edge of the desk. The polished toe of Stan Raab's wing tip arced over it. She inched the strap in.

"We'll look at that Worldco folder, Joe, and at least your dad will be satisfied that everything's in order on this end. The way this thing is framing up, the SEC will be camping out here. I'd better get a handle on our documentation before they come in and roll out the filing cabinets."

They started walking away.

Raab asked, "You're still coming to Morgan's birthday party on Sunday, aren't you?"

"Sure."

"And your mom and dad?"

"Pop loves Disneyland. And you know how he is with kids."

"That's right, number one son. When are you getting started on a family of your own?"

"I'd like to, but it's hard to level with somebody about the family business. I don't want to lie." After a pause, Joe changed the subject, "We're meeting at ten o'clock on the Castle Bridge, right?"

They'd moved inside Stan's office. Iris had sat at her desk and listened to Stan enough times to recognize the pitch and resonance his office walls gave his voice. She slowly shoved out her desk chair, wincing at the noise it made rolling on the plastic floor protector. She crawled forward and raised her head over the top of her cubicle wall. She could barely see into Stan's office.

"A tough, New York Italian guy like your dad getting a kick out of Disneyland."

Iris looped her shoulder bag across her chest and crawled on her hands and knees down the corridor, staying close to the cubicle walls. She almost caught her knee in her pearl rope, which dragged on the carpet. In the lobby, one of the cleaning crew was dusting a glass-topped coffee table. He looked at her curiously. She put her index finger to her lips. Quiet. He continued cleaning. At the entrance, Iris stood up quickly and opened the glass doors just wide enough to squeeze through. She didn't breathe freely until the elevator doors closed and she was on her way downstairs.

Jacket, purse… what am I forgetting?

This filing cabinet is unlocked," Stan said.

"Did you forget to lock it?"

"I guess I could have. Here's the Worldco file. Wait. It's empty." Stan displayed the empty folder to Joe. "How could it be empty?"

"What's this knife doing on top?" Joe picked it up.

"Someone broke into my filing cabinet."

"With a knife?"

"I've seen the secretaries do it when they've lost a key. Someone pried open my filing cabinet and took all my Worldco documentation."

"Why didn't they take the whole folder?"

"So it'd be in its place? I looked at it… yesterday afternoon."

"We were the only ones from McKinney signed in downstairs."

"The security in this place is abominable. The guard isn't there half the time. Did you see that bag lady in the doorway? Anyone could walk in here."

"But who?"

* * *

Iris turned the ignition key and the TR's engine roared in the empty garage. She shook out her jacket, folded it neatly, and laid it across the passenger's seat. She took out the pull-out stereo from where she'd hid it beneath the driver's seat and slid it into its chassis. She examined the knees of her stockings.

Jacket, purse ...

She started to laugh. She laughed harder and harder, high pitched and uncontrolled. Tears popped into her eyes. She doubled over and held her ribs. She replayed the cleaning guy's expression again and rubbed and laughed at her bruised knees. The laughter subsided into chuckles. She threw the TR into reverse and remembered with a clear vision.

"The knife!"

She stopped laughing. *No matter. Just a knife.*

Fourteen

It was Saturday afternoon. A bank building said it was 101 degrees Fahrenheit, 69 Celsius. Lankershim Boulevard was hopping. Street vendors sold tropical flavored Popsicles from refrigerated carts. Salsa dance music blared from record stores. Merchants showed goods on the sidewalk. People walked.

John Somers left the jacket of his good navy blue suit in the car, rolled up the sleeves of his burgundy-striped shirt, and loosened his striped rep tie. He pulled open the smudged glass doors of the Café Zamboanga and went inside into barely air-conditioned heat.

An old man with carefully pressed khaki pants belted around his chest and a plaid shirt looked up with dull eyes from a newspaper. His fedora, decorated with a bright feather in the brim, was on the counter near the crooked handle of his cane, which hung from the edge. Somers nodded and he nodded back.

A little girl ate ice cream, dripping chocolate, swinging her legs from a tall counter stool. Her mother gave Somers a sidelong glance, then looked away.

Somers sat at the counter, straddling the stool to accommodate his height.

"What can I get you?" The waitress wore a pink dress, crisp for the hot day and drab surroundings. A pink flower swung from the end of her long braid. A plastic nametag on her dress said CARMEN. She squinted at Somers. She'd seen him someplace before.

"I'll have what she's having." Somers nodded toward the little girl.

The waitress sat a small bowl on a chipped saucer and pulled a silver scoop from a milky bath.

"What's a summer day without ice cream?" Somers smiled.

Carmen responded with a tight smile. She dished chocolate ice cream from a cardboard vat with her back to Somers. The old man looked up over his newspaper. The little girl openly stared. The ancient air-conditioning unit whirred. The glass doors muffled the outside noise.

"Make it two scoops?" Somers asked.

Carmen rolled the spoon into the vat again and smashed a second scoop onto the first. She placed the bowl in front of him. The ice cream's edges were already melted and creamy.

"Something about ice cream on a hot summer day that makes you feel like a kid again, doesn't it?"

Carmen gave a quick nod.

"Say, Carmen," Somers began, "did you wait on the man who was murdered last week?"

"No."

"You're not on days?"

"I was off that day."

"That waitress's name was Carmen, too."

She looked at him, her brown eyes outlined with heavy liner. "I saw you at Alley's funeral. You're a cop."

Somers nodded and rolled the ice cream on his tongue.

Carmen shook her head bitterly and turned back to her work, sponging down the chrome-lined linoleum counter. The yellow marble pattern was printed with faded silver star bursts.

The little girl was still watching Somers. She brought a dripping spoon of brown ice cream soup to her mouth.

Somers winked at her and then asked the waitress, "What did you see that day, Carmen?"

"I already told that other one. The short one and another guy. They wrote it all down. Don't you talk to each other?"

"I want to hear it from you."

"You don't look like a cop."

"I'll take that as a compliment." He showed her his shield and handed her his business card.

Carmen looked the card over. "Okay. All right. This is how it was. He came in. Five-fifteen, about. Like he did every weekday. He had coffee. He looked at the newspaper."

"He didn't have pie that day?"

"Coffee. That's all he ever ordered."

"He always only had coffee?"

"His mama made his dinner. He was waiting to meet her bus."

"Did you speak with him?"

"I asked him how his mother was and he didn't understand. He finished his coffee. He paid. He left."

"What was he wearing?"

"The same thing they took him to the morgue in. Don't you read your own reports?"

"What was he wearing?"

"His navy suit. With the pinstripes. A light blue shirt."

"He had other suits?"

"*Cabrón.*"

"He had other suits?"

"A plain navy one and a plain gray one."

"Charcoal gray?"

"Yes. Charcoal. This going to help you find his killer?"

"Did he have his briefcase that day?"

"I don't remember."

"What happened after he left the café?"

"A *vato* stopped him in front. I was washing dishes with my back turned. I heard screaming. I ran out. He was on the sidewalk. Blood was everywhere. I went inside and called nine-one-one."

"With his briefcase."

"No."

"Wasn't he carrying a briefcase with him?"

"I told you I don't remember."

"Didn't he always carry a briefcase?"

"Sometimes. Maybe. I don't remember."

"You're pretty observant, aren't you, Carmen?"

"I know what's going on."

"You know Alley's wardrobe and what he was wearing that day and what he ordered that day and every other day and you can recite the conversation you had with him. Pretty impressive."

She shrugged.

"But you can't remember whether he was carrying his shiny aluminum briefcase that his coworkers say he was never without. Something's not right here, Carmen. Does it seem like something's not right to you?"

Her cheeks flushed.

"Seems like you would have noticed if he *wasn't* carrying his briefcase. You would have wondered whether the murderer took it. You would have looked around for it. Wouldn't you? Carmen?"

She squeezed the damp sponge over the sink and threw it on the counter, then marched into the galley on rubber soles past the cook, who was mopping up. A door opened. Things were jostled. Padded footsteps returned. She hoisted the briefcase onto the counter.

"You try to do something nice for someone…"

"What's in it?" Somers asked.

"Junk! It's full of junk. Here." She clicked the lid open. "See."

Somers put his big hand on the lid and closed the briefcase with a snap. "Did you remove anything?"

"I wouldn't take anything from a dead man."

Somers stood and the little girl twisted her head to look up at him. "Carmen, thank you for your cooperation." He placed a few bills on the counter.

Carmen folded her arms over her chest and leaned against the coffee station.

"If you are ever unfortunate enough to be at a crime scene again, please don't remove evidence."

"I was going to take it to his mama after the funeral."

Somers nodded. "I know you were." He patted the little girl on the head, said "Ma'am" to her mother, nodded at the old man, and left. He unlocked the trunk of his car, which was parked in front of the café, and put in the briefcase. He looked up at the bright sun, which was beginning its downward arc in the lengthening afternoon.

He took a few steps and squatted on the sidewalk. He looked north up Lankershim to see what Alley had seen, turned to look the other direction, then looked at the cement. The blood had been washed away, probably by a tidy shop owner. He opened the blade of a pocketknife and scraped at a chocolate-colored substance that had settled in the sidewalk cracks. He circled around while squatting and scanned the sidewalk and gutters. He used the blade to stir wrappers and cigarette butts that had worked up next to the storefronts, then crept crablike to the gutter and dragged the blade around in the refuse there.

He got up and looked at the surrounding storefronts and upstairs apartment windows on both sides of the street. Then he started walking, zigzagging down the sidewalk, looking at the pavement, then up at the windows, then down at the pavement, squatting to dig at refuse and stopping to stare into storefront windows. He continued down the street like that until he reached the corner of Lankershim and Hortense. He looked up and a curtain in a third-floor apartment window dropped closed.

Somers entered the building and walked up two flights of stairs onto a small landing covered with a threadbare carpet in a faded floral pattern. The air smelled of dust and mold and, very faintly, of lavender. He rapped on the door. No answer. A shadow passed in front of the peephole.

"Hello! This is Detective John Somers with the police department. Please open the door." He held his shield so that it was visible through the peephole.

A shrill voice asked, "What do you want?"

"I'd like to ask you a few questions about the murder outside the Café Zamboanga last week. It'll only take a few minutes."

"How do I know you're with the police? Anyone can have a badge. Can buy one at the dime store."

"You can call my office, ma'am."

"Call your office? So what? Could be your friend sitting there pretending like he's the police."

"Ma'am? Can I ask you some questions?"

"Sure, go ahead. But I'm not opening the door."

"That's fine. Can I have your name, please?"

"What do you need my name for? Isn't this about the boy who was murdered?"

"Yes, it is. Did you see the murder?"

"Saw the whole thing. So what? So did everyone else on this street. Why are you bothering me?"

"Could you please tell me what you saw?"

"One of these young toughs walked up to the little crippled boy. You know, those toughs. You know how they do. I don't even carry my purse any more. I pin my money and keys inside my clothes." She was shouting now. "The way things are today. Terrible! Kill you just to look at you."

"What happened next, ma'am?"

"I guess you are a cop. No one says 'ma'am' anymore."

"Will you open the door for me, ma'am?"

"No!" she yelled.

"What happened next, ma'am?"

"They talked, then the tough stabbed the crippled boy and ran down the street and around the corner there onto Hortense and got into a car."

"He got into a car?"

"That's what I said, isn't it? You hard of hearing?"

"Where did he get into the car?"

"Around the corner, there. Around on Hortense. I went to my bedroom and saw it out the back window. There was a car parked there and that young tough got into it."

"What kind of a car?"

"A big, black car. Like a big, old Cadillac. Almost looked like a hearse."

"Do you think it was a hearse?"

"No! It was big like a hearse. I think it was a Cadillac. With black windows—you know how they do."

"Did you see who was driving?"

"The windows were black. I just told you that. Now don't try my patience."

"Ma'am, thank you very much for speaking with me."

"Now, I didn't get a good look at that young tough. And I didn't see that car too well, either. So don't come around here and expect me to identify anyone. I'm an old woman and I don't see too well and I'll tell that to anyone from the police who comes around here. You understand, young man?"

"Yes, ma'am. Have a good day."

"Good as can be expected."

Somers jogged down the stairs and out onto Lankershim Boulevard and down the street to his car. A breeze blew hot, churning the refuse on the sidewalk. He bought a mango Popsicle from a street vendor, sat in his car, turned on the ignition, turned the air conditioner all the way up, and rubbed his temples. He took the wrapper off the Popsicle and held the Popsicle between his teeth as he pulled the car away from the curb.

Fifteen

Twenty-five-eighteen Camille was a tiny wood-framed bungalow with a wide porch and a low roof, built in the California craftsman style common in houses of the twenties and thirties. An overgrown palm tree stood in the front yard, shooting fifty feet straight up, its trunk shrouded with yellow fronds, its base covered with ancient ivy, thick with spiders, their webs white against the surface of the dusty dark green leaves. Aluminum chairs with patched plastic webbing were on the porch. A jangle of plants hung from the porch eaves in macramé slings strung with small shells. Iron bars covered the windows and an iron gate replaced the screen door. A glass wind chime tinkled in the breeze, which teased with promised relief but blew hot.

Two mongrel dogs ran across the yellowed lawn and barked at John Somers's heels, the hair on their necks up. A watchful shadow appeared in the doorway of the house across the street.

Somers rang the bell, then knocked on the door's wooden frame when the bell didn't sound.

A man Somers guessed to be about thirty and whom he recognized as one of the pallbearers at Alley's funeral came to the door wearing a sleeveless T-shirt tucked into dark suit pants. Inside the house, Somers heard a television broadcast in Spanish and a jumble of conversation in two languages. He showed his shield and the man unlatched and opened the iron gate.

"I'm Efrain Muñoz, Alley's cousin," the man said, holding out his palm. "I saw you at the funeral." A faded gang tattoo was on the inside of his wrist.

The living room was crowded with people, sitting thigh to thigh on the couch, on folding aluminum chairs from the yard, and on chrome-and-vinyl chairs from the kitchen. Somers recognized faces from the funeral but there were more children here. They must have been kept at home.

"This is a detective from the police," Efrain said to the group.

There was loud silence. Everyone looked at Somers, appraising his red hair and freckles, his imp's nose on the face of a big man, trying to reconcile his discordant image with the detectives they knew from television and the streets. A wide man with pomaded hair, another one of the pallbearers, got up from the couch, a gold tooth in his broad smile, and grabbed Somers's hand with one of his and slapped his back with the other.

"Welcome to this house, Detective." He smelled of drugstore cologne. "The police are welcome here. You guys stopped a robbery in my store on the boulevard. I could have been killed."

An old woman sitting on a Naugahyde lounger in the corner crossed herself.

"But, grace of God, the police got the guys."

"*Tió* Tito, why don't you tell him about when they cracked Flaco's head open for no reason," said a young man sitting on the couch. He was wearing a sleeveless T-shirt and his arms bore several blue tattoos, probably done by the local street artist with a blue ink pen. There was a cross emitting sun rays on his right biceps, a heart pierced by an arrow and dripping blood on his left, and CIRRUS STREET in three-dimensional block letters on the inside of his right forearm. A girl with long black hair, ratted high on top of her head, wearing white lipstick and heavy black eye makeup was sitting next to him, her fingers entwined with his.

"Hello, Chuy," Somers said. "And Blanca. Long time."

"Not long enough, *azul*."

"Quiet, *hombre*. I won't have that attitude in my house," Tito said.

Chuy stood and slowly sauntered out the front door without saying anything, trailing Blanca.

"My nephew," Tito shrugged. "Acts tough, him and his homies, because they don't got nothing. Care about nothing. Detective, sit down." He pulled over a chrome-and-vinyl chair and placed it near Somers.

Somers sat.

"Can I get you a beer, a soda? Have something to eat. My mother made tamales."

"A glass of water would be great, thanks."

A woman standing in the doorway of the kitchen quickly moved to get the water. She handed Somers a well-worn glass tumbler painted with washed-out yellow flowers.

"Detective, what can we do for you?" Tito asked.

"I came to talk to the people who were close to Alley, to try to put the pieces together. Who else lives here?"

"Alley's mother, who is my sister, my wife and two daughters, and my mother, too." He gestured toward the old woman on the Naugahyde lounger. She nodded at Somers regally. "We brought Alley and his mother from Mexico ten years ago so that he could go to go to deaf school here."

Other conversation had stopped except for whispering behind hands. Somers looked over the furnishings, which included a sofa and love seat in burgundy velour, a smoked-glass coffee table with a chrome base, and a chrome-and-glass wall unit, all sparkling new. The wall unit's fluorescent lights spotlighted a flamenco dancer doll in one cubicle, dressed in stiff pink chiffon, and a gold plaster bull in another. A clutter of framed photographs was on a center shelf. A crucifix hung over the door. Two black velvet paintings of bull fighting scenes were on a wall above the television, which was a wide-screen model and new. So were the two videocassette recorders and the stereo with compact disk player that Somers had priced himself and decided was too expensive for him.

"Mr. Muñoz, you said you have a store."

"Clothing store. Fifteen years."

"You look like you're doing well for yourself."

"Yes, yes. But we all work. Me, my wife, and Alley's mother, Maria. And Alley. He made good money, especially after he got promoted."

"Promoted?"

"Oh, yes. They made him director of their Mexico business. Big job. They sent him to Mexico and everything. Very big job." Tito nodded to emphasize how big the job was.

"Who sent him?"

Tito shrugged. "His bosses."

"Which boss? Who did he talk about?"

"Oh, he talked, you know. He talked about lots of people. He loved his job. He was so proud when he got that job, Detective." Tito put his hand on Somers's thigh and leaned closer. "He got up so early in the morning. Put on his suit. Took his briefcase." Tito puffed up to show how Alley looked. "I told him he could work in the store with me. But no. Not Alley. He'd say, 'Tío, my future is there,' and he'd point downtown.

"Mr. Raab was the big boss. He gave Alley a gold pen with his name on it for Christmas. Alley was so proud of that pen. Put it in his pocket, here, he said, just like the big shots. Jaynie was his supervisor. There was Iris. Iris was his special friend. There was, ahh... let's see... Teddy. I can't keep them all straight."

"Why was Iris his special friend?"

"She knew the sign language. Alley could talk, you know. But if you didn't know him, he was hard to understand. And he was very proud. He knew he didn't sound right. The way people looked at him. That hurt him. So with Iris, he had someone he could talk to in his language."

"What did he do on his trips to Mexico?"

"Business." Tito raised his palms. "He wasn't supposed to say. It was confidential."

"He never told you what he did in Mexico?"

"Took take care of business. If they told him not to say, he wouldn't say. That was Alley. But he'd always visit his hometown and see his friends there."

"Where was that?"

"Oaxcatil."

"W-A-C-A…"

"No. O-A-X-C-A-T-I-L. Oaxcatil. Same name as the volcano there."

"How many trips did he make?"

"Let's see. Three . . no… two. He was getting ready to go again then… you know. I'll show you."

Somers followed Tito down a narrow hallway with two rooms off each side and a small bathroom at the end. Tito opened the last door on the right and they walked into a small, sunny room, hot with the afternoon sun. The windows were covered with light blue curtains and the bed had a navy blue spread. A small bookcase held books in Spanish, mystery novels, Spanish and English dictionaries, a book on taking charge of your life, and a few general business textbooks: *Marketing, Business Mathematics*, and *Introduction to Finance*. A worn wooden desk stood against a wall. A "From the desk of…" pad was squared beside a pencil holder that held new pencils and a small red, white, and green Mexican flag. A stuffed iguana crawled by the wall and a small flamenco dancer doll danced next to it, a sneer molded onto his plastic face.

Tito took down one of the business texts. "See. Always working to make himself better. That was Alley. He took business classes at the junior college over on Vermont Street." He paused, smiled wistfully, and shook his head.

"Did Alley do well in school?" asked Somers.

"Very well. He was a very bright boy."

"*Qué pasa*, Tito?"

"Maria, we woke you up?"

"I not sleep." She looked at Somers. "I know you from my son's funeral."

"I'm Detective John Somers. I'm investigating your son's murder."

Maria Muñoz nodded wearily. "What you doing here, Tito?"

"The detective wanted to know about Alley's trips to Mexico. I came to show him this."

Tito pulled an airline envelope from beneath the pencil holder and showed Somers a computer-printed itinerary. Alley was flying into Mexico City on Friday night and back home again on Sunday with a driver to Oaxcatil arranged on Saturday.

"Did he always fly over the weekend?"

"Yes. He said he had to work the weekends now."

"Detective, tell me, what happened to my son," Maria sat on the bed, her hands limp in her lap, her shoulders curved forward. A few threads of gray hair were woven through the black.

"What do you think happened, Mrs. Muñoz?"

She sighed and her shoulders curved deeper. "I don't know. Something not right. Too much money."

"Maria, his promotion. He was doing well," Tito said.

She waved her hand and blew out air. "No one gives a handicapped deaf boy that much money."

"Oh, Maria. You read about it in the paper all the time. Those bankers there, those stockbrokers, they earn millions. This is a great country."

"They give my son money over a white American. A whole American who hears and speaks? This country not that great."

"He worked harder than the rest. That's all."

"Mrs. Muñoz," Somers said, "do you think your son could have been involved in something illegal?"

"I don't know. I ask him, *Mijo*, what you do? Why you have so much money? You doing something wrong? You tell me. He say, 'Mommy, I don't do anything make you ashamed of me.' I say, 'Okay, just remember, you have to face God,' and he say, 'That's okay, Mommy, I always do the right thing. I work hard. I want you to be proud of me.' I tell him it's not money that make me proud of him.

"My boy, he had a hard life. People so mean, you know—they make fun of him. And he is very proud. So when I hear from Oaxcatil, how he acting down there, spreading the money around, I know he trying to tell them something."

"Did Alley hang around with the Cirrus Street gang? Could they have put him up to something?"

"Detective," Tito said, "I tell my good-for-nothing nephew out there that I kill him and I kill his homeboys too if I find out they're behind this. He says I insult him. That Alley was blood."

"My boy knew the difference between right and wrong," Maria said.

"What do you think happened, Tito?"

"He wasn't someone from the neighborhood. Everyone tells me. I don't know. I guess it was God's will."

"God's will that my boy dies on the street like a dog. I not understand this God." Maria got up and walked out the door, her blue terry cloth slippers shuffling on the carpet. Somers guessed she was about forty but she moved like someone much older.

Somers looked through Alley's drawers and closet and under the bed without finding anything pertinent. He turned down another offer of food and drink, shook hands all around, promising to do his best, then left. Outside the house, Somers approached Chuy and his girlfriend, who were sitting on the curb. The air smelled of marijuana.

"Chuy, who killed your cousin?"

"You find out, *azul*, and we'll take care of him."

Somers watched two girls playing hopscotch on a chalk grid drawn on the sidewalk. One of the girls stood at the end, knees together, feet together, toes barely outside the line, and threw her rabbit-foot-and-trinket marker. It hit the cement with a scrape and a jangle.

"I'll keep in touch, Chuy." Somers got in his car to drive home.

Sixteen

"Is John Somers there, please?"

"Who's this?"

"This is Iris Thorne. Who's this?"

"I don't have to tell you who I am. You called here."

"Is John there?"

"He's here."

"Can I speak with him, please?"

"Yeah. Hang on."

The telephone receiver banged once, twice, then several quick times as it swung from its cord.

"Dad! That Iris lady is on the phone."

Iris bristled. "John, hi... I'm on my way over, but I lost the directions to your house." She forced a chuckle.

"Oh. You still want to come?"

"Of course I want to come. I... they must have fallen out of my pocket. I don't usually lose things, but lately..."

"Well, don't feel obligated. I know you've had a long day."

"Don't you want me to come?"

"Of course I do. But if you're tired or if it's not good for you, it's okay. I thought maybe I put you on the spot today in the parking lot."

"Not at all. I've been looking forward to it. Tell me again where you live. Was that your daughter?"

She lost the directions to my house. She doesn't really want to come over.

Somers sat at his desk in the den. He chose the blue dry erase pen and wrote *Alley* at the top middle of a white board that was nailed to a wall. Down the left side, he wrote: *Uncle Tito, Mrs. Muñoz, Chuy/Cirrus St., Carmen, Lady Upstairs.*

He drew a horizontal line and wrote: *briefcase, ice pick, Oaxcatil, hearse/Cadillac.* Down the right side he wrote: *Stan Raab, Teddy Kraus, Joe Campbell, Billy Drye, Jayne Perkins, Iris Thorne.* He put a question mark next to Iris's name. Then he circled her name and circled it again.

He took the photo of Alley that he'd enlarged from Alley's California ID card, a somber Alley with serious eyes, and stuck it to the white board with a magnet shaped like a pineapple that said HAWAII. Then he opened Alley's briefcase.

There was a plastic package of tissues. A book on time management. Some seashells in a Ziploc bag. A brown paper bag with an apple and a napkin and a neatly folded, used piece of aluminum foil. A pocket calculator. A magnifying glass toy from a box of Cracker Jack. New pens and pencils. Junk, just like Carmen had said. He lifted and prodded the contents with a letter opener from his desk.

He pulled a tissue from the plastic package and folded it over his fingers. He pulled a memo pad from the file compartment. "From the desk of… Alejandro Muñoz." He held the pad by the edge and turned it so that the surface caught the light. There were writing impressions, but he couldn't make them out. He put the pad back. An opening in the face of the file compartment held business cards. He took one out. They were imprinted with the McKinney Alitzer logo and read: "Alejandro Muñoz, Director, Mexican Operations."

Somers looked out the den window at the afternoon shadows, then looked back at the card, flicked the stiff paper with his thumb, and put it in his wallet. He looked at his watch, closed Alley's briefcase, and moved it to the center of the desk. He noticed a chocolate-colored smear on a corner.

Somers examined his face in a Coors mirror over a couch. A blue-and-white mountain stream splashed around one edge. He unbuttoned his Levi's and tucked in the white cotton shirt woven with blue ticking stripes that his daughter had given him for his birthday, probably picked out with the help of his ex-wife. It seemed as if he had always been dressed by women.

Iris'll probably have me in Armani suits. Hold on. This is just dinner. Anyone can lose directions and it's just dinner.

He prodded the soft circle of flesh that rolled out a little over his belt. He ran his hand over his chin to check for any prickly spots.

Maybe I should wear slacks. Too formal. Or shorts. Wait. It's just dinner with an old friend.

Iris brought the TR to a crawl and squinted at the street signs, looking for Cat Canyon Road where she was supposed to turn left after she'd passed the junction of Old and New Topanga Canyon boulevards. Cars and motorcycles sped around the twisting road that connects the arid San Fernando Valley to the east with Malibu over the hills and on the other side of the canyon to the west. The canyon road was lined with ersatz western shops, patchouli-and-clove-scented health food restaurants, cozy Italian restaurants with dangling Chianti bottles, funky rock-and-roll boîtes with Harleys parked outside, woodcraft studios cluttered with pelican and dolphin sculptures, and clothing boutiques where tie-dye was miraculously in vogue again. Folks sold fruit and vegetables from roadside stands and carpets and framed pictures and shorts out of car trunks.

The middle of the canyon was far from anywhere—far from the freeway, the malls, the beach. Parts of it were wooded and laced with creeks, home to coyotes that roamed at night and picked off careless house cats, home to deer, a few mountain lions, tortoises, and skunks and snakes. Home to people seeking a country flavor in L.A. Home to the counterculture residue.

Iris found Cat Canyon and turned, crossing a wooden bridge built over a small creek, dry from the drought. She found Withered Canyon, the second turn, and wound her way up and up. The pavement ran out and turned to dirt scattered with pebbles. She followed the road to the end and parked in an unpaved clearing overlooking the summertime-browned Santa Monica Mountains and the blue Pacific. The fault line beneath the mountains had crumpled and folded the earth so that the brown hills looked like a bedspread after a restless night.

Residents had nailed wooden placards painted or carved with their names to a post at the bottom of the road. Ramshackle wood-frame houses with homemade stained glass windows, wind chimes made out of metal tubing, and dogs sleeping in beds of fallen pine needles stood next to newer structures of cement and greenish glass blocks or dark wood and smoked glass that looked like those in feature articles in architectural design magazines. "*Haut Style* on a Narrow Lot in the Wilderness."

Iris walked up the road, which got steeper and steeper, the heels of her pumps slipping on the gravel and poking small, round holes in the dirt. She balanced on one foot and grabbed the other to examine the damage to her Bruno Maglis. At the top of the hill, she saw a steel mailbox on a post painted with John Somers's street number and primitive daisies. She climbed a neat path bordered with sturdy, spring-blooming ice plant and small boulders and finally saw the house when she reached the crest. It clung to the hillside, built in several stories descending the side of the hill, and was wood, stained to look like redwood.

Iris pressed the doorbell. No answer. She tried the door. It was open.

"Hello?"

A muscular, white bull terrier burst through the door, barking. Iris stood still. She watched the dog and the dog watched her with one blue eye and one brown eye. He growled.

"Buster, stop it."

The girl followed the dog out the door. She was of indeterminate adolescent-girl age, somewhere between eleven and fifteen. She was almost as tall as Iris, lean and tan, with curves that looked out of place, as if the dolls had hardly been put away. She wore baggy, knee-length jams, an oversized T-shirt with the sleeves rolled up, rubber, rainbow-hued flip-flops, and several frayed and dirty friendship strings tied around her wrist. Her fingernails and toenails were painted with badly chipped rose polish, an attempt at glamour without the discipline to maintain it. She had long, thick hair, pulled back in a ponytail, in Somers's auburn color.

"You're Iris," she stated.

"Yes," Iris said, feeling unwelcome. "Are you John's daughter?"

"Didn't he tell you about me?" She patted the dog's head.

The dog narrowed his eyes at Iris, raised his muzzle, and sniffed the air in her direction. His throat rumbled and the fur on the back of his neck stood up.

"He… sure, he…"

John Somers rounded the side of the house. "Iris." His voice came out in a light bubble. He cleared his throat. "You found it. And you met Chloe and Buster."

"Sort of. Hi, Chloe."

"Hi." Chloe whipped around and walked into the house. The dog followed. She started to pull the door closed, then popped her head out. "Dad, I'm going to Courtney's house."

"Okay, but you're coming back for dinner."

"But Daaaad…"

"We've already talked about this."

Chloe sighed theatrically and closed the door hard.

John looked at Iris and shrugged. "Thirteen."

"I don't think she likes me."

"Chloe? Of course she likes you."

"Does she live here?"

"No, she lives with her mother in the Valley but comes here as much as she wants, which means she practically lives here during the summer. Come in. Let me show you around."

John pushed open the front door, which was inset with stained-glass panels. They creaked down a wooden hallway into a living room with a high beamed ceiling and knotty pine walls lined with built-in bookshelves crammed with books, records, and knickknacks. A coffee table made out of a resin-covered slice of tree trunk was flanked by two well-worn sofas. Sunlight streamed through a glass wall opening onto a wooden deck that extended the length of the house. The deck had a hole in the center to allow the trunk of a broad oak tree to pass through. Its branches grew over the house, shading and littering it with fallen leaves.

They poked their heads into the den and then into an upstairs bathroom, where an orchid with a single long stem heavy with spotted flowers grew on the windowsill. He pointed down a narrow staircase to the bedrooms. They walked through a sunny kitchen, trimmed in yellow and magenta tiles, that overlooked the canyon. It was a working kitchen. Wooden spoons, spatulas, scrapers, tongs, and chopsticks, all stained from use, were crammed into a ceramic bin.

John took two glasses and a bottle of wine from the refrigerator. They walked out the backdoor and down a sloping yard to a flat terraced area where rows of tomato plants heavy with fruit grew in mesh cones next to well-tended rows of carrots, radishes, and tall corn. The dog was lying in the corn, the leaves brushing his back. An old peach tree spread thick branches covered with fruit and dark oblong leaves over a far corner of the yard. John and Iris scattered the birds that were eating the fallen fruit.

"Nice place," Iris said.

"You like it, really?"

"Sure. Are you surprised?"

"It's sort of… rustic. It doesn't seem like it would be to your taste."

"I like things rustic. How long have you lived here?"

"Ten years."

"Your wife didn't want the house?"

"No. She said it was too much me." *Good move. Let her know how little Penny thinks of me.* He turned and walked into the vegetable patch. "Help me pick some tomatoes. I'm doing a tomato salad with basil and olive oil."

She walked into the soft earth. "That's right. You said you were a good cook."

"Yep. You?"

She shrugged. "No. But, I like it when men are." Her heel sunk deep into the dirt. When she tried to free it, her foot came out of her shoe and she toppled forward. He caught her, grabbing her forearms.

"Be careful."

He looked down at her and met her eyes, which looked very blue with the deepening sky. She laughed nervously and looked back at her shoe, which was embedded in the ground three feet behind them. He released her arms and held out a hand.

"Hold on. I'll pick it up."

She put her hand in his palm and he leaned over and dislodged the shoe. He tapped the dirt out, dusted it off against his Levi's, and presented it to her like Prince Charming at the ball. She supported her weight on his palm and bent over to put the errant shoe back on her foot.

He looked down at her long-boned hand that crossed his palm, at her narrow, enameled nails, felt her warmth penetrating through his skin and savored a sweet remembrance. *Her hands and feet were always warm.*

"Sorry. What a klutz."

"Well, you're not dressed for crawling around in the dirt."

"I wanted to change clothes, but I had to do something and I ran out of time."

She stood on both feet and slid her hand from his palm. He closed his hand as if to hold her touch. She walked back to the grass.

"These tomato plants remind me of my father," she said.

"He was my inspiration."

"No kidding?"

He squatted in the soft dirt by the row of tomato cones. He lifted a tomato away from the vine and turned it in his hand until it released.

"Seedless beefsteak tomatoes. I remember your dad out in your backyard, walking around with a hand pump, spraying them with God knows what. Carrying the little green worms he found in the palm of his hand, jingling them like coins. How is he?"

She watched the line of Somers's back through his shirt, which was pulled taut and tucked into jeans that were stretched across his muscular hips and thighs. "Crazy as ever."

"We forgot to pour the wine."

"I can do it."

"You never used to touch the stuff."

"You never used to have a daughter."

He walked out of the garden, cradling tomatoes in his arms against his chest. He looked at her and laughed. "That's true."

She took one of the tomatoes, held it to her nose, and breathed the ripe sugar. A piece of vine with leaves was stuck to it. She crumpled the leaves in her fingers and pressed them against her nose, inhaling the pungent green aroma. "Boy. This brings back memories. Nothing like it. It feels like July and I'm standing in my backyard in shorts and bare feet. Funny, isn't it? Years go by but something remains."

"The smell of tomatoes?"

"Well, that, and I feel comfortable here."

"I'm glad. I'm sorry if I made you mad the other day."

She shrugged. "Forget it. Let's not talk about it. I haven't imagined Alley dead on that sidewalk for a whole hour."

"Deal. Speaking of comfortable, you'd probably fit into something of Chloe's."

"That's okay. I don't think she'd want me wearing her clothes."

"I don't think she'd mind."

"I don't want her wearing my clothes." The leaves of the old peach tree rustled and Chloe backed down a branch, stepped on a lower one, swung from it with both hands, then dropped to the ground.

"Chloe, have you been up there the whole time?" John asked.

"I always sit there. It's my place."

"You should have told us you were there."

"I wasn't listening."

"All right. Please take these tomatoes to the kitchen."

"I don't want her wearing my clothes."

"John, I have some running stuff, shorts and tennis shoes and a T-shirt in my car," Iris said. "I'll run the tomatoes up to the house and change."

Iris carried her black linen suit and silk blouse folded in her arms and dangled her pumps from her fingers. She looked out the window of a bathroom tiled in black-and-white checkerboard and saw John and Chloe bent over the carrots, pulling them from the ground.

Iris sat the bundle of clothing on one of the living room couches and wandered with her hands behind her back, her sneakers squeaking on the wood floor. She looked at the crowded bookshelves. There was a framed picture of a clean-cut John Somers looking official in a midnight blue LAPD uniform and a more recent one of Somers and Lewin and some other men in tuxedos. Someone's wedding. Then there were pictures of Chloe. Toothy school portraits, as a baby in the arms of a roan-bearded, frizzy-haired John Somers, in a party dress at the front door of this house with several other girls.

Iris wandered into the darkened den. She saw a desk lamp in the dim light and turned it on. The light shone on Alley's briefcase. She jerked back and bumped into a floor lamp. She turned and steadied the lamp with trembling hands, then saw the white board.

"You're not supposed to be in here."

"What?" Iris turned.

"This is my father's office."

"I was just looking around... I wandered in."

Chloe walked assuredly to the desk and put her hand on the briefcase. The dog walked into the room behind her, its nails clicking on the hardwood floor.

"This man was murdered." She pointed to Alley's somber photograph. "And this is his briefcase." She pointed to the chocolate smear. "Know what this is?"

Iris pressed her hand over her mouth. She closed her eyes.

Chloe pointed to the white board. "He was stabbed with an ice pick."

Iris grabbed her stomach and turned away.

"Chloe, what are you talking about?" John walked into the room.

"I found her in your office, Dad."

"Iris can go wherever she wants. She's our guest. How did you know about the ice pick?"

Iris looked at him wide-eyed. "It's true?"

Somers looked at her without answering.

"I have eyes and ears, Dad," Chloe said.

Iris left the den and picked up her clothes from the couch. She heard John's voice low and Chloe's higher, whining. She stood in the doorway of the den with her clothes in her arms. John stopped in midsentence and looked at Iris.

"John... I can't. You've been hospitable and nice, but Alley, I..."

"Iris, I'm sorry. I didn't mean for you to see this."

"It's my fault. I was snooping. Maybe Alley's just another homicide to you, but he was my friend. They buried him today." A tear rolled down her face.

John winced.

"Maybe you can separate it. I can't."

"Iris, let's eat something..."

She looked past him. He followed her gaze. She was looking at her name on the white board.

"Iris, your name's circled because you haven't been interrogated yet."

"See?" She walked to the front door and opened it. "This isn't going to work, John."

The sun shone through the colored stained glass in the door and made a pattern on the wood floor. Iris tiptoed around the colors. She looked at John and pointed at the ground. "It's like at Alley's funeral. 'Bye, John. Chloe."

She closed the door and the colors shimmered on the floor.

John watched the undulating lights. Chloe put her arms around him.

"That's all right, Dad. You still have me."

Seventeen

"I've got Alley's briefcase."

"Let me change phones."

Somers heard Lewin's voice from across the room. "Jason, hang up the phone after I pick up, will ya?"

There was heavy, moist breathing into the phone. A young hand was holding the receiver too close.

"Jason, you can hang up now. From where?"

"The waitress. Carmen."

"Carmen."

"You have to have the right touch, Shamus."

"Guess she has a thing for goofy redheads. So what's in it?"

"Thanks, partner. Mostly a lot of junk."

"Great find."

Somers told Lewin about Alley's business cards, about *Tió* Tito's house with the expensive toys and new furnishings, about Alley's so-called promotion and his trips to Mexico, about the noise back from Oaxcatil, about Chuy vowing to get the *cabrón* who did Alley, about the Lady Upstairs and the big car.

"Huh," Lewin said. "Drug courier."

"Remember what the guys at the office said."

"Wait. Jason, put the phone down! Damn kids. Go to school and thrill their friends."

"Chloe too. Could be all the brains had to do was include Alley. Tell him he'd be one of the boys. Invite him to the frat party. Throw him some cash for pain and suffering."

"Seems like a lot of cash."

"Maybe Alley got greedy. Then Alley got dead. But it could be sweeter than that. Look at the obvious. Ambitious yuppies with megabucks passing through their hands every day. Avaricious, willing to sacrifice anything and anyone for the almighty greenback."

"Get off the soap box, Professor. But it's worth following up on. What did Ms. Thorne have to say?"

"About what?"

"Don't be coy, Professor. You were going to interview her today."

"Didn't come off. We had a scheduling conflict."

"Uh-huh."

"C'mon. What did you bring to the party today?"

"We're not talking about me. We're talking about you. About you and *Ms.* Thorne."

"Why do you say her name like that?"

"It's her name, isn't it?"

"What do you have against her?"

"I never said I have anything against her."

"You don't have to."

"I just want to know what her angle is on this case. And I'm getting tired of you making excuses for not facing her down." Lewin's voice rose.

"Ease up. There's no reason for you to get upset."

"You're avoiding talking to her about the case because of some prior relationship you had with her. Don't deny it."

"Look. If I can't get what we need from Iris by Monday morning, she's yours, okay? No reason to get bent. It just didn't happen today, okay? This case is moving forward just fine. She probably can't even add anything that we haven't already found out."

"It's principle."

"I don't like my credibility being questioned. We've worked together a long time."

"My point exactly, Professor. I want to go on that way."

"Goes without saying. What else you got in mind?"

"I think I'll drop by and see Teddy Kraus. See why we make him so nervous. See him without his buddies around so he can't goof for their benefit. Wanna come?"

"No, I've got Chloe."

"Here's something for you. Jayne Perkins sought a restraining order against one Teddy Kraus."

"Office lovers?"

"Looks like. Ms. Thorne could have told us that three days ago."

"You already made that point. You'd think Jayne would have better taste."

"So, big Saturday night?"

"I might call the police down in Oaxcatil, Mexico. See if they have any skinny on Alley."

"And you're working on Ms. Thorne's tail. I mean, trail. Ooops, another call coming in. Damn 'call waiting.' Hang on."

"I'm done."

"Okay, Professor. Keep low and drive slow." Lewin clicked the other call in. "This is Lewin."

"Detective, this is Stan Raab—"

"Stan, what's up?"

"—from McKinney Alitzer?"

"Sure, sure. Of course. What can I do for you?"

"I'm sorry to bother you at home—"

"No problema."

"—but you said to call if I thought I had information pertinent to the case. Well, something unusual happened today after the funeral."

"Yeah…"

"I went back to my office, downtown?"

"Yeah…"

"And I found out that Iris Thorne, one of my sales reps, had been there."

"Is that unusual?"

"Well... no... She comes in on Saturdays sometimes. I know she was there today because she dropped a program from the funeral on the floor inside my private office."

"What's the problem?"

"I think she pried open my filing cabinet. There was a knife on top of the filing cabinet and the cabinet was unlocked."

"Anything missing?"

"A file, for one of the firm's accounts."

"Why would Ms. Thorne be interested in this account?"

"It's... one of our larger accounts. A big... unique account."

"The name?"

"Sorry?"

"The account's name?"

"Oh... Worldco."

"Could your secretary have taken the file?"

"She could have. Yes, that's possible. She could have taken it."

"Could anyone else have been in the suite?"

"The cleaning crew was there when I came in."

"So, they could have been in your office."

"Yes... yes, they could have."

"Stan, I'm a little confused. Does this file have something to do with Muñoz?"

"No. It was... just an account file. This sounds ridiculous, doesn't it? I'm sorry. I'm on edge. I'm seeing the bogeyman everywhere."

"How do you know the funeral program was Ms. Thorne's?"

"She'd written on it. I recognized her handwriting. She wrote directions and an address. Here, it says: Twelve Withered Canyon Road. And there's a phone number. I think she was going to this place tonight. It says six o'clock."

"Well, isn't that damn interesting?"

"Really, why?"

"Stan, you still haven't said why she'd want this file."

"You know, you're right. My secretary was in my filing cabinet on Friday. I'm making a big deal over nothing. I'm just rattled. I shouldn't have bothered you."

"No bother at all, Stan. You never know. Cases sometimes break from oddball information. Call anytime."

Lewin hung up the phone. "Damn interesting."

Eighteen

Paul Lewin parked across the street from Teddy Kraus's house in a quiet West L.A. neighborhood where real estate inflation had made the modest, older homes too rich for most working folks. The lawn was paid-gardener neat and Lewin guessed that the interior would be paid-housekeeper tidy also.

Freaking yuppies, Lewin thought. *Life's just one big Hacky Sack game.*

He watched the house for a few minutes out of habit, then opened his car door to get out.

Teddy came out of his house just then and got into his paid-hand washed clean, candy-apple red Beemer. The electronic chirp of the car alarm being disengaged joined the other clear noises of the late summer L.A. night. The sweet fragrance of night-blooming jasmine hung thick in the air. A few stars and a three-quarter moon shined weakly through the smoggy sky.

What the hell. It's Saturday night. Lewin followed Teddy.

The traffic on the Five south was light on Saturday night. Monday through Friday, the southern leg of the Golden State Freeway is owned by big rigs in the very early hours and by

Orange County-to-L.A. commuters other times, everyone rolling down the old asphalt, which doesn't seem up to the task.

Tonight there wasn't much action on the Five. Teddy chewed up the asphalt.

Damn, Lewin said to himself.

When they exited at Florence Avenue, Lewin felt the bass of Teddy's stereo through the steel chassis of his wife's minivan. He saw Teddy drumming his hands on the steering wheel in time with the beat.

A car full of girls out on Saturday night pulled beside Teddy. Happy days. He stared at them and they ignored him and he stared at them and they finally turned and giggled. Teddy half-stood through the open sunroof and blew them a kiss. They drove off, giggling. *Ladies, ladies! You don't know what you're missing!*

The facade of the Four Queens Card Club was lit up like a Christmas tree in red, green, and white neon. Christmas every day. Blinking white lights swirled around and around—a drunk's nightmare.

Lewin parked one car away from Teddy and watched through the windows of the car between them. Teddy hadn't seen him. Lewin figured that Teddy probably wouldn't notice him unless he went right up to his face. Teddy was that kind of a guy. Full of himself.

Teddy took a snort off a vial.

Get some courage, baby.

Teddy lit a cigarette with the Beemer's lighter and then got out. He hitched his pants up over his belly and started toward the club. The Beemer chirped twice behind him.

The place was packed. A low cloud of cigarette smoke hung in the air. Waitresses wearing short, poufy skirts buzzed past, balancing trays of drinks. Chip attendants wearing red shirts with the Four Queens logo embroidered across the back hopped from table to table, buying and selling poker chips. A hypnotist did a show in the lounge. Laughter and applause spilled out.

Lewin pictured people doing stupid things like acting like strippers or as if they were in love with people they didn't know.

What a crock.

The reservation hostess's voice carried across the main room.

"W.R. for five-ten stud, smoking. W.R. for five-ten stud."

There wasn't much talking. There was a buzzing white noise of poker chips being jiggled in palms, tossed onto felt, stacked on top of one another. A clattering hum of plastic on plastic.

Teddy made his reservation and walked to a cash machine. He took out his wallet, pulled out a stack of credit cards, and examined each one.

"Not you, not you. Limitsville for you. Whoa! Come to Daddy. Five-thousand-dollar limit. Just sign on the line."

He slid the card into the machine and it handed him cash. Magic.

Lewin ordered a scotch on the rocks from a passing waitress. *Coke and gambling. Could definitely change things.*

The hostess called Teddy's reservation. "Follow Frankie to your table."

Teddy hip-hopped over to Frankie, who glared at him from across the room, holding a walkie-talkie in his left hand like a broken bottle.

"Frankeeebuddeee," Teddy said.

"Asshole," Frankie said.

"What have I ever done to you, Frank-eee?"

"They let you back in here, huh?"

"Eddie and I go way back, Frank-eee. Way back."

Frankie started walking.

Teddy sauntered after him to a table where eight men were already seated—four blacks, three Asians, and one white guy. The dealer was middle-aged and white, with graying Elvis hair. He rolled a poker chip up and down over the tops of his fingers and looked bored.

"Sit," Frankie ordered.

"Here." Teddy tried to hand him a ten-dollar bill.

Frankie glowered at him. "Get out of my face."

Teddy turned to the group. "Gotta love this guy."

The three Asians smoked cigarettes and drank from glasses of beer on little round tables positioned between every two chairs. The white man had thin gray hair deeply parted at the side and combed over his bald patch down the center of his head. One of the black men had neat, short-cropped, salt-and-pepper hair and was wearing a cotton crew-neck sweater with the sleeves pushed up. The other three blacks looked to be in their early twenties and were wearing designer jogging suits with the jackets zipped open and no shirts, beepers clipped to their waistbands. One of them had his hand inside his jacket and was absentmindedly stroking his pectorals. They looked at Teddy impassively.

"Men!" Teddy said. "I'm Teddy Kraus the third and I'm pleased as hell to meetcha all." He smiled like a scout leader at a jamboree.

The other players either ignored him or looked as if they didn't know what to make of him.

"Friendly group," Teddy said. "Boys, just don't spend the rent money. You'll have hell to pay at home. Dealer, let's party."

"Don't deal," Frankie said, walking up to the table. "Get up. You're done here."

"Awww, maann!" Teddy swatted his chips. They flew across the felt table top. "Guys, play in Gardena. You can stick a fork in this place, it's done."

The chip attendant gathered Teddy's chips and handed him cash. Teddy grabbed it from him, pushed Frankie aside, and strode ahead.

"Don't let the door hit you on your way out," Teddy heard someone say behind him. His face flushed red.

Sally Lamb was sitting in Eddie's white leather chair with his hands folded over his lean belly. His loose facial skin sagged into a world-weary expression. Jimmy Easter paced the floor behind the chair where Teddy was sitting, walking slowly, watching Teddy with each step, passing close enough so that Teddy could feel, or thought he could feel, Jimmy's leather jacket brush against his hair. Teddy angled his head slightly from side to side, trying to keep Jimmy in his line of vision.

"Gambling with my money out there?" Sally asked.

"You guys said Friday," Teddy said. "Bring the money Friday. It's only Saturday. I have almost a whole week."

"Go home," Sally said. "No gambling for you."

"But I'm feeling lucky tonight."

"We're going to Gardena after this and if I find you there, I'm going to have Jimmy kick your ass."

"You can't tell me what to do. I'll go wherever I want." Teddy shifted his shoulders uneasily as Jimmy paced behind him. "Tell him to sit down."

Sally continued. "Teddy, if I don't get my money on Friday, I'm going to have to move on you. Much as I like you, business is business. I'm being up front with you."

"You'll get it Friday." Teddy scooted forward to sit on the edge of the chair. "I've got this scam on penny stocks. It's beautiful." He rubbed his palms together. "Your portfolio earned nine thousand bucks in one day. Hey, you know, a guy like you should invest in the market. You ever think about that?"

"You know, Teddy, since you brought it up, I have been thinkin' about this securities thing you're in. It seems like it's got a lot of business opportunities. Nine large is good money for a day's work. With a little management, you could do very well."

"That's a one-time-only thing, Sally. Just to get out of this jam."

Sally held his palms together and pressed them against his lips. "Look, I'll cut twenty grand off what you owe me if we do some business. Or you can pay me. It's real simple."

"I can't do a scam long term! I'll get caught. I'll lose my license."

"I'm just tryin' to help you out. You decide. Tell me on Friday."

Jimmy stood close to Teddy's chair. He stroked Teddy's cheek with the back of his index finger.

Lewin watched Teddy come out from behind the mirrored door, slamming it behind him. He watched Teddy cross the floor and go up the stairs, passing within inches of him, and walk out of the card room into the lobby. Lewin started to follow him when he saw the door to the back office open. He drained the last of the scotch rocks and walked toward the mirrored door.

This is getting damn interesting.

"Sally Lamb," Lewin said. "And... lessee... Jimmy Easter. Ha, haaaha. You guys slay me. So. You boys leave any more souvenirs in the canyon for me?"

Nineteen

Iris Thorne took a cool shower that should have refreshed her but only solidified the bad way she felt.

She stood in her walk-in closet and clicked the hangers. She pulled out an ankle-length white cotton nightgown trimmed in eyelet and hand embroidery, which she'd forgotten she'd bought. The price tag was still on it. The price made her gasp. Then she figured that buying it probably had been the right thing to do at the time. She wouldn't second-guess herself. She wouldn't start that tonight. At least she hadn't headed straight to the mall. She'd come straight home from John Somers's house. That was good.

She lay on the goose-down comforter on her bed, shoving lace pillows out of the way, and closed her eyes. Twenty seconds later, she got up.

She wrestled with the cork on a champagne bottle and it finally gave with a pop. She filled a Baccarat flute, started to bring it to her lips, then filled a second one, and left it sitting on the sink. She clinked the two glasses together.

"To Alley, wherever you are."

She gestured around the room as if he was floating there, somewhere.

"May death be kinder than life. At least quieter. I guess it was already too quiet for you."

She drank most of the glass, then topped it off again. She ran her finger across the dust that had gathered on a revolving herb and spice rack that someone had given her as a housewarming gift and made a mental note to speak to her cleaning lady. She looked at the herbs and spices that had paled with age. She'd never had the occasion to open any of them.

She started to leave the kitchen and went back and took the bottle of champagne with her. She tucked the cordless phone under her arm and went onto the terrace. The sea wind tickled the air like it always did and the cotton nightgown fluttered against her legs. She gave the philodendron a drink of champagne and sat in the wooden Adirondack lounge chair that she had ordered from the company in Maine.

This is living, she thought.

She punched in Steve's number and his phone rang several times before his answering machine clicked on. She hung up.

She called back again, waited for the phone message to end, opened her mouth to speak, then hung up again without saying anything. She started to speculate about where he could be on a Saturday night, then stopped.

She called her mother.

"Come over, honey," her mother said.

No. Her mother would somehow pull the unhappiness out of her and Iris would cry and end up confirming her mother's feeling that she should be worried about her and it would make Iris think that indeed she had made the wrong choices.

But she told her mother about Alley. She only told her who Alley was and what happened to him and the about funeral that day but none of the other stuff about the money and the stock and the ice pick and Somers and now Joe Campbell's father.

But it was enough for her mother to sense the wolf at Iris's door and she started to worry. And the weight of her mother's worrying added to Iris's burden.

She went inside, got the bag from the Rodeo Drive boutique, sat cross-legged on the Oriental area rug in the living room, and dumped out the cash. She took the rubber bands off the bundles. There were mostly hundred-dollar bills. She rubbed them around on the carpet. Then she started counting.

The microwave sang and John Somers pulled out the ballooned bag of popcorn. He grabbed the opposite corners of the package, pulled it open, and reached in, fingers dancing around the steam. He tossed a kernel to the dog who expertly snatched it out of the air, then stood at attention for more.

"Does that have tropical oils in it?" Chloe said.

"I don't know. It's good." Somers handed her the bag.

"It has palm oil in it. Says right here. Mom says you'll drop dead in your tracks, the way you eat."

"Have your mother make the arrangements."

"Why do you always call her that—'your mother'?"

"Isn't she?"

"It just sounds so official, or something."

"She's not getting my Dead albums when I drop."

"Philip doesn't like the Grateful Dead."

"I'll bet old Phil doesn't."

"He likes to be called Philip."

"Figures."

"*He* doesn't eat tropical oils."

"I bet your mother thinks I could take a lesson from old Phil, right?"

"She says some men never grow up. With your tree house and cops and robbers."

"What do you think?"

"I like this house, Dad. It's fun."

"I like it too. Tell your mother that your father says to have fun this week, okay? She forgets sometimes."

"Okay."

"That's good for your heart, too."

Somers threw another kernel to Buster, high this time, and the dog snatched it out of the air, his jaws closing with a snap. Somers walked into the living room, Chloe and the dog following like a quail family. He reached to the top of a bookshelf and pulled down a stack of oversized books that were lying on their sides. Dust rolled off the top.

"Ugh," Chloe said, "dust bunnies. Don't you ever clean up there, Dad?"

Somers sighed, looked at his daughter, and hoped she'd grow out of it.

"Let's go downstairs," he said. "There's a movie starting that I want to see."

"Wait. Is it in color?"

"Let's see. Yes, it was made in color."

"Okay, is it in English?"

"It has… English subtitles."

"Awww, Dad! Not subtitles. Puleeese, no subtitles."

"But I named you after the girl in the movie. Don't you want to see it?"

"Wellll, okay. What were you going to name me if I'd been a boy?"

"Claus."

"Claus?"

"Good strong name. Claus. No one messes with Claus."

Somers walked down the stairs followed by Chloe, then Buster, the dog's nails clicking on the wood floor. Chloe threw herself on Somers's water bed, creating undulating waves. The bed was covered with a patchwork spread and was in a heavy wood frame with high posts. Somers propped up a pillow and sat next to his daughter. He put the popcorn between them and spread the books out, wiping dust off the covers with his hand.

"Here it is, *'Carta de México.'*"

He handed it to Chloe. "Find a town called Oaxcatil for me."

"Waka what?"

He spelled it for her.

"Where is it, about?"

"I forgot to ask."

He clicked on the television just as the opening credits were starting. He threw another kernel to the dog, who waited longingly with his head stretched up onto the bed. Somers looked through the other books he had taken from the shelf and pulled a photo album onto his lap. He opened the album cover and felt a rush of nostalgia.

The first picture was of Iris. It was on Santa Monica beach, looking north where it curves into Malibu, in winter under gray skies. Iris was bundled up in sweaters and she was smiling. She was smiling at him.

He turned the album pages. The paper was brittle. Children had been born and half grown and paper had dried up.

He turned a page.

He'd never thought about love until he fell in love with Iris and it felt pretty great. It felt like the real thing from what he could tell when he was twenty years old. He hadn't quite felt that way since.

He turned a page.

Then he thought that maybe he was trying to recapture something that belonged to the past. Like people wearing vintage clothing. It looks authentic but it's still just a show. And who really wants to go back, anyway?

He turned a page.

But then he saw a picture of a day he'd forgotten about. He might have gone the whole rest of his life without remembering that day. It was a day when he felt transported. When everything had made crazy sense. When he had meshed with the crazy scheme of things. When his mind had been clear and his senses open.

It was a Sunday in late summer and they'd driven to East Los Angeles in his MG with the brakes almost gone. Easlos, she'd called it. The Santa Ana winds had blown hot and hard all night, raising the crime rate, bewildering sailors, shoving the smog to the ocean, enervating everyone, circling the city with slate mountains, cleansing the sky to a brilliant blue that was hard to look at, reminding everyone of what a glorious place Southern California must have been once upon a time.

The freeways shone white, the silicon in the asphalt sparkling like cut jewels. There wasn't as much traffic then. You could get on the freeway at certain times and there'd be hardly anyone else there. And he drove the freeway with the MG with bad brakes with the top down, Iris Thorne at his side, driving through thin, blue air, cruising on brilliant concrete and steel. It made you feel as if you were on the pipeline to anywhere.

Iris's house was on top of a hill in a worn lower-middle-class neighborhood that had changed hands from the Jews to the Japanese to the Mexicans, who had it still. Iris's father had moved there before it had been claimed by anyone and bought a lot of the cheap, rolling land. Some roads were still unpaved. Some streets still didn't have sidewalks. Some people had chickens and ducks and rabbits in their backyards. There was undeveloped land all around, only fifteen years ago. Great hills covered with tall, dry yellow weeds that swayed and rustled in the wind, home to tortoises and road runners and snakes. It was like a day in the country.

The air was hot and dry and Indian summer brittle.

Iris took Somers inside to greet her parents. Her mother, forties-movie-star pretty, hanging clothes out to dry in the backyard with wooden clothespins. Her father, sunburned nose, his flat, straight hair looking like a wind off a Texas plain had just blown through it.

They were in the house for ten minutes, had been sitting on the flowered sofa for ten seconds, tinted aluminum tumblers of pink fruit punch and ice in front of them, television on, when Iris turned to show him the pink moustache she'd made on her upper lip with the fruit punch and he'd laughed and she'd pulled his arm to go.

They walked up the great yellow, weed-covered hill, dragging a cardboard refrigerator box that someone had left for the garbage man. The dog ran ahead and looked back to wait for them, then ran ahead again. The weeds stood four feet tall, heavy with pointy seeds that caught on everything.

They positioned the refrigerator box at the crest of the slope, the bottom facing downhill. Iris slid in front and he straddled her, wrapping his arms around her waist, feeling her ribs through her cotton T-shirt, as narrow as a sparrow's. They pressed their faces against the half-inch opening in the box bottom where the flaps came together. He pushed off, down the hill. They smashed through the slick weeds, gaining momentum, the rocks and dirt clods sending the box on a wild trajectory, the dog running alongside barking, both of them screaming, seeing only a flash of yellow weeds. They hit a hole that sent them flying out, ten feet in either direction, and they rolled down the hill until they finally stopped.

He rolled onto his back and laughed at the blue sky.

Iris stood over him, trailing the battered box by a flap, grinning, panting, then falling in the tall weeds that hid them from the world. They tore handfuls of weeds from the ground, dirt clods dangling from the ends, and lay on them and looked up at the sky, the dry wind troubling the weeds around them.

"Shhhh, listen!" Iris said.

She put her ear against the ground and he did the same. The weeds beneath his ear rustled and clicked and whirred.

"It's a different world."

Their legs were covered with shallow cuts, bloody and caked with dirt. He kissed her bruises, which were already starting to come up, purple against her ermine skin. He kissed her face and stroked her tangled hair. She put her hands under his T-shirt and laid her cheek against his chest. She pulled his shorts down and sat astride him. They made love, with him staring into a sky that was so bright it made his eyes hurt, feeling as if he was one with the lizards and spiders below and crows and pigeons above and the dog panting and drooling next to them and with Iris. Every pore was open, every nerve sensitized. It was simple and perfect. He wanted to hold on to Iris forever.

Iris pulled the frosting off a Sara Lee butter pecan coffee cake. She picked off the pecans and dug out the cinnamon filling with her fingers, washing it down with champagne. She clicked through the five million cable stations. An Asian man pounded on a desk, his Korean translated into rows of Mandarin, Vietnamese, and Tagalog characters at the bottom of the screen. A hospital promised relief. Kids out of control? Wife depressed? Husband alcoholic? Stash them here. A nature program showed baby sea turtles breaking out of their eggs and scampering down the sand to the sea. Iris started to weep.

She clicked to a movie where people were talking and smoking a lot. It had a flat art-film texture and was in French with subtitles. The girl called the man "bourgeois." Iris remembered when it used to be an insult.

She remembered seeing every French and Italian movie that came out in college, yearning in the dark for crumbling buildings, old art, thick coffee, stinky cigarettes, neat aperitifs, and sultry-eyed men with suggestive manners. Ooohhh-la-la.

Somers had been great. He was fun. He was a pal. But he was just so... homespun. Big and freckled with a face as wide open as the grain belt. You didn't live for the moment with someone you met in the cafeteria dishing up mystery meat, did you?

She remembered taking Somers to this same movie and they made love afterward in his dorm room with the sun streaming in the single window and his roommate at an afternoon lab. She'd learned every inch of his body, exploring with the curiosity of the new and the leisure of youth, where the only penalty was missing the four o'clock lecture. Then they'd slept, Somers's holding her in his arms so that she wouldn't roll off the narrow dorm-room bed, and she'd dreamt of faraway places.

Iris picked at the coffee cake with her fingers and watched the movie. Chloe, the protagonist, whom Iris once had thought free-spirited, bohemian, and impossibly chic now seemed lonely and adrift. The man, the bourgeois, just seemed to be a guy trying to make a nice life for his family and having a midlife crisis. And Iris felt a pang for those afternoons with Somers in his dorm room and second-guessed herself and wondered how she had got here from there.

"Dad, isn't that Iris?"
"Yes, it's Iris."
"When?"
"In college."

"You didn't tell me you knew her in college."

"It didn't come up."

"Were you boyfriend and girlfriend?"

"Yes."

"Did you sleep with her?"

Somers looked at his daughter, started to lie, then backed off. "Yes... but we were in college. We were almost adults. We *were* adults. And careful. Safe... you know?"

"I get the point, Dad. Why did you break up?"

He sighed. For a time, he had shared Iris's bright dream and imagined a life as something other than another cop in the family. His grades hadn't been good enough to join Iris in the European study program and he saw this as only the first time she would leave him behind. But he hadn't tried very hard to go with her. He'd said he preferred staying put. Who cares about going over there anyway? He'd hidden his fear of the unknown under a cover of macho bravado. It seemed stupid now, but that was how he felt then. He'd been young.

He'd dated other people, as they'd agreed, and Penny had become pregnant. They'd been careless, as he and Iris had never been, but Iris had held onto her future with clenched fist and would never have made such a trivial mistake. Somers had done the right thing, got married, put the past behind him, provided for his family, and thought he was happy. He was busy and didn't have time to dwell on what could have been or even what was. But reflective moments had crept in since, uninvited, and although he loved his daughter and would never have undone the events that created her, he'd wondered about those careless encounters with Penny and why he'd let himself slip so easily into a familiar lifestyle. It was as if the dangers of being a cop weren't as scary as the exploration of his own potential.

"We grew in different directions."

"Oh. Here's Oaxcatil. It's north of Mexico City—here." She pointed to a small dot on the map.

"Looks like a cow town. I wonder if Camarena with the Tijuana police can help me out." He looked at his watch. It was 9:00. "I'm going to try him at home."

He went upstairs to use the phone in the den.

Camarena was home and was glad to hear from him. Buddies forever, after that case they'd worked on together. Somers made plans to drive down to Tijuana the next day, Sunday. It would make communications with Oaxcatil easier than trying to have a three-way conversation. He'd spend the day. They'd do it up. Dog races, everything.

He climbed back onto the bed. "Done."

The phone rang.

"Iris. What a surprise. How are you?"

"I'm fine."

"What's up?"

"Look, I'm sorry about leaving today. You're just doing your job."

"It's okay. I know my job's weird."

"It must be hard, day in and day out."

"We have a sick sense of humor about it."

"Really?"

"But I'll spare you."

Laughter. Silence.

"Look, John. I have to tell you something."

"I'm all ears."

"Joe Campbell's father might know something about Alley's murder."

"Joe Campbell's father? How did you come up with that?"

"I… heard something. I think you should look into it."

"What did you hear?"

"I just heard something, okay? Can't we leave it like that?"

"Why won't you tell me?"

"It's just something that someone said. I can't even remember it exactly."

"C'mon, Iris. I've been doing this a long time."

"No, honestly."

"Who are you trying to protect?"

"I'm not trying to protect anyone."

"Who are you protecting, Iris?"

"No one."

"You don't trust me to do my job."

"John, I don't want to fight. I'm just trying to help."

"You'd help a lot more if you'd tell me what's going on."

"I can't."

"Why not?"

"Because you've discounted Alley. Look at what you told the newspaper."

"You're discounting me. I told them something based upon experience."

"Alley wasn't that way. You don't know."

"I'll tell you what I know. I know a guy who got involved in a lot of money somehow, probably because he let somebody sweet-talk him into thinking he was a big shot. Played on this pride that everyone's been talking about. That's the Alley I know."

"That wasn't Alley. I know it wasn't. And I won't sell him out."

"Iris, this is wearing a little thin."

"Look. Just listen to this. Joe Campbell and his parents are meeting Stan Raab and his family at Disneyland tomorrow."

"That's nice, I hope they have a good time."

"They're meeting at ten o'clock. On the Castle Bridge."

"You expect me to go on some wild-goose chase? Why not make it easy and just tell me what this is all about?"

"Joe Campbell's father has some connection to Alley."

"Iris, I don't have time to fool around with citizens trying to be cops."

"If that's the way you feel about it, fine. I only have one more thing to say."

"Go."

"You're wrong about Alley."

"Thank you for that unsolicited insight, once again."

"And it was good that things turned out the way they did between us. You always accepted the status quo. You never challenged yourself."

"Oh, I didn't? Well, why don't you think about why you're obsessed with Alley's murder?"

"Because no one else will be his friend."

"No, that's not why. Solving this murder has become bigger than life to you. It's your cause, your purpose. It makes you feel needed and not so alone. Maybe I'm not the only one who should do some thinking. Let Alley go, Iris."

She slammed down the telephone receiver.

He smashed his thumb on the TV remote control and changed the station. "I hate French movies."

Iris finished the bottle of champagne and fell asleep on the couch.

Twenty

Stan Raab stood on the bridge to the castle with his arm around his wife's shoulders and watched the swans swim in the moat and his children play. He compared his family to the ordinary folks walking around and found his brood to be a cut above. This was what his hard work had earned.

"Kyle, Morgan!" Susan Raab yelled. "You're going to get dirty before anyone gets here. C'mere." She leaned down and swatted the knees of their Baby Gap overalls, adjusted their matching painter's caps, and raked her porcelain nails through their spiked, pop-star haircuts, her wedding-ring rocks splitting light like prisms.

Stan smiled at Morgan, the birthday boy, and thought about the price tag on this Disneyland birthday soirée. The contractors' final payment on the Tahoe house construction was due this week. As well as the boys' tuition. The family vacation to a Caribbean resort was coming up. Insurance had refused to pay anything on Susan's liposuction and tummy tuck. He hated worrying about money. No matter how much you had, it was never enough. There were always so many hands in his pockets.

"There's Vi and Vito and Joey," Stan said. He stood straighter.

"Joey's alone?" Susan said. "I thought he was bringing a date."

"He's weird about bringing women around his family. Remember that girl he was engaged to who got cold feet after he told her about the family business?"

Joe Campbell stood tall and lean, looking like Hyannis Port in crisp khaki slacks and a loose white shirt with the sleeves rolled up. His mother, Violetta, held his arm and was bright and happy, talking and smiling, being escorted by her son. She was petite with auburn-tinted hair cut in a cute bob. She wore white pants, a bright print shirt, and practical tennis shoes for the day of walking.

Joe's father walked a little apart from Joe and his mother, his hands behind his back, turning to watch a uniformed worker efficiently brush a cigarette butt and a candy wrapper into a dustbin, nodding with approval, like a *patrón* stepping his acreage. He wore a forest green polo shirt, buttoned to the neck, tucked into dark slacks, and dark sunglasses, which hid eyes that could quickly turn from warm to menacing.

Stan met his friends halfway down the bridge, radiant with family good cheer. "Vito, Violetta, Joey! So good to see you."

There was hugging and kissing.

Susan gathered her squirming children under each arm.

"Look at these fine boys," Vito said, bending over to their level.

Susan Raab beamed. "Say hello to Uncle Vito, boys."

The seven-year-old murmured, "Hello, Uncle Vito."

Joey's father laughed and took a lollipop out of his pocket.

The boy took it, muttered his thanks, and darted away.

"And here's the birthday boy," Vito said.

"Morgan, say hello to Uncle Vito," Susan said.

The four-year-old saw the dark glasses loom close and buried his face in his mother's legs.

"Morgan," Stan scolded.

"Vito," Vi said. "He's scared by your sunglasses."

Vito laughed, "Heh, heh, heh," and firmly patted the boy's head. He handed Susan the other lollipop he'd brought. "Such fine boys."

Susan beamed a bonded smile, "It won't be too long before Joey will have some grandkids for you to play with."

"Tch," Vito sucked his teeth.

"Joey's just a late bloomer, Vito," Stan Raab said.

Vito faced his son. "Family is nothing to this one. This is the boy who changed his family name."

"Not here, Pop," Joe said.

Vi leaned toward Susan. "They've been at each other's throats all morning."

"How would you feel, Stan, if your boys changed their family name?" Vito asked.

"Don't drag Stan into this," Joe said.

"Listen to how my son talks to me."

"Let's put whatever is going on between you two behind us today, okay?" Vi said.

"Vi, this isn't your business," Vito said.

"Don't talk to my mother that way," Joe said.

"This boy knows everything," Vito said. "Tell me, since you know everything, since you know so much, you must know how to fix that offshore thing by now. Just yes or no."

Stan paled.

Joey shook his head. "I don't believe this."

"That's it," Vi said. "That's it. Finished. Susan, come on. Let's go. We'll leave them here." She swept Susan and the boys along with outstretched arms.

"I'll go with you," Joe said.

Stan waited until they were out of earshot. "Vito. I'm glad we have a chance to be alone."

"Joey said you and he talked."

"I feel responsible."

"Stan," Vito turned the dark sunglasses toward him. "It's done. Don't beat yourself up."

"I'm the manager of the department." Stan threw up his hands. "I feel like I have to do something. Did Joey tell you what happened yesterday?"

"Your Worldco papers were stolen. It's someone in your office. We figured that."

"Vito, I think I know who took the papers." Stan pulled a snapshot from his pants pocket and handed it to Joe's father.

Vito shoved his sunglasses up onto his forehead, where they rested. "Good looking girls. Fat guy."

"It was taken at a company picnic. Everyone got a set of pictures. They're all McKinney employees."

"This is the guy?"

"No." Stan tapped the photo. "I think this woman, Iris Thorne, stole my Worldco file."

"The woman?"

"She broke into my filing cabinet yesterday. I have proof. She was closer to Alley than anyone else at the firm. If anyone could have put Alley up to something, it's Iris."

"Huh."

"Vito, I feel like I have to do something. We go way back, Joe and me. He trusted me. You trusted me."

Vito patted him on the back and put the photo into his rear pocket. "Stan, you've been a good friend to my son."

"Iris is one of my top people. I keep asking myself how she got involved in this. I don't want to put her in danger."

"Stan, I just want to find out what happened. That's all." He patted him on the back again.

"You won't tell Joe?"

"You've come to me in confidence. Enough business for Sunday. Let's go on that ride with the singing dolls." He chuckled, put his hand on Stan's back, and guided him along.

"What do we tell Joe we were talking about?"

"Flowers. For your spring garden."

Jimmy Easter was talking to two high school girls, smiling a winner's smile, charming them with his smarmy good looks and his just slightly over familiar manner.

Sally Lamb came back with ice cream bars and told the girls to beat it. They looked scared and hurt and scurried away.

"I'm tired of gettin' in trouble because you can't keep your dick in your pants," Sally told Jimmy.

"I'm gonna forget how, the long hours we've been working."

"Just watch the man. If we don't stay straight and keep our noses clean, we'll end up in the canyon."

"Sleeping with rattlesnakes."

"You'd better believe it."

Well isn't this a stupid waste of time?

Paul Lewin shoved popcorn from a cardboard box into his mouth, scattering puffs on the ground. A young man in a crisp uniform swept up the puffs as soon as Lewin walked away.

I end up on the Ice Princess's wild-goose chase so that the Professor can down tequila shooters in Tijuana.

Lewin crossed the Castle Bridge, keeping a safe distance behind Stan Raab and his party.

People. Somers and this Thorne broad. Go figure it. At least he's wised up. Probably found ice cubes up there.

Lewin watched Joe Campbell's father laughing at the costumed Mickey Mouse and Goofy characters that were walking around. A crowd of kids were following the plush costumes, pulling on everything they could pull on.

I know that guy.

Joe and his father stood on either side of Goofy and Stan framed them in his instant photo camera. Joe's father put his arm around his son's shoulders and pulled him close. Joe returned the hug.

Campbell's father. From where?

They gathered around Stan and watched the magic as the photo developed in Stan's hands.

"Aw, Joey," his father said, "You got your eyes closed. Why d'you do that?"

Joey said nothing.

"No problem," Stan said, "We'll just take another one."

"Take off your sunglasses, Vito," Vi said.

Vito?

Stan walked to a trash bin and dropped the in the snapshot.

Vito pulled on Goofy's arm, brushing away the kids that were gathered around. "Sorry kids. Goofy's gotta come here for a minute."

Everyone was pleased with the second try. Vi put the snapshot into her handbag. The group walked to the carousel, where Stan's kids were circling astride painted horses.

Sally Lamb and Jimmy Easter watched from twenty feet away. Jimmy dropped his spent ice cream stick on the ground and a uniformed worker rushed to sweep it up.

Lewin went to the trash bin and dug around until he found the discarded photo.

Vito Campbell?

A tall man wearing an Hawaiian print shirt with a camera around his neck watched him.

Lewin approached him. "Hey. You're security, right?"

"Sir? I'm just visiting the park."

"Get off. I'm LAPD. You an off-duty?"

"You're a police officer?"

"A homicide detective. Are you an off-duty or what?"

"Sheriff's Department."

"Good dough?"

"Not too shabby."

"Tell me something." Lewin showed him the snapshot. "You know this guy here? Does he look familiar to you?"

"Yeah. I see him all the time."

"Yeah?"

"Sure, it's Goofy." The man laughed at his joke.

"Wiseass."

The man laughed some more.

"So you don't know him?"

"He kind of looks familiar, but I couldn't name him. What are you doing here today?"

"Just visiting the park."

"Why are you interested in this guy?"

"Just visiting the park, sir."

"I could put you outside."

"I'm following up on some half-baked lead."

"You got a card?"

"No."

"You don't have a card?"

"No."

"Just thought I might be able to help you out, that's all."

"Thanks anyway."

"This is a family place. I gotta keep track of what goes on here."

"Nothin's goin' on. Nothin's goin' down. Okay?"

"Okay."

"Well, see ya around." Lewin turned and walked straight to Sally Lamb and Jimmy Easter.

"Good afternoon, scum," he said to them.

"If it isn't the long arm of the law," Sally said.

Jimmy laughed and dug his hand into Lewin's box of popcorn, scattering it on the ground.

The uniformed park employee eyed the dropped popcorn but stood a hesitant ten feet away with his dustbin and broom.

"And you brought the psychopath with you. Jimmy Happy Easter Bunny."

"Catch me if you can," Jimmy said.

"So, who's paying you to be on the Vito circuit today?"

"Who?" Sally asked.

"Vito." Lewin showed him the photo.

"Hey, Jimmy. Look, it's Vito. He's here, too."

"Nice sunglasses," Jimmy said.

"Didn't he just get outta jail?" Lewin asked.

"Vito? Not Vito Camelletti. You must be thinkin' of someone else. Vito's a legit businessman."

"Vito Camelletti." Lewin nodded, finally recalling the name. "You're working for Vito now, huh? You'd think he could afford better muscle than the likes of you two."

"Working? We're seeing the sights." Sally raised his chin. "Why are you on our ass all the time lately, chief?"

"This is a family place, Lambertini. See that guy over there?" He nodded toward the man in the Hawaiian shirt who was watching them. "That's what he just told me."

"You got nothing on us." Sally glowered at him.

"Good. We're even. I'm going home. I'll be in touch. Smile for the FBI."

The man in the Hawaiian shirt took their picture.

Twenty-One

Iris Thorne put her arms through the straps of her backpack , hoisted it onto her shoulders, then swung her leg up to mount the bicycle. She started pedaling and the wheels turned with their soothing *click-click-click-click*.

It was Sunday morning and the air was fresh with a chill on it that goose-pimpled her bare legs below the hem of her Spandex cycling shorts. She turned down the hill that led to the beach and started picking up speed. The light at the bottom changed to green and she sped through it, not hitting the brakes once.

She raced between the cement posts separating the street and the beach and turned left down the bike path, her tires skidding on sand. She changed gears and started to pedal.

The bike path, like the freeway, always has traffic. In a few hours the path would be crowded with visitors on rented wheels, cops in shorts, beach bunnettes in teeny bikinis, dudes in psychedelic jams with pirate kerchiefs tied around their heads, and little kids in sand-packed swimsuits all elbow to elbow with street people, street performers, street saviors and doomsayers, and anyone else who came to warm their face in the sun and dig their toes in the sand and escape the inland asphalt heat.

On weekend mornings, the locals took the air and the path was transformed. Strangers that tailgated and cursed and snubbed each other on freeways and in office buildings and stores smiled and said, "Good morning," as in friendly small-town anywhere. The party animals sat in beach chairs on their patios and toasted the early risers, the locals, their people, holding the first beers of the day in foam insulators. Everyone was full of vigor and good will. Life in Southern California.

Iris pedaled hard.

Good morning, good morning.

"Left." A guy cycling faster than her signaled he was passing.

The breezy quaintness of Santa Monica gave way to the funky weirdness of Venice to the tony newness of Marina del Rey. Iris stopped at a store and picked up croissants, a ripe melon, and Brie, and shoved the groceries into her backpack.

Inside Marina del Rey, weekend boaters sat on their decks sipping coffee. You didn't even have to hassle with taking the boat out. It was great just sitting in it. A breeze rustled the sailboat halyards, clanging steel shackles and blocks against aluminum masts.

People nodded.

Good morning, good morning.

Iris got off her bike and unlatched the gate that led to the slip where *Sympa* was docked. Steve was standing on her undulating bow in bare feet with a sailor's grace, at ease on moving ground. She looked at him with affection. The companionship was good. The good times were good. The sex was great. But it was all crumbs. Steve was what he was and it was up to her to take it or leave it. And she couldn't seem to get up the energy to make a move.

Steve was talking to the owner of the large power boat docked in the slip next to *Sympa*, a bankruptcy attorney with a boat named *Chapter 11*. The weekend sailors liked talking with Steve, trading nautical war stories or debating about sports. Steve knew all of the them, watched their boats during the week, hired himself out for maintenance work. They trusted him. They should. And they went back to their offices on Monday morning with stories about Marina life and Steve was part of the local color. Steve, whom they'd never seen wear shoes, who wore this dangling turquoise earring and was tan year-round and wore shorts in winter and was strong and lean and had long hair that he pulled back into a ponytail and somehow made it all look good. Just a really great guy. Would take off, go sailing for months at a time. And the women he has coming and going off that boat. Then the weekend boaters would pick up their phone messages and go in their offices and turn on the computer and wonder if they'd trade it all to be like Steve.

Iris walked her bicycle down the wooden dock. Steve waved. *Chapter 11's* owner said hello and gave her a once-over. Steve gave her a quick kiss on the lips and she ran her fingers through the curls cut short on top of his head, bleached almost platinum by the sun. She couldn't resist. Steve gazed into her eyes with affection and lust. *Chapter 11's* owner excused himself. He'd have some great Steve stories to tell on Monday.

"I brought breakfast," Iris said.

She took her sandy tennis shoes off before climbing onto *Sympa's* pristine wooden deck. She pulled off the heavy backpack, tossed it into the cockpit ahead of her, then boarded and sat down on one of the benches that flanked both sides of the boat. She stretched out. "I'm pooped."

Steve sat on the other end of the bench, pulled her foot onto his lap, and started massaging it.

"Alley's funeral was yesterday. Mmm... Remember I was telling you?"

He kissed her big toe, then the next one and the next one, then circled his hand around her ankle and held her foot between his chest and the crook of his chin, cradling her leg like a baby.

"It was weird. These cops were there and everything. Raab pontificating and Drye being an ass. Teddy freaked out and threw up on the steps. I met Alley's mother. She was beautiful, like Alley."

Steve caressed her leg as he watched her talk, moving her hands, her conversation self-propelled. He watched her and smiled. He liked this Iris Thorne.

He rubbed his smooth cheek against her foot, then kissed the bottom of it.

"I knew one of the cops in college. We dated. Well, it was more than just dating. But he's on this case, can you believe it? And, he told me he wants to be, like, *friends* again, you know? We had dinner… sort of. But there's nothing left. There's really nothing. I'm not attracted to him at all. It's over. It was over. It's been over."

"Doesn't sound like it's over."

"It totally is! There's nothing left. It just makes me uncomfortable. He's *around* now. And I don't like the job they're doing. I didn't tell you about Joe's father and EquiMex and Worldco. It's just a mess. Everything's all screwed up." She let out a long sigh of sorrow and fatigue and the burden of the world.

"And I called you last night and you weren't home."

He stroked her leg and looked at her with sparkling hazel eyes with green flecks and smiled a small smile. "I'm here now."

He was here now. She knew that was all she could expect.

They stared into each other's eyes like people in love or anger. She touched his hair where it curled to his shoulders and circled her fingers around the curve of his ear and ran fingertips across his collar bone and the dip in his throat on his bare chest and stroked the delicate skin there. She smiled the small smile back.

She pulled her foot away, got up, and walked down the steps to the cabin without looking behind her or saying a thing. He followed her, closing the cabin door behind them.

Iris stood in the galley in bare feet. She put slices of Brie inside the croissants and heated them in a toaster oven until the croissants were toasted and the Brie melted. "Cholesterol sandwiches, coming up."

She went onto the deck and sat with her feet in Steve's lap, drinking coffee from a stoneware mug, eating the croissants with strawberry jam, scattering papery crumbs on her clothes and around her mouth. She realized she was starving. She fed Steve bits of croissant with her fingers. The cool air raised goose bumps on her legs and arms. Everything tasted great. Her legs were comfortably fatigued from the bike ride and Steve. Life wasn't so bad sometimes after all.

The morning wind in Marina del Rey was light, but they sailed instead of motoring out of the channel anyway, tacking *Sympa* back and forth until they cleared the breakwater and reached open water, zigzagging around power boats, called stink pots by sailors, that were carelessly cruising in the sail lane, *Sympa* turning on a dime around them with a flutter of sails and swoosh of ropes, propelled only by wind, water, sail, rudder, and skill.

Once they had cleared the channel, Iris cranked the main halyard and raised the mainsail, struggling against the winch handle on the last few clicks. She secured the halyard with a cleat hitch, a sailor's knot Steve had taught her and that she'd practiced over and over. She also knew the bowline, the figure eight, and the clove hitch, each knot having its own function. Good sailor's knots, quickly done and undone.

She rolled the tail of the halyard into a neat coil on the deck and released the main sheet until the wind filled the sail, then fastened the sheet in the cam cleat with a firm downward snap. Then she raised the jib, adjusting the sail until it was smooth and full, at the correct angle with the wind.

Steve fine-tuned the sails with a master's touch, releasing the cunningham to make the mainsail fuller in the light wind, releasing the clew outhaul to reduce tension on the foot of the sail, sliding the traveler into position on the block. The wind had picked up, and they retrimmed the sails and traveled close-hauled up the coast in the slot.

"Where to?"

"Away," she said.

They changed course and sailed on a beam reach in a perpendicular line from Santa Monica, toward the horizon.

Iris sat on the bow and leaned against the rail. Steve sat on the stern, holding the wheel with his feet. They finally passed most of the Sunday boat traffic and waded through the brown sewage crud floating in the bay. They took turns at the helm, silent for long periods of time, lulled by the sun and salt water, listening to the boat cut through the waves. Land disappeared and they had seagulls, pelicans, porpoises, and sea lions for company.

She went below deck and came up with the plastic bag from the Rodeo Drive boutique. She pulled open the drawstring, took out the pair of miniature leather cowboy boots, and chucked them overboard.

A seagull dove for them, then left them floating on the surface after getting a closer look.

Iris took out the graying white chocolate rose on a wire and tossed that over. Then came the tin of lemon drops and the brass angel. Then the dried carnation, which stayed on the surface, like a floating wreath.

She dusted her hands, wiping them clean. It was done. Finished. Except for the cash.

Steve watched her without saying anything. She'd talk when she was ready.

She moved to him, open the plastic bag, and announced, "Two hundred thirty-eight thousand dollars."

Then, for the first time since she'd opened Alley's envelope, she explained. She told Steve about the key and the message, "Open this. You will know when to." She told him about the safe-deposit box and the EquiMex stock that wasn't traded publicly. About the cops. Paul Lewin, who hadn't like her from the get-go. Calling her "Ms. Thorne" all the time. Real sarcastic. And John Somers.

She told him about how she had decided to see what she could find out on her own because the cops were so off-base. How she'd overheard Stan and Joe talking about Alley stealing ten million dollars from Joe's dad and from Worldco, or at least Alley's name was on everything. About how money had been transferred from Worldco to EquiMex, which turned out to be an offshore corporation where Alley was a director. And Teddy, coked up, scamming on penny stocks, freaking out about the cops at Alley's funeral. Cutting off Jaynie's head in the snapshot. And Somers saying that Alley had been stabbed with an ice pick.

Iris felt released.

"How much of this do the police know?" Steve asked.

"They know that Alley was murdered with an ice pick. At least that's the only thing I've found out they know. They don't know about Worldco or EquiMex or the safe-deposit box. I did tell them to watch Joe Campbell's father, that they might learn something."

"Is he a mobster?"

"He's a guy with ten million dollars in an offshore corporation. Stan and Joe said something about a family business. Maybe the police will figure it out, if John follows up."

"Why are you taking this into your own hands?"

"Because if I gave the police the safe-deposit box stuff, they'd say 'Great! Case solved. Alley was a doper, just like we thought'. I know they're trying to do a good job, but Alley told me that things aren't the way they seem. If I tell the police, they won't look beyond the obvious. The person behind Alley's murder will go free. That's the reason. In spite of what John Somers says. Jerk."

She watched five dolphins gliding in the water near the boat, dipping up, skimming under.

"I remember the first time I saw Alley," she said. "He was in the lunchroom and was trying to get something out of the snack machine. He was crouching down, trying to pull open the sliding door, which I didn't realize could only be opened by sliding it from the front. Alley couldn't get his hand in the right position to slide it, so he'd contorted himself, trying to hook his finger around the door. Once he had it open, he couldn't hold it and grab the snack at the same time.

"I reached to help but he shuffled faster and managed to get out his potato chips or whatever. He smiled at me with that warm smile, then he had a spasm and his smile got all twisted. It surprised me and I was sorry that he saw my reaction. When I was leaving, he held the door open for me. He had to maneuver around to get his hand on the doorknob. It took him a while, but I waited.

"After I started signing with him and got to know him, he became just Alley. The Boys' Club came after him, goading each other on, telling Alley 'Spit it out' and 'What have you got to say for yourself?' Billy Drye bought this toy wind-up penis—you know, one of those little toys that hops along on two feet, sadistic bastard—and put it in Alley's briefcase. The thing kept showing up—in Alley's pocket, in his desk drawer. Those idiots laughing and laughing. Alley tried to laugh with them, which just made them laugh more.

"Alley still wanted to be their friend. He kept trying. It's like the men's clubs that won't take women members. You know one of their reasons? Women's voices are too high. It would spoil the ambience. I have no interest in spending five minutes in there, but I'd be a member in a minute if I could. You always think that once you get power, you'll change the rules. You play *their* game, right? Then they'll be playing *your* game. But what happens is you become some sort of mutant. You have feet in both worlds and you're not part of either anymore. Then you wonder if it's worth it but you're too stubborn to give up because you've sacrificed too much and maybe you can't go back even if you wanted to."

She looked at the sun setting on the horizon, at the ocean and the curve of the earth and the sky and the first stars, and felt comfortably minuscule.

"At the office last year, I started to get familiar with one of the reps who's not there anymore. You know, just drinks, talking, lunch. But I could see one thing leading to another. I really liked him. It felt like it could be something, I mean... you know..."

"You don't have to explain."

"Then Alley told me about this bet that the Boys' Club had, about who could sleep with me first. Alley knew everything. He read lips well. People forgot that. Alley hinted around, hinted around until I finally got it out of him.

"So I asked this guy about it. He turned beet red and swore he had nothing to do with it. He probably didn't, but I thought, it's not worth the risk. And I thought those guys were starting to warm up to me." She laughed. "What a fool. I owe Alley. I owe him for that."

She took the plastic shopping bag below deck, turned on *Sympa's* running lights, then came up a few minutes later wearing a fleece-lined jacket against the evening chill.

They jibed, changed direction by turning the boat through the eye of the wind, ducking when the boom swung from starboard to port, and started heading back, wing on wing.

She put her arms around Steve's tight waist and leaned against him as he steered with his arm around her shoulders. The temperature had dropped with the setting sun.

"Iris, come with me to the South Pacific. We could leave next week."

"Just leave?"

"Just leave. Head for warm water."

"What about my job?"

"Leave for a year. Think about what you really want to do."

"My condo?"

"Give your mom the keys."

"It's not that easy."

"Don't complicate it."

"I can't."

"You can. Leave all the bullshit until everything blows over. Let the cops solve this thing however they can. You won't have sold Alley out. Alley wouldn't have wanted you being this upset. He got involved in something bad. He was probably murdered for it. Maybe that's what he meant by 'Be smart.' Get the hell out. Take the money he left you and live on some island in Micronesia and open a shell shop."

"But it's not my money."

"Who's then? It's dirty. C'mon, I could use a first mate. The trip of a lifetime. Open sea, birds, fish, the boat, and you."

"And you, Popeye."

He wrapped his arms around her and squeezed and squeezed tighter and tighter until she squeaked and laughed and laughed and forgot about herself.

Twenty-Two

"Paper or plastic?"

Iris had taken the plastic and felt guilty. A plastic shopping bag dangled from each handlebar of her bicycle. The bike was unsteady as she rolled it down the carpeted corridor to her condo.

Her front door was open.

She put her key in the lock and the door just pushed open. She knew she hadn't been that scattered, too scattered to forget to lock, to remember to even close the door.

The automatic timer on the lights had already lit the room. The drapes billowed back and forth through the open sliding glass door. She hadn't left that open either. She also hadn't done what had been done to her place.

Everything was everywhere.

She carefully took the grocery bags off the handlebars, slowly set them on the floor, pulled down the kickstand with her foot, and balanced the bicycle, operating in a sort of surreal hyperspace. She looked at the billowing drapes and started to walk toward the terrace, stepping through the albums and CDs strewn across the floor. The terrace was a mile away and she walked on legs that weren't hers, walking to the gates of hell.

Midway across the room, she bolted and fell on the drape pulls, whimpering while she fumbled for the right one. The drapes rose and fell. She finally found the pull and let the world in.

The terrace was empty.

She sighed in relief.

Then she stood stone still and listened. She heard her heart beating and the blood rushing in her ears and the rolling ocean outside and they were the same noise. She wished they'd stop. She needed to hear better. She stood still for a long time—longer, she figured, than anyone else there could possibly remain quiet. Then she stood quiet even longer and didn't hear anything and decided that whoever had done the dirty deed must have left.

She walked into the kitchen, rolling the little round bottles from the splintered spice rack out of the way. She wasn't cleaning that rack now. Some of the cupboards were scraped clean, their contents covering the counters and floor. Others looked like the stuff inside had just been moved around. She thought it looked like the work of two creeps—one neat, one frenzied.

The smash-master must have done the china hutch. Most of the china and crystal was on the floor, most of it broken. It must have made a wonderful clatter.

Iris was pragmatic. Now she wouldn't have to worry about the earthquake doing it.

The empty champagne bottle from her Saturday night party for one poked up through the mess. She lifted it by the neck. The base was broken. She held it in front of her, business end out, saw a bloody image of someone using it on her, but took it anyway.

Now armed, she walked assertively toward the hall, flipping on the hall light without stopping, marching into the bedroom, jumping when she saw a figure silhouetted against the bedroom window, relieved when the light turned it into her bathrobe.

Her goose down comforter had been thrown off the bed, her Laura Ashley sheets slashed, the mattress stuffing pulled out in tufts and scattered across the room.

The walk-in closet was three feet deep in clothes, shoes, purses, belts, hats, and luggage. *Quelle soirée.* Her new Anne Klein suit lay on top of the pile. She held her breath as she picked it up. It wasn't slashed. At least they hadn't been sick enough to slash her new Anne Klein.

They had been sick enough to play with her lingerie. All of it was pulled out and displayed on top of the other mess. She looked through it, lifting each piece by her fingernails, thinking maybe they'd left behind a surprise wadded inside.

At least they weren't perverts.

Then she saw the sign scribbled on the bedroom mirror with a lipstick, her new shade.

NATSY, it said.

"Natsy?" Iris said.

The police arrived in eight minutes. It was Sunday night and the action in the neighborhood was slow. Iris put her lingerie back, then called John Somers's house after she'd called the police, then threw the telephone across the room when she heard some hokey music click on and his voice over it. She retrieved the phone and called his office. He wasn't on that night. It wasn't their business to keep track of him.

She threw the phone across the room again.

She put the couch back together, sat on it cross-legged, and watched the police poke around. They'd asked her if anything was missing. She did a quick inventory. Nothing was.

Well, why was her place trashed?

How the hell did she know?

She sat with arms crossed and legs crossed and sulked.

Then Paul Lewin came in. Just breezed in, wearing a plaid short-sleeved shirt buttoned over his belly and jeans that were too baggy in the seat.

"You don't knock?" Iris asked.

"This is a crime scene, ma'am," Lewin said.

"So, crooks *and* cops own my privacy."

"Just conducting my business, Ms. Thorne."

"No bodies here, Detective."

"The station said you called for Somers. Thought I'd follow up."

"Where is he?"

"On police business, ma'am."

"What business? Isn't this his case?"

"I can't discuss it, Ms. Thorne."

"Please stop calling me ma'am and Ms. Thorne."

"They're terms of respect."

"Somehow you don't make it sound that way."

"I'm sorry you feel that way, ma'am."

Iris blew out air and shook her head. She scraped the polish off a fingernail with the thumb of her other hand. "Doesn't matter. Guess he didn't believe me."

"Ma'am?"

"John. Something I told him."

"I followed up on your Disneyland lead."

"He told *you?*"

"We're partners, ma'am."

"What happened?"

"I can't discuss a case in progress."

"But I'm the one who told John."

"How did you come across that information, Ms. Thorne?"

"What information?"

"Ma'am, this isn't a game."

"You know who Joe Campbell's father is. Tell me."

"I suspect you already have that information, Ms. Thorne."

"Who is Joe Campbell's father?"

Lewin put his hands on his hips and looked around the room. "It's police business. Judging by the looks of this place, I'd advise you to stay out of it."

"Why don't you like me?"

"Ma'am?"

"Is it because of John?"

"I'm doing my job. Whether I like you or not doesn't have a thing to do with it." He left the room.

Iris sank her head down lower. She started scraping another nail.

After a few minutes, Lewin strolled back into the room.

"Ms. Thorne, are you involved in any political organizations—" he searched for the right words—"any... movements?"

"Movements?"

"Abortion, whales, skinheads..."

"What does that have to do with anything?"

"They're calling you a Nazi."

"Who is?"

"On the mirror, in your bedroom."

"Nazi?" Iris was incredulous. "That doesn't say Nazi."

Lewin put his hands on his hips. "Why don't you tell me what it does say? Ms. Thorne."

"It doesn't say anything."

"What's it doing there?"

"You're the detective, Detective."

He looked out the open glass door at the phosphorescent white caps on the rolling sea. He turned to face her.

He stared.

She stared back.

"Ms. Thorne, what have you got that someone's looking for?"

She stared. "Nothing."

"Who are you protecting?"

"No one."

"Teddy Kraus?"

"No one."

"Joe Campbell?"

"Seriously? No."

"Yourself?"

"You'd love that, wouldn't you?"

"You're only endangering yourself."

"You hung Alley out to dry."

"This doesn't look good for you, Ms. Thorne."

"My condo gets trashed and I'm the bad guy."

"This is no coincidence. Is Alley worth it?"

She didn't say anything.

"Sleep well, Ms. Thorne. And don't leave town."

Steve stood in the open doorway and watched Iris iron. It was after midnight.

"Iris, why is the door wide open?"

"Everyone in the world's coming through anyway. Why make it hard on 'em?"

"Look at this place."

"Yeah, look." She smashed the iron against a blouse draped over the board.

"What are you doing?"

"Ironing something to wear to work."

He picked his way through the clutter, took the iron out of her hand, set it on its base, and put his arms around her.

She sank into them.

They managed to put enough stuffing back into the mattress to sleep on it. She set the alarm for 4:25 in the morning. She watched Steve sleep, his eyes fluttering beneath his lids, his face calm. What was he dreaming? Of her? Of another woman? Or was he just at peace with himself?

She picked up the gold-and-midnight-blue velour Crown Royal whiskey bag from her nightstand and took out the handgun that was inside. Steve's gun. Protection from pirates. He thought she should have it. Steve had taught her about guns, first at sea, then at a shooting range. She held it up and aimed it at the NATSY message, then at the Rodeo Drive shopping bag with the two hundred thirty-eight thousand dollars in it, then at her own head, just to see how it felt. Then she put it away and lay down and did not sleep.

Twenty-Three

"Steve." Iris stroked his bare shoulder. "Steve, wake up. There's a problem with the TR."

"Prince of Darkness?"

"Electrical's fine. It's dripping fuel. There's a big puddle on the drip pan."

"Need a ride to work?"

"Please?"

"I'll run the TR to the shop."

"Thank you."

"Want me to pick you up later?"

"That's okay. I have an appointment in Century City. I'll get there and home somehow."

Steve pulled up in front of Iris's office building in his beat-up Volvo and ponytail and earring and suntan and Iris felt like she was standing on the street in her merry widow and G-string. She put on her jacket, grabbed her briefcase, kissed Steve, patted his sun-bleached hair, watched him drive away, and wished she was going wherever he was going.

She was late. It was Monday morning and the market had been open for forty-five minutes. The office was buzzing.

Iris stood tall and held her briefcase with a firm hand and her head high and ignored her grainy eyes and took sure steps, making eye contact all around and smiling and forcing a spring into her stride.

She smiled at Joe Campbell. He fumbled a greeting and averted his eyes. She kept smiling.

She smiled at Billy Drye. He pointedly looked at his watch. She flipped him off, shielding it with her briefcase. He winced and mouthed "oohhh." She kept smiling.

She smiled at Stan Raab. He watched her from his office and didn't look at his watch but Iris knew that he knew that she knew what time it was. She kept smiling.

She smiled at Teddy Kraus. She rubbed his bald spot for luck and he smacked her hand away without looking at her, too hard to be just fooling around. She kept smiling.

She threw her purse into her desk drawer, flipped on her computer with her workday one-two motion, sat down, and took out a pad and pen. She held the telephone receiver to her ear, listened to the dial tone, stared at the fake wood-grain desk top, and tried to remember what she did there.

It came to her. She talked on the phone. She made deals. She earned money for people with money. She got paid for good and bad decisions, both ways. She built paper empires. She sold promises.

She got up to get coffee. Stan watched her. She smiled. She knew that he knew that she hadn't produced today. She hadn't used her telephone relationships to make paper wealth. She was off quota. She didn't care.

John Somers was wolfing down two eggs, two strips of bacon, and two pancakes. Paul Lewin spooned a bowl of bran cereal with 2 percent milk and eyed Somers's bacon. Somers was talking.

"The Oaxcatil police had wanted to talk to us, too. They figured the drug cartels had found the perfect courier. Someone everyone notices but no one suspects."

"But Alley's going 'Par-*ty*'" Lewin said. "*Fiesta. Baile.*"

Somers explained. "They think Alley was bringing down cash in suitcases or something, then handing it off or depositing it in a bank down there that's not curious about cash. Then it was probably transferred through a bunch of Caribbean shell corporations and finally wired back here as clean money.

"They were going to nab Alley on his next trip down. When I told them he was offed, they figured he got caught in the cookie jar. But it was beautiful while it lasted. Alley kept a prostitute down there, name of Mariposa. Butterfly tattoo on her breast. Seventeen years old, if that. Decked out in clothes her sugar daddy brought from *el norte*. Alley's requests were pretty plain vanilla, except for a few times..." Somers shook his fingers as if they were hot.

Lewin dropped his spoon in the empty cereal bowl with a clatter. "So, Teddy uses too much and gambles too much and gets in deep with Lamb and Easter. They offer to work something out. Courier this dough across the border. But Teddy won't soil his hands. He recruits Alley, who'd do anything to be his friend. But Alley skims off the top and the geeks put the heat on Teddy for it. Or maybe Alley threatened to blackmail Teddy. Or maybe Teddy planned to off Alley as soon as the job was done and it all came off like planned."

"Murder for hire doesn't fit Teddy."

"He's got money trouble. He's got drug trouble. Not losing face is important to a guy like that."

"He's a knucklehead. Look at his show at the funeral. That wasn't the move of a calculating criminal. He's as wide open as an all-night convenience store," Somers said.

"He felt guilty. Don't forget he's threatened his ex, Jaynie."

"A crime of passion, yeah, but Teddy's too sloppy for something planned. He keeps bad company. He says stupid things. He's volatile. So what? Nothing ties it back to Alley."

"Except Ms. Iris Thorne."

"Go on," Somers said.

"Alley couldn't resist bragging to his lady friend."

"Okay."

"She puts him up to stealing a hunk off the top."

"No."

"How do you know?"

"Iris wouldn't do that. I know her. I've known her for years."

"You knew her. We all said our prayers before going to bed back then."

"It's worth something."

"Why did she put us onto that Disneyland thing? Oh... check this out." Lewin opened his wallet and took out the Polaroid folded inside. "Joey and his papa."

"Vito Camelletti."

"Was Vito Camelletti. Word is, he's retired."

"We should check OCU," Somers said.

"I've checked Organized Crime, and he's clean."

"Like Joe Bananas was clean."

"That's the way it's done now. The old stuff's penny ante. The big money's on Wall Street. No muss, no fuss. Just send a few faxes, tell a few lies, forge a few signatures, fudge a few numbers. No ring around the collar."

"My son, the securities expert. Sweet deal for the old man," Somers said.

"Probably changed his name to avoid the underworld rep."

"He'll have to do more than that to get out. Who do the geeks work for?" Somers downed his last piece of syrup-soaked bacon.

"Lamb and Easter? Camelletti. At Disneyland, they were busy keeping the man safe from opportunists. You didn't give me any bacon."

"You're not supposed to have any."

"It's probably Camelletti's dirty money going through the laundry and Ms. Thorne stumbled on the connection between Camelletti and McKinney Alitzer."

"Try this," Somers said. "Alley bragged to Iris, but she's afraid Campbell and his father will find out she knows about the laundry. So she tips us off, we find out on our own, and no one knows she knows."

"But what's her angle? Why put herself at risk?"

"Wrong place, wrong time," Somers said.

"Wake up and smell the coffee, Professor."

"You're not coming to this party empty-handed either, Shamus. You won't let go of Teddy Kraus when the only thing we have on him is that he's a jerk. But he pissed you off. And Iris pissed you off. But Raab's such a great guy that his name doesn't even come up. What about that missing file? He jumps all over Iris and you let it lie there."

"He said he was just seeing the bogeyman."

"Why didn't he just ask Iris about it? Why call you at home? And why was Raab schmoozing with Camelletti? All this stuff is going on and he doesn't know anything about it? But he makes an accusation about Iris and you're ready to hang her."

"Hey, Stan's been more than helpful all down the line."

"Then he should be really glad to see us again."

Iris poked her head in Jaynie's office. "Hi. Can I bug you for a big favor?"

"Sure."

"The TR's at the mechanic near your house and I can't get there before they close because I have an appointment in Century City. Could you pay the guy and park it on the street? I'll write you a blank check."

"No problem. How are you going to pick it up?"

"I'll take a cab."

"That'll cost a fortune. I'll get the TR and pick you up."

"That's a hassle for you."

"It's fine. I need to get out."

"What's up?"

"Teddy was parked outside my apartment the whole night. Iris, what am I going to do?"

"Take the cure… shopping!"

"Let's buy something foolish and expensive."

"And eat French fries and onion rings."

"And chocolate chip cheesecake at that place. Where should I meet you?"

"Five o'clock in front of the Tower Building."

"Great." Jaynie's phone rang. "Iris, Stan wants you in his office."

"Probably wants to give another one of my accounts to Billy Drye. See ya."

Iris left and the receptionist appeared in Jaynie's doorway.

A Hispanic woman wearing a pink waitress's uniform and a long ponytail stood behind her. The woman turned to watch Iris speed past.

The receptionist said, "This lady would like to talk to someone about Alley."

Jaynie stood, smiled brightly, and extended her hand. "I'm Jayne Perkins."

"I'm Carmen Garcia." She formally shook Jaynie's hand, appearing to feel as out of place as she looked.

"Please sit down," Jaynie said.

Carmen was holding a large manila envelope, which she abruptly handed to Jaynie. "Please take this."

The envelope was stuffed full and heavy. A label on the front was addressed to Iris Thorne at the McKinney Alitzer address. Jaynie recognized Alley's handwriting.

"I'm delivering this for Alley," Carmen said.

"Where did you get this?"

"From Alley's briefcase."

"You have his briefcase?"

"The police have it now. But I took this out first. Alley was killed in front of the coffee shop where I work. I saw everything. I picked up his briefcase. I wasn't thinking. I just wanted to give it to his mother. Then the police came for it…Was that Iris? I remember her from the funeral, but there were too many police that day."

"The police should have this."

"Oh, lady. They're mad at me already. Please, lady. The police don't need his stuff. He's dead already."

"Well, I guess there's no harm. I'll make sure it gets to Iris."

Jaynie got up and looked for someplace to put the oversized envelope. Her desk was covered from end to end. She tried balancing it on top of her filing cabinet, but it slipped off of the pile of reports and books stacked there. She pulled back the floor-length drapes that covered the window behind her desk, leaned the envelope against the wall, and pulled the drapes over it again.

"Carmen, thank you for taking your time to come here. Can I validate your parking ticket?"

"I took the bus."

"Oh, the bus. Well, I'll show you out."

Jaynie turned down the corridor with Carmen in front of her as Billy Drye stomped down the opposite direction with a sales assistant on his heels.

"I'm sick of shit-for-brains screwing me up!" He jabbed a finger in the air at the sales assistant.

"He told me thirty-four and a half. Then he saw he made a mistake and blamed me," she said.

"Bullshit! I want this bimbo out of here," Drye yelled.

"*Enough*," Jaynie said. "Let's discuss this in my office. Sit down and I'll be with you shortly." She turned to finish walking Carmen out, but she was already gone.

Iris sat in one of the stiff-backed antique chairs facing Stan's desk with her legs tucked underneath the chair while she waited for him to finish his telephone call, politely pretending not to listen. Stan winked at her and grinned. She grinned back and sat straight to look purposeful and alert. He shrugged to show he was sorry about the call. She waved him on. No, no. No problem at all. Take your time.

He finally hung up. He clasped his hands on the desk and leaned forward across the polished wood.

At least it wasn't a remove-the-barrier-of-the-desk conversation.

"Iris, could you flip the door closed, please?"

But it was a close-the-door. Billy Drye watched her close the door. She smiled cheerfully at him.

"Iris." Stan rubbed his chin thoughtfully. He locked his eyes on hers. "We've always been able to speak freely, you and me."

"We're both up front, Stan."

"Then, I won't beat around the bush. I called you in today because I'm concerned about you."

Iris sat straighter and relaxed her face to show there was no reason to be concerned. "I know I was late. My car——"

He raised his palm.

She stopped talking.

"Iris, it's not that." He rolled his fist into a coil and pressed it against his lips. "You seem to be extremely upset about Alley. More than one would expect."

"All due respect, Stan, but how upset should I be?"

"He was, after all, only a work friend."

"Stan, since we're speaking freely, why don't you tell me what you're getting at?"

"Something's bothering you and it's affecting your performance. I have an obligation to the firm."

"I don't agree that my personal affairs are the firm's business."

"Iris, I've always considered us to be... closer than just boss-employee. I've thought of us as friends."

She looked in his eyes.

"Tell me what's hiding that pretty smile?"

She weighed the possibilities.

"I only want what's best for you... and the firm."

She found a piece of skin on her finger to pull.

"Iris, I know that what's bothering you is not just personal."

She tore the skin from her finger.

"I can help you if you'd let me."

"Stan, I can't address what's on your mind if I don't know what it is."

He pulled open the top drawer of his desk. It slid out silently on oiled rollers. He took something out and tossed it across the desk. It was the funeral program.

Iris picked it up, rubbed her forehead, and laughed humorlessly.

"You broke into my filing cabinet on Saturday."

"Yes, I did."

He stood, walked to the floor-to-ceiling window, and faced it with his back to her. "Why are you interested in Worldco?"

"Okay, Stan. I overheard you and Joe in the supply room on Friday talking about Worldco and something to do with Alley. I decided to do some looking around on my own to find out what was going on. But the stuff in the Worldco file was gone before I got here."

Stan moved to sit in the chair beside her. He leaned his elbows against his thighs and dropped his clasped hands between his knees. "Iris, let me help you." He touched her arm.

She pulled her arm away. "Help me? I haven't done anything."

"The detectives are coming back today. What should I tell them?"

"So that's what this is about." She stood and walked to the door. "If you're worried about what to tell the police, give them this." She sailed the funeral program across his desk. "It's evidence. They'll be thrilled. Tell them I stole your file. Tell them I put Alley up to siphoning funds from Worldco."

Stan shot from the chair. "What did you hear? You haven't told me everything!"

She put her hand on the doorknob. "Never show all your cards, Stan." She opened the door. "You taught me that."

"Iris."

She stopped without turning around.

"If you need me, call."

She walked back to her desk. She furiously tapped on her keyboard, checking the status of her portfolio. She'd won a little. It was enough. She started cashing out her accounts.

Teddy looked over. "What? You crazy? The market's down."

"Doesn't matter. The cost of living is cheap in Micronesia."

Twenty-Four

Stan Raab flicked the corner of the business card with his thumb, testing the snap of the paper.

"I have to hand it to whoever thought of this. It's very creative. Alley, Director of Mexican Operations." He laughed and shook his head. "The position doesn't exist."

"What did Alley earn?" Lewin asked.

"I don't know—less than twenty grand, I imagine."

"Did he receive any sort of salary increase or promotion in the past few months?" Somers asked.

"Maybe an annual bump. Let me get Jaynie to help us with these questions." Raab picked up the telephone receiver, punched in three numbers, and murmured into it. "She'll be right down. Detectives, I'm confused about the money angle. Was Alley involved with money?"

"We can't say, Stan," Somers said.

"I can tell you have new information. The specificity of your questions has changed." Raab looked at Lewin and smiled. "Am I right?"

Somers answered. "The investigation's just a few days older, Stan. Does anyone in the office drive a large black sedan?"

"A black sedan?" Raab laughed and rose from his desk chair. He walked to the window and looked out at the brown sky. "Someone saw Alley in a black sedan?"

"We can't discuss that, Stan," Somers said.

"No. Of course you can't. No, I don't know anyone here who drives a black sedan."

Jaynie walked into the office holding a manila file folder.

"There she is," Raab said. "Our little organizer. Jaynie, you know our detectives?"

"Yes. Hello again."

The detectives stood and extended their palms. Jaynie shook Lewin's hand first, then Somers's, holding it a second too long and giving him a quick, appraising smile.

His face colored slightly.

Lewin gestured for Jaynie to take his chair. He leaned in the corner against the filing cabinet and spotted Billy Drye at the water cooler outside Raab's office. Drye filled a cup, drank it slowly, then filled another. Lewin walked to the door, leaned out, and glanced around. He spotted Teddy standing in his cubicle, looking at Raab's office. He raised his thumb and index finger, shot Teddy, then turned to Drye.

"It's good to drink water," he told Drye. "Flushes out the system." He pulled the door closed. Drye's face flashed with disappointment.

"Stan, I overheard you mention a black sedan," Jaynie said. "I remember seeing a black Mercedes with tinted windows in our parking section once or twice. I can't remember in whose spot it was parked."

"Do you have records of employees' cars?" Somers asked.

"Yes. Employees list the cars they may be driving for the garage."

"Can you see if anyone drives a large black, sedan-type car?"

"Certainly. I'm in the middle of something that has to go in the mail by three o'clock, so later this afternoon?"

Somers fished a card out of his pocket. "Call me?"

Jaynie took the card and smiled. "Be happy to." She slipped the card into her skirt pocket. "You wanted to know about

Alley's salary?" She opened the file folder. "He was earning eight dollars an hour at the time of his death which is sixteen thousand, six hundred a year. He received a merit increase of fifty cents an hour about two months before that... about a thousand more a year."

Raab again sat at his desk.

"May I?" Lewin reached over to take the business card that Raab was still holding. "Jaynie, what do you make of this?"

She turned it over and looked at Raab, bemused. "Is this a joke? Director of Mexican Operations. Alley didn't even have a business card for his own position. Guess he could have ordered these cards himself. He filled out purchase requisitions all the time, but they need a signature."

"Who signs off?" Somers asked?

"Any of the managers, or Stan."

"How about Iris Thorne?" Lewin again leaned in the corner.

"She's not a manager. But it all depends on how closely the people downstairs look at the request."

"But Alley could have forged a signature," Somers said.

"Sure. I can have someone go through the copies of the purchase reqs. I'll call you with that and the car information."

"Thank you, Jaynie," Somers said. "We'll let you get back to work."

Raab watched Jaynie close the door and sat silently, holding his chin between his thumb and index finger, until he saw her walk past the windows of his office. Then he clasped his hands together on his desk and leaned forward.

"Detective Lewin," Raab began in a confidential tone, "you mentioned Iris Thorne in relation to this business card. You must suspect her involvement."

"Her involvement in what, Stan?" Somers frowned.

"In this Alley thing."

"Alley's murder?" Somers asked.

"Well... not exactly."

Somers raised his eyebrows. "What's on your mind, Stan?"

"It's nothing. It's an internal matter. Forget I brought it up, gentlemen."

"Go ahead," Lewin said. "Let us decide what's important."

Raab made a triangle with his hands, "We've had problems with the transfer of funds between accounts. A considerable sum of money has been... misdirected."

"Embezzled?" Somers said.

"No, not embezzled. I wouldn't use that word. We just can't locate it. Gentlemen, this is really an internal matter. We're conducting an audit now. It's probably just a transposition of numbers or something like that."

"The Worldco file that's missing wouldn't involve these misdirected funds?" Somers asked.

"Yes, it does."

"What does this Worldco company do? What's their business?"

"It's an offshore corporation, a holding account set up in the Caribbean for tax purposes. It encompasses many different business ventures. Gentlemen, not that much money is in question. Just about... ah...ten thousand dollars. In this business, a sum like that's not even material. I'm just seeing the bogeyman everywhere, like I told Detective Lewin the other night."

"Seems like whenever you see the bogeyman, Iris Thorne is around," Somers said.

Raab laughed. "Yes, it does, doesn't it? Poor Iris."

"You're insinuating that Iris had something to do with these missing funds and that Alley had some involvement as well."

"Well, all the Worldco documents have disappeared and this was left behind in my office." Raab reached to hand the funeral program to Somers.

Somers folded it, put it in his jacket pocket, and avoided looking at Lewin.

"Iris's handwriting is on it," Raab said.

"So, it's not just a case of a transposition of numbers," Somers said. "A crime was committed."

"If you put it that way... yes."

"Why did you say it was an accounting error?"

"It's embarrassing. It reflects on the integrity of my department. But our first level of investigation is an internal audit. Gentlemen, let's leave it like that."

"Why didn't you tell us about the missing money before?" Lewin asked.

"I just found out myself."

"Stan," Somers said, "you appear to have a good relationship with Iris. You said she's one of your best people."

"That's true."

"Why not approach her with these concerns?"

"I did. This morning, in fact. She became very upset."

"Stan, we're just a couple of street cops," Lewin said. "This stuff is a little too highbrow for us. I think we should notify the Securities and Exchange Commission."

"I couldn't agree more, Detectives. But that step is premature. Like I said, we're in the process of completing our own internal audit. Calling the SEC at this point is like asking the IRS to find an error on your taxes. I'm sure you appreciate my position."

"We have an obligation to report any crime, Stan," Somers said. "I'm sure you appreciate our position."

"But that's my point. I'm not sure a crime occurred. I don't want to call the SEC until I've exhausted all possible avenues internally."

"What's your relationship with Joe Campbell?" Lewin asked.

"Joe?" Raab was out of his chair again. "You guys hop around, don't you?" He faced the window, his back to the detectives. "I've known Joe since college. We were fraternity brothers. You saw this picture." Raab crossed room and squinted at the photograph of fresh faces that hung on the wall. "Second row."

"You know his family?" Lewin asked.

"Sure. New York Italian. Moved out here when Joe and his sister were little."

"What kind of business is Campbell senior in?" Lewin asked.

"Food distribution, mostly to restaurants. Gourmet meats, vegetables, deli items. He's done well."

"Mob connections?"

"Ha!" Raab ran his hand through his hair. "This *is* interesting." He sat on a corner of his desk and looked down at the detectives. "You guys slay me."

"Please answer the question, Stan," Somers said.

"No." Stan picked up the frame with the silver pins off his desk and rolled his fist against it, watching the undulating impression it made on the other side. "No mob connections."

"We'd like to talk to Joe," Somers said.

"Sure. I'll take you to his office."

Raab moved to take his jacket off a hook on the back of the door. He put it on, pulling his shirt cuffs down so that they extended one quarter inch beneath his sleeves. He held the door open but the detectives stood aside to let him go first. He walked to the office directly across from his in the opposite corner.

Joe Campbell was on the phone. He saw the detectives and said, "I'll have to get back to you on that," and hung up.

"Joe," Raab said. "Our detectives asked to speak with you."

Campbell gestured for the detectives to sit in the two chairs facing his desk. Raab stood inside the office and started to pull the door closed.

"Stan," Lewin said. "We want to talk to Joe in private."

"Of course." Raab gave Campbell a meaningful look.

Campbell's eyes revealed nothing.

Raab left, closing the door behind him.

Campbell pushed the cap back onto his pen and slowly clipped it inside his shirt pocket.

"Joe Camelletti," Lewin began.

"Yes."

"Why did you change your name?"

"It's too ethnic. Too hard to pronounce."

"Wouldn't have anything to do with Vito?" Lewin asked.

"Talk to my attorney." Campbell flipped through a Rolodex on his desk. He took the pen from his shirt pocket, pulled off the top, and wrote on a notepad. "Wendell Ellis. In Beverly Hills."

"But Joe," Somers said. "You don't even know what we want to talk to you about. We can probably resolve this right here and save all of us a lot of time. Tell us about your father's underworld connections."

"My father is not involved in the underworld, to use your word."

"C'mon, Joe," Lewin said. "It's well known."

"Some overzealous prosecutors have made wild accusations, none of which have been substantiated."

"I'll bet he can thank this Wendell Ellis guy for that."

"Detectives, I'm very busy. Please make your point."

"Tell us about Worldco," Lewin said.

"It's one of the firm's accounts. What about it?"

"Stan Raab said that some of Worldco's funds were... what's the term he used? Misdirected."

"He said what?"

"He made a connection between the missing funds, Iris Thorne, and Alley Muñoz."

"What does that have to do with me?"

"Your father must be pretty proud of you, a son working in an organization like this," Lewin said.

"What are you insinuating?"

"Let's see," Lewin said. "McKinney Alitzer buys and sells securities for a shady offshore corporation called Worldco. Raab says the corporation's documentation and money disappears. A mailroom boy named Alley makes trips to Mexico; a female trader, who may have stolen the documentation, is cozy with the mailroom boy; and another trader is the son of a known organized crime figure. The mailroom boy ends up dead, the female trader is harassed, and you wonder what it has to do with you. Your father wouldn't, by any chance, own Worldco, would he, Joe?"

"I have things to do. Please leave." Campbell got up. The meeting was over.

The detectives walked to the door.

"Thank you for your time, Joe."

Campbell stood silently, holding his desk with both hands as if he were about to fall into an abyss. When the detectives were gone, he quickly walked to close the door. He picked up the phone and punched in a number.

"Pop, the police were just here. They suspect a connection between Worldco, Alley, and you. It's just speculation on their part at this point. I told you it would catch up with us. Trading securities isn't the same as fencing goods from stolen trucks. That *is* your history. I don't want to it blow up, I'm just telling you what happened. Even if the police drop this angle, the Worldco money laundry can't continue. It should have never started."

The detectives stood next to Teddy's cubicle. Somers looked at Joe Campbell's closed door. Lewin looked around the suite.

"Kraus left," Billy Drye said from across the room. "When you guys were in with Raab."

"Iris gone too?" Somers asked.

"She had an appointment in Century City."

Drye walked over to the detectives. "Maybe if you tell me what's going on, I can help you."

"Thanks," Somers said. "We'll let you know."

"Everyone's acting dumb today." Drye said. "Iris cashed out her accounts and the market's down."

"Why?" Somers asked.

"Teddy said that she said that life was cheap, or something like that."

"Life's cheap?" Somers said.

"Yeah. Something like that."

"We'll be in touch, Mr. Drye."

"Anytime."

Twenty-Five

Jaynie Perkins drove the canyon road from the Valley to Century City with the top down on the TR, swinging the little car around the curves and feeling the wind in her hair and the sun on her face. It was 99 degrees at 4:30 in the afternoon, the city was having a stage-two smog alert, and it all felt great. People looked at her in the red car. It felt like California and she felt like a California girl. She'd hardly ever done anything reckless, except maybe dating Teddy, and while she was driving she forgot about Teddy, at least between the red lights.

She found a parking spot in the street in front of the Century City Tower Building. What luck. It had turned out to be a good day, after all, after such a bad start when she saw Teddy sitting in his car outside her apartment at five in the morning.

She looked up at the tower's black eyes and thought about Iris in there somewhere. Conducting business. Making deals. Shaking hands. Jaynie wished she'd finished college. When she was married and playing house, she'd forgotten about her career ambitions and some of her personal goals as well. Now she was divorced and bored and getting older and wishing she'd been more focused. She'd done okay for herself, but she felt trapped in Human Resources and Administration, the velvet ghetto. She could see across the next thirty-five years of her working life, a straight shot. It took guts to change, and determination. Iris had that. In spades. Jaynie decided she could do it, too. She'd go back to school. That's what she'd do. Good. It was a good day.

A car drove up and parked next to the curb behind her. Jaynie heard the car door slam and saw a shadow on the sidewalk approaching the TR from behind. She didn't think anything of it until the shadow covered the TR's shiny hood and she felt someone at her left shoulder. She looked up.

"Hi," he said.

"Hi." The sun was behind him and Jaynie squinted. "Can I help you?"

"You're coming with me."

"What?"

"Get out of the car."

"Why?"

"Just do it."

"I'm not coming with you."

She reached for the key in the ignition. She felt something hard against her arm and looked down to see the barrel of a gun peeking out from under a jacket that was thrown over his arm.

"Get out of the car."

Jaynie turned the ignition key and forgot about the clutch. The car lurched forward six inches. He jumped forward after it. He pulled on the driver's door, reached inside to unlock it, then pulled it open.

"What are you doing!" Jaynie screamed.

A few people were walking on the street, but mostly there were commuters in their cars with the windows up and the radio and air conditioner on. They might have heard Jaynie's screams and looked over, but everyone's so loud in L.A. anyway. They'd rushed to windows enough times because someone was screaming just to hear the screams turn into laughter. You feel like a fool. The guy was well dressed and cleaned up. If he were something else, they might have paid more attention. It looked like these two were just talking in a groovy, showy, L.A. sort of way.

Jaynie undid her seat belt and lunged for the passenger door. The stick shift hit her in the middle and she tried to angle around it. He grabbed her by the arm and pulled her back.

"Just relax. Just come with me. Nothing's gonna happen."

"Why do you have a gun?"

"To get your attention. C'mon. Get outta the car."

He held onto her arm and pulled her toward him. She stood up on Silly Putty legs. He pressed the gun into her side and walked her toward the car parked behind her. Maybe she'd kick him. Yell. Or maybe she'd humor him until she could get away. That's it. She'd go along. They weren't going anywhere fast in this traffic, anyway. She'd keep her wits about her. He'd be careless. She'd find a moment. That was all she needed.

Iris came out of the office building and saw the TR parked. She figured Jaynie was just taking a walk. Probably wanted to clear her head. Poor kid. Iris's blood pressure rose when she saw the keys dangling from the ignition. She looked up and down and around for Jaynie and didn't see her anywhere.

"She's got a hell of a lot of nerve."

Iris punched her fists into her waist and stared lasers at the ignition keys. Then she saw Jaynie's purse tucked behind the passenger's seat. Her stomach sank. This was not right. This was not right at all.

Iris looked through Jaynie's purse. Everything seemed to be there, even cash. She sat in the TR and waited, watching the cars clot and flow through the intersection. An hour passed. She pulled her cuticles into rags. She got out of the car, went back in the building, and called the police.

The cop who answered said he was sorry she was concerned, ma'am, but the police couldn't do anything about someone who'd only been missing an hour. He understood about the boyfriend, but unless there were signs of a struggle, they couldn't consider her a missing person.

Iris persisted. "But she wouldn't have left her purse."

The cop said he understood she was worried, but he couldn't do anything at this point. "If she's still missing tomorrow, ma'am, give us a call."

"I'm going to bean the next person who ma'ams me." She slammed the phone down. "Probably thinks I'm PMS crazy lady. Jerk."

Iris sat until 7:00. The traffic started to clear a little. She started the TR and took the One-oh-one to the Valley and knocked on the door of Jaynie's apartment. No answer. Her car was in the carport. The apartment was dark.

She drove home. She called John Somers's office. He wasn't available. Was there a message?

"Yes, there's a message. Help me!"

Twenty-Six

The sound of car tires crossing the bridge connectors echoed in the canyon like a Ping-Pong game played in an empty gymnasium. Police spotlights illuminated the crisscrossed bridges in white daylight, the art deco trim of an older, unused lower bridge throwing open-weave shadows on the underside of the concrete freeway built over it. Yellow plastic police ribbon encircled a section of the canyon, crossing a creek that babbled a narrow foot of water in defiance of the drought.

"The way I figure," Lewin said, "she was kneeling about here..." He stood near the body and bent his knees. "Then, he stood here, and..." Lewin raised an imaginary gun. "Boom. Lights out."

Somers looked down at the body. He'd seen lots of murder victims but remembered a forgotten horror and felt that if he'd just worked harder, been more on top of his game, paid closer attention, listened better, he could have prevented this one.

Jaynie was on her back, her legs bent in a way that would have been uncomfortable in life, her arms casually dropped by her sides, her head in the shallow creek, her blonde hair flowing with the current. The bullet had made a small hole in her forehead. The back of her head had been washed down the creek. She was wearing the black-and-white houndstooth check dress she'd worn to wear to work that morning. One of her black patent leather pumps had been freed from her foot and was on the grassy bank beside her.

Somers turned to a uniformed officer. "What did those kids have to say?" He inclined his head in the direction of four teenagers huddled together on the steep canyon bank.

"They came down to neck and drink, saw her, and climbed back up and called us. They're scared because one of the boys has a coupla cans of spray paint on him."

Lewin squatted on the muddy bank of the creek. It was covered with short grass. "Professor, how many sets of footprints you see here?"

"Hard to tell. Mud's soft. There's Jaynie's. One man... maybe two. Smooth-soled shoes."

"I want Teddy picked up," Lewin said. "Hey," he called to a police photographer. "Take one from that angle looking across and I want one from the top of the hill up there." He turned back to Somers. "That's the jerk who messed me up last time."

"More and more bullshit. Every time we turn around," Somers said. "Iris Thorne is talking. Today. You notify Jaynie's next of kin. I'm going to Santa Monica."

"You're the man, Professor."

Somers knocked on the open door of Iris's condo.

"Anyone home?" He walked across the parquet entryway into the living room, stepping over the clutter. "Iris?" The room was illuminated by a lamp that had been put back in its place on an end table, the shade crushed on one side. "Hello?"

He walked through the kitchen, checked the terrace, then walked toward the bedroom, turning quickly to check the bathroom first. The bathroom was empty. The bedroom was empty. The light in the walk-in closet was on. Something rustled inside.

Somers stood ready to draw his weapon. "Iris?"

"Who's there?"

Somers looked inside the closet and saw Iris standing thigh-high in a pile of clothing.

"John?"

"I yelled, but… why is your door open?"

"Let 'em in if they want in. Look. They threw every last thing on the floor."

Somers surveyed the closet and the portable clothes rack that stood outside the door, crammed with clothes. "Why do you have so much stuff?"

"Why?" She shrugged. "Because I can, I guess." She started digging through the pile surrounding her knees.

"Iris, I came to tell you something."

"You got my message?"

"What message? At home?"

"At the office. You didn't get it? Here's what I'm looking for." She grabbed a long nylon webbing strap and walked backward. A large canvas duffel bag popped free. She threw the bag onto the bed, unzipped it, and started packing a small mound of clothes that were piled outside the closet door.

"Going somewhere?" Somers asked.

"Yep."

"Where?"

"The South Pacific. Sailing."

"For long?"

"Maybe."

"That's why you cashed out your accounts."

"How did you know about that?"

"At your office today."

"Talk about life in a fishbowl. At least I won't be under scrutiny day and night."

"Leaving's not a good idea, Iris."

"It's the best idea I've had in a long time."

"The case… everything's unresolved."

"It won't stay that way. You'll find a solution, and whatever it is, it'll be the right one. Then everything will be fine. Back to normal. Status quo. Except I'll be sitting under a palm tree somewhere. Finally being smart."

"Typical Iris."

"Typical Iris, what?"

"Never lets any grass grow under her feet."

She glared at him. "What's *your* problem?"

"The going gets a little tough, and she's outta here."

"Where do you get off coming into my home and saying those things? You don't know me. You don't know anything about me."

She walked into the closet, bent over the pile of clothes, and threw a bunch into the room behind her. They landed near his feet.

"I know you, Iris. You left a situation fifteen years ago and didn't care about what you left behind then, either."

"You were Mr. Sour Grapes. 'Who wants to live in Europe anyway? Who cares?' You couldn't see beyond your own backyard. Then you stopped writing me. I found out you got married from my girlfriend. Talk about bailing out of a situation." She threw more clothes behind her.

"I made a wrong decision," he said. "It wouldn't have happened if you hadn't left."

"So it's my fault? Nothing like taking responsibility for your own actions, huh, John?"

"That cuts both ways. Your girlfriend filled in the details you left out of your letters, about your affair with that French guy, what was his name? Poopoo? Fifi?"

"Real close, John. Loulou, a nickname for Louis. An affair. You make it sound so sordid. He was just a guy in my class. We decided not to be tied to each other that year, remember?"

"You traveled with him."

"So what! You got married! Got married and moved away and didn't even have the guts to tell me. Big macho cop."

She pulled a black Chanel handbag from the pile, twisted backward, and threw it at him with a quick overhand toss. It hit him squarely on the chest then fell at his feet.

"Dropped out of school. Real tough guy."

Somers looked down at the purse with his mouth open, then looked back up in time to dodge a taupe Coach leather clutch that sailed past his left shoulder. His face turned red. He clenched his fists. She stood staring at him, still twisted backward, her hands dug into her waist, her jaw tight and her face seething.

He took one heavy step toward her, paused, took one more, wrestled for control, then swiveled and walked to the doorway. He held on to the top of the door frame with one hand and rubbed his other hand across his face.

"You found me after fifteen years, remember? Come into my life and criticize how I live and what I do. Forget the message I left. I don't need your help. I don't need anyone's help. I'm the only one I can count on. That's the way it was then, and that's the way it is now."

"What was the message?"

"Jaynie's disappeared. The police blew me off."

Somers pulled his hand away from his face. He caught a glimpse of himself in the bathroom mirror at the end of the hallway. His shoulders slumped. He couldn't do it anymore.

He turned to Iris with his hands out, palms up, apologizing in advance for the bad news.

She stopped packing. "What is it?"

"Iris..."

"What! What is it?"

"Jaynie's dead."

Her legs gave way. She dropped onto the pile of clothes.

"She was murdered. We just found her body. I'm sorry. I'm so sorry." He took a step toward her with palms open but empty, without solace.

She got to her feet and waded out of the closet, waving him away. She drifted to the bed, sat on a corner, and stared straight ahead. She folded her hands in her lap and worked her knuckles, breathing hard and slow. Then her breath caught and the tears started to flow. She covered her face with her hands. "My God, my God."

He knelt on the floor beside her and put one hand on her knee and the other around her waist.

"She wanted to pick up my car. Wanted something to do." She wiped her nose against the back of her hand.

He went into the bathroom, pulled a length of toilet paper from the roll, and handed it to her.

She got up and walked to one side of the room, turned, walked back, then retraced her steps, back and forth, trailing the toilet paper behind her. "My God, Jaynie."

"She was driving your car?"

"She picked me up. The TR had keys in the ignition… with her purse. I told the police. I told them."

"Iris, tell me what you know about Alley. What you know about any of it."

"It was supposed to be me, wasn't it? Jaynie had the TR. We looked like sisters… what everyone always said." She searched his face for an answer, then turned and walked with her hands limp at her sides. "What have I done?"

He pulled a chair out from the desk and flung it around to face the room. "Iris, sit down."

She paced, her body jerking with hiccupping sobs.

"Iris, sit down." He grabbed her arm on the next turn and pulled her down into the chair.

She inhaled tremulously.

He put his hands on her shoulders. "Iris. Trust me."

She breathed in short gasps with each hiccup. "Should have been me. They wanted me."

"I don't know why you're protecting Alley. You don't know the kind of person he really was."

"He really was?"

He put his face within inches of hers. "Alley was a thief."

She sobbed. "He wasn't."

"Oh, no? He made trips to Mexico, passed himself off as an executive of your firm, threw money around. Big show. You know the Mexican police were going to arrest him? They think he was part of a money-laundering scheme."

"Wasn't a thief." Her arms dangled at her sides and she shook her head back and forth. "I knew him."

"Did you? Did you know he kept a prostitute? A real racehorse. She told me Alley had a couple of weird requests, but she got used to it, being a pro."

"Sadist."

Somers pulled a desk lamp around and turned it on, twisting the neck so that the light blazed onto her face.

She covered her swollen eyes with her hand. "Turn it off. Think you're in some old grade B detective movie?"

"Where did Alley get the money? Did you help him?"

She held her hand in front of her face and squinted at the light coming between her fingers. "Bastard. Trust me, you said."

"Tell me what you know about Alley and I'll leave you alone. Forever."

"I don't know anything."

"What kind of a fool do you take me for? Your name comes up in every conversation. You're onto Joe Campbell's father. Your condo's been trashed. Jaynie's murdered after driving your car. Your boss insinuated you've embezzled money. I've defended you down the line, Iris. It's time for you to do something for me."

"How much money did Stan say was missing?"

"Ten thousand dollars."

She looked at the Rodeo Drive shopping bag and stopped crying. "Oh, really?"

"He said you broke into his filing cabinet and took the Worldco file."

"And you believe him."

"Tell me what the truth is."

"You stomp in here saying how you know Iris Thorne. Bullshit."

He put his face in her line of vision. "Iris, you're in a world of trouble. Let me help you."

"Did Stan say who the money belonged to?"

"Joe Campbell's father."

"Stan wouldn't tell you that."

"Joe Campbell told me."

"Bull. Bull, bull, bull. Lie, lie, lie. Liars! All around me. Damn you!"

"Iris, clear it up for us."

She wiped her nose on the toilet paper and glared back.

"Tell me what happened."

"Trust you? I'll carry it to my grave first."

"Okay, Iris. Fine. We have plenty of time. I have an obligation to stay here anyway if someone's trying to kill you."

He sat on the edge of the bed and watched her. He thought about the irony of finally being in her bedroom again when he heard footsteps. He moved his hand to the gun in a holster on his belt.

Steve entered the room, balancing takeout containers on each hand.

Somers released his grip.

"Hi," Steve said. "The door was open, so I just walked in. Am I interrupting something?"

Iris punched out a laugh. "Steve Grant, this is Detective John Somers."

Steve put the container in his right hand on top of the one he held in his left. He reached to shake Somers's hand. "Nice to meet you."

"Howya doin'?" He walked over and kissed Iris on the lips. A casual "I'm home" sort of kiss.

Somers watched.

"I thought I'd help you pack. I brought sushi. With your kitchen messed up… anyway, there's plenty for three."

Steve set the containers on the dresser, opened one, took out a white rice rectangle with a slab of dark pink raw fish on top, and held it up to Iris's lips. "The maguro's really fresh."

She held Steve's hand and took a bite from his fingers.

Somers watched.

The sushi crumbled into grains of rice, pungent green wasabi, and fish into her hand. She tried to mash it back into a rectangle. She tipped the mess into the box and rubbed her hands together. "I can't eat right now. Thanks, Steve. You go ahead."

He looked at Somers and then at Iris's tear-swollen face. "Maybe I should go. Looks like I came at a bad time."

"That's all right," Somers said. "I'll leave. I can see you don't need my help, Iris, just like you said." He left the bedroom. At the front door, he loudly said, "I'd advise you to keep this door locked," and closed it hard behind him.

Steve asked, "What's going on? I just came over to see if you needed any help packing."

"Steve, I need time to think. I can't think. I need to be alone right now."

"No problem. I'll be on the boat if you need me. I'll put the food the fridge, okay?"

"Okay. Thanks."

He kissed her on the forehead and rubbed his forefinger against her cheek. He walked out and she heard the soft soles of his deck shoes squishing on the linoleum as he opened and closed the refrigerator door and then went out the front door.

Iris sat slumped in the desk chair. Time passed. She didn't move. After a long time, she sat up straight. She blew her nose into the damp wad of toilet paper.

"Okay. Enough."

She got out of the chair, dropped to her knees, and started digging through a pile of books and magazines on the floor. She threw magazines across the room, their slick covers sliding on the carpet. She finally found her personal telephone book. She flipped the pages, her fingers sticky, then held a page open with one hand and punched numbers into the telephone with the other.

"Hi, it's Iris."

"Iris. What a surprise."

"I have to talk to you. Can you meet me?"

"Of course. Where?"

"The office in half an hour."

"I'll see you there."

Iris opened the top drawer of her nightstand and took out the blue velour Crown Royal bag and the box of cartridges. She untied the yellow braid at the neck of the bag, pulled the gun out, and loaded it. She unzipped her purse and crammed the gun inside, slipping the box of cartridges in after it. She slung the purse over her shoulder, zipped the Rodeo Drive shopping bag with the two hundred thirty-eight thousand dollars into her backpack, scooped up her keys, and jogged to the front door.

She started to close the door behind her, then flung it open, so hard that it banged against the door stop and almost slammed closed again on its own momentum.

Twenty-Seven

John Somers drove the arced junction of the Ten and the Four-oh-Five, holding the inside curve of the banked road, swinging past the towers of Westwood toward the darkness of the Sepulveda pass, going home to his tree house. But he was too unsettled to go home. Then back to the crime scene. But it'd be cleaned up by now, and dark. There was only one place to go.

He slammed the steering wheel with both hands.

"Damn her!"

He sped across two lanes of traffic and exited at the next off ramp. He turned left, underneath the freeway, and got on again in the opposite direction.

"Somers, you idiot."

He took the stairs to Iris's condo two by two and rapped hard on the door with his knuckles. It swung open silently.

"Iris!" He slammed the door closed behind him. "Keep this blasted door locked. What the hell is wrong with you, anyway?"

He strode through the kitchen, dining room and bathroom, his long legs making quick work of the condo's floor space. He flung the shower door open and it rattled in its frame.

"Iris!"

In the bedroom, he walked into the closet and kicked through the pile of clothing. The duffel bag was still on the bed. He sat next to it and worried its nylon webbing strap in his hands, looking furiously around the room for some idea of what to do next.

He saw a dog-eared telephone book on the bed. It hadn't been there before. Iris had doodled a scallop around the edge of the museum print on the cover. Somers held the book and stared at the cover as if a breeze would blow through the window and flutter the pages open to the last one she'd looked at. He picked up her telephone to see if it had an automatic redial function. It didn't.

She went with him.

He flipped the book open to the Gs. "Goss, Greene... Grant, Steve. P.O. Box blah-blah. *Sympa* at D-Basin. Panay Way, slip eighty-nine. *Sympa.* Must be a boat."

He pocketed the telephone book and started to leave the condo when he heard someone open the front door. There were tentative steps on the parquet entryway. Something lying on the floor got kicked out of the way and skidded against the wall.

Somers drew his gun. He crept down the hallway with his back to the wall, holding his gun close to his chest with both hands. He inched closer to the doorway that led to the living room, reached it, then started to swing into it with weapon raised when he heard a voice.

"Iris?"

It was a woman's voice. The tone was uncertain.

"Iris? Where are you?"

Somers peeked his head around the doorway, then put his gun back in his holster. She was older, but she still looked pretty much the same.

"Mrs. Thorne?"

"Yes?" She walked over to him and looked into his face. She struggled with recognition. "Johnny Somers. My gosh."

She held out both hands and he extended his. She took his hand between hers and held it. "Johnny, what happened? Where's Iris?" She nervously looked around the room.

Somers didn't have a good answer.

Mrs. Thorne walked into the kitchen, her hand pressed over her lips.

"What happened? All her china and crystal. Lord. I knew something was wrong. I just knew it. Where is she, Johnny? Is she all right?"

"She's with her friend, Steve Grant."

"Oh. The sailor. Well, as long as she's all right."

His face burned with the lie.

"What are you doing here, Johnny?"

He didn't have a good answer to that one, either.

"Mrs. Thorne, I think you should go home. I'll have Iris call you as soon as she can."

"She's in trouble, isn't she? What's happened?" Her hands trembled against her lips.

"Iris is fine, Mrs. Thorne. I just saw her. Let me walk you to your car. Don't worry, okay?"

"I feel better knowing you're looking out for her."

Somers sent Mrs. Thorne home and got in his car. She felt better. People should feel better when he was around. He protected and served and made folks feel safe. It came with the territory. They didn't know that sometimes he made it up as he went along, that sometimes he hid the helpless feeling reeling in his gut. That seemed to come with the territory lately, too.

Sailboat halyard fixtures clanged against aluminum masts in the light breeze that blew through the marina. The wind carried the sound, like shallow church bells, across the water. Laughter and music and the tinkle of ice cubes in glasses came from the balconies of apartment buildings that edged the marina, where tenants paid dearly to overlook the boats, hear those nautical sounds, and sleep close to the edge of the world.

Somers opened the unlocked gate that led to slip 89 and walked down the dock, his heavy-soled shoes echoing on the wooden planks. A light burned inside *Sympa's* cabin. Somers walked down the wooden finger beside the boat, his weight making the finger undulate in the water. He had never been comfortable with the unstable feeling of walking on liquid ground.

There wasn't any place to knock, so he loudly called, "Hello, Steve Grant?"

Steve poked his head out the open cabin door. "Hello? Hi. John Somers, right?" Steve heaved himself over the steep set of stairs to the cabin without touching them and stepped onto the deck. He was barefoot and wearing red jogging shorts and a tank top smudged with grease.

"Come on board. But take your shoes off. Those soles'll mark the deck."

Somers removed his shoes and socks, feeling naked in his bare feet and suit and tie. He grabbed onto the stanchions on either side of an opening between the lifelines and hoisted his leg over the side. The boat tipped a little with his weight and he reached to grab something to steady himself. Steve held out his hand. Somers felt the sureness of Steve's grasp and the hardened skin of his palm. Steve's palm felt like he'd never had a helpless moment in his life.

Somers pulled his other leg over and stood on the deck wide-legged, finding his sea legs. "It's been years since I've been on a boat."

"You'll get your sea legs. Come down. I just made coffee." Steve hopped down the stairs and Somers picked his way after him. The surface of the deck felt cold and damp and foreign beneath his bare feet.

The cabin was wide and comfortable. The shelves lining the walls were packed with dry and canned food. A two-inch lip ran along the edge of each shelf, to keep the contents from sliding out when the boat heeled. Fruit swung in a net hammock suspended above the galley. Framed pen-and-ink seascapes were hung on the walls. Curled maps and charts were scattered across the cushioned benches. A map was spread open on a wooden table that had been pulled down from the wall. A protractor, a pencil, and a ruler held down one side of the map and an amber beer bottle filled with water and a fresh rosebud held down the other side. The table was lit by a small gooseneck lamp bracketed to the wall.

The door to the bow berth was open and Somers could see down the narrow, wood-paneled corridor past a door that must have been the head and into a spacious cabin where a cushioned area was made up with royal blue sheets, fluffy pillows, and a light-blue-and-white striped feather comforter.

A wooden hatch was pulled away beneath the cabin stairs and a flashlight in a square case sat on the floor, shining on the workings inside. Chrome tools were spread out on two shop cloths protecting the wood floor, laid out by type and in descending order by size, as precise as surgeon's instruments.

There was no Iris.

Somers sat on an upholstered bench that ran the length of one side of the cabin. Steve poured Somers coffee into a stoneware mug, then spread a towel down before sitting across from Somers on a small, wood-framed sofa that had been strapped to the side of the boat with leather thongs around the rear legs. Steve looked at Somers's hands.

"I got grease on you." He took a clean shop cloth from a stack on the floor and dipped a corner into an open can of a slippery concoction. He handed the cloth to Somers.

"Sorry about that. I was fine-tuning the pumps. I'm leaving tomorrow morning for the South Pacific. What can I do for you? Mind if I work while we talk?"

Somers wiped the grease from his large hands, which seemed clumsy and pale next to Steve's, which were nimble, efficient, and tanned. Somers picked up a black leather portfolio from a corner of the bench. It was embossed with the initials I.A.T. Iris Ann Thorne. He rubbed the insignia with his thumb.

"Go ahead. Steve, I'm looking for Iris."

Steve selected a crescent wrench. "She's not at home?"

"No. I went back to her place and she was gone. The door was wide open."

Steve laughed and shook his head. "Iris."

"I thought she'd left with you."

"No. After you left, she said she wanted to be alone. I put the food in the fridge and split. I'm surprised. She needs to get her gear together to leave at sunrise."

"I'm investigating the murder of someone who worked in her office, a man named Alejandro Muñoz."

"Sure. Iris talked about it." Steve fastened the wrench around a nut and winced while he tried to turned it. "And she talked about you."

Somers watched him labor over the mysteries of the boat works. "I guess she doesn't think too much of me."

"Iris appreciates the job you have to do. But she's just stubborn, man. Once she latches on to something…" Steve laughed.

"I guess you know her better than I do."

"Well, she'll be out of the picture and you guys can follow up on the money."

"What money?"

"She still hasn't told you?" Steve smiled and shook his head, his ponytail brushing his shoulders. "I told her that if she didn't come clean before she left, she'd have a tough time coming back. These aren't nice people she's dealing with."

Somers didn't respond. He was irritated with Steve's familiar tone regarding Iris.

Steve loosened the nut and finished unscrewing it with his fingers. "Gotta admire her determination, though."

"Somebody's trying to kill her."

Steve placed the wrench on the shop cloth in its place and rolled back on his heels and met Somers's eyes. "I thought it might come to something like that." He sat cross-legged on the floor. "Iris came on the boat yesterday with two hundred-odd grand in cash crammed into her backpack."

"Where'd she get it?"

"Alley gave Iris a key to a safe-deposit box. Before he was murdered. He just handed her an envelope and told her to 'be smart.' She blew it off until… you know. The box had the cash and stock certificates for some company called Equi… something and a bunch of stuff… dried flowers, trinkets—"

"A ring."

"A ring, right. Iris thought Alley knew something might happen to him and he knew things would appear to be different than they really are. She starts to check around and overhears her boss and this other guy, Joe Campbell, at the office talking about money being transferred out of one of the company's offshore accounts, Worldco, into this Equi... Mex, that's it, another Caribbean corporation. So, Iris gets the idea to check into Worldco."

"But the documentation's already gone," Somers said.

"Right. While she's at the office, Raab and Campbell show up. She hides underneath a desk and hears them talking about ten million dollars missing from Worldco, which turns out to be owned by Joe's dad. And EquiMex is owned by Alley—or at least his name is on everything."

"Not ten thousand?"

"No. It was definitely ten million, because Iris and I were speculating as to what kind of business Joe's dad could be in to have so much dough. Then Iris hears about the Sunday doings at Disneyland and you know the rest."

"Did they find the safe-deposit box money in Iris's condo?"

"No. She'd brought it here to show me. After they broke in, I gave her my forty-five."

"You gave her a gun?"

"She knows how to use it."

Somers rubbed the leather portfolio that he still held in his lap, then set it aside and stood, bending his head to keep it from hitting cabin ceiling.

"She called someone before she left her condo tonight. Any idea who?"

Steve stroked his chin. "Knowing Iris, she's might want to settle the score before she left. Turn in the money and stock, sort of 'Stop hassling me.' Maybe she went to see Campbell. It's his dad's dough."

Somers climbed onto *Sympa's* deck and stood facing the marina lights. Patches of oil and gasoline on the surface of the black water diffused the light into swirls of violet and green.

Someone on an apartment balcony laughed. Someone else let out a rebel war whoop. Somers looked at the black water and thought of Alley beneath the ground and was irritated at Iris for closing the distance between him and his homicide victim, for taking his objectivity.

"He's relieved from his suffering now. His death wasn't a struggle," someone had said.

Somers looked out at the blackness and imagined the sea and imagined being rootless. He was a root maker. Iris was not. Whatever. He still had work to do, a daughter to raise, and a dog to feed.

He took Iris's telephone book from his inside pocket and looked at the cover. He touched something pasty on the corner and held it to his nose. Wasabi paste from the sushi she'd eaten. He opened the cover and smelled the first page. Then he turned over the next page and smelled it. Then the next one and the next one. He finally found it. Raw fish and wasabi. The page Iris had turned to for a number.

Somers stuck his head back inside the cabin and saw Steve lying on his side on the floor, digging at the boat's guts.

"Steve, phone?"

"Just been disconnected because of the trip. There's one outside the Ship's Store."

Somers put his socks and shoes back on and ran up the dock, fishing for change in his pocket. A man who looked like he'd wobbled down from one of the balcony parties was using the phone. Somers showed him his shield. The man ended his call, suddenly sober.

Somers opened Iris's phone book to the page and furiously punched in numbers, talked briefly, ran to his car, switched on the siren, and sped toward the freeway.

Twenty-Eight

The One-oh-one flows north from its mouth in downtown Los Angeles, rises above Hollywood, transverses the San Fernando Valley, where it's fed by tributaries—the One-seventy and the One-thirty-four and others—then drops into Camarillo and continues to Santa Barbara, San Luis Obispo, Salinas, San Francisco, Eureka, then up into Oregon, past sequoias and rugged coastline and pockets of population gathered at its banks as in ancient times, then into Washington, where it disperses in Olympia, running with the Five. Of the Southern California freeways, the One-oh-one is the most traveled.

Teddy drove it with the Beemer's sunroof open, the metal station's volume up and the bass down. Slower drivers, which was almost everyone, spotted the Beemer's buffed candy-apple lacquer up their tailpipes and stubbornly held their positions at first, not ceding the road—No way—sick of all the aggressive creeps empowered by tons of steel—Go around, jerk—until Teddy got so close that they closed their eyes and they remembered the freeway snipers looking for an excuse and they figured, Let him have it if it's that important to him. And Teddy grinned even more and waved merrily as he shot up the tailpipe of the next driver.

The CHP motorcycle spotted the red Beemer west of the junction with Sunset Boulevard. It looked like the car. The cop swung out of his hiding place in a nook of a putty-colored retaining wall and closed in on the Beemer to get a closer look. MAKE ME. It was him. The cop radioed for backup.

"Turn it up and piss off your neighbors!" the D.J. yelled in a whiskey voice. Teddy obeyed. He twisted the bass down and the treble up but they were already maxed out. He wrapped his big chest around the steering wheel and steered with his shoulders and drummed his paws against the dash in time.

He drove up the tailpipe of a new Japanese compact.

The driver changed lanes.

"Wimp!" Teddy waved his hand in a V out of the sunroof anyway. Have a beautiful day.

Teddy bore down on a woman with henna-red hair driving a new Jaguar and talking into a car phone.

"Get that exhaust-spewing relic from a faded empire out of lane one!"

The woman glanced in the rearview mirror with the smallest shift of her head, her tinted designer glasses camouflaging her eyes.

"Hyped-up yuppie," she sneered.

"The fast lane means fast, bitch!"

The woman ended her call and looked full on in the rearview mirror. She flipped Teddy off with a porcelain-tipped nail.

Teddy laughed. "A Pink Coral Frost bird. I'm scared now!" He blew her a kiss. "Go home to Calabasas! Close the gate! Keep the Mexicans out! Except Thursdays when they do the lawn."

The woman looked at her speedometer. Teddy had inched her up to eighty. She saw the red Beemer nervously swerving back and forth in the lane behind her like an itchy trigger finger. Goddamn. You go along, minding your own business, and turn around and there's some guy dressed in battle fatigues carrying an assault rifle or some guy on your ass on the freeway because he doesn't like your car.

She turned on her signal indicator.

Teddy gave her two thumbs up. No hard feelings. She *should* yield to superior German technology. She *should* yield lane one. He waved two fingers at her through the open sunroof. Peace and love, baby.

The CHP motorcycle swung in behind Teddy. Backup was on the way. A black-and-white was already cruising two miles ahead. You could never tell. This guy could go down easy, meek and mild, or he could want a fight. The APB said he'd just put a bullet through some girl's head. The motorcycle decided to clear the freeway.

Teddy sidled up next to a topless jeep with zebra-striped seat covers. The driver was female and blond and tanned and fetching in that sun-kissed, twisted-hair, strawberry-ice-cream, Southern California sort of way. She raked her long mane with her hand and tossed her head, over and over again. I'm young, I'm beautiful, I have a Jeep.

Teddy gave her a drop-dead, come-hither look. Yo, baby.

She looked at him sidelong, up from underneath her eyebrows, pushing her glossed bottom lip out, affecting every ad in *Cosmo*. She raked her hair again and breathed fire.

The yellow halogen lights lining the freeway sparkled on the Beemer's fresh hand-wax job. It looked beautiful. Teddy's chest swelled with pride. He sat tall, sucked in his gut, and angled a crooked smile at her. He was Brando, he was Nicholson, he was going for it. You're beautiful, baby. I love you. Make me forget.

An American-made sedan, going about twenty miles per hour slower than Teddy, slipped in front of the Beemer.

Teddy slammed on his brakes. The Jeep sped away on the right, out of his life. He saw her hand go up. Was she waving farewell or raking her hair?

Teddy narrowed his eyes at the American sedan and assessed the driver. Male, forty-something, short hair, white shirt, driving with his left hand at 12:00 the steering wheel, his right arm draped lazily over the empty passenger's seat. A plastic cup holder hanging from the passenger window held a jumbo-sized Styrofoam coffee container that probably had a corner of the plastic lid torn off to sip and drive. Small boxes were scattered across the shelf beneath the rear window.

Recognition washed over Teddy. Samples. The boxes were samples. He was a salesman. A freaking salesman driving a freaking company car.

Teddy flashed his high beams. "Get off the road, peddler!"

The man wearily raised his hand, made a formidable bird, then dropped his arm back across the passenger's seat. It'd been a long day.

Teddy flashed his high beams again and again, then left them steady on.

The man slowly raised his resting arm and flipped his rearview mirror to the "night" position, deflecting the glare of the high beams onto the ceiling of the car. He punched another radio station and held his speed steady at sixty-five miles per, his left hand at twelve o'clock.

Disarmed of his high beams, all Teddy could do was bear down.

Two motorcycle cops five miles behind Teddy started to slow traffic by swinging back and forth across all lanes. The black-and-white two miles ahead was ready. The motorcycle following Teddy decided the time had come. He whooped his siren once.

Teddy didn't hear. He was focused on the American sedan's rubber-faced bumper. He was half an inch away. It was a feat of nerve, skill, and timing and Teddy was king. The salesman's arm didn't move from the passenger's seat. He knew better. The yuppie wouldn't damage his fine German car on his white-bread company sedan. The expensive car implied weakness.

The motorcycle cop turned his spotlight on Teddy and whooped his siren again.

Teddy was momentarily blinded and took his foot off the gas, losing ground. He looked in his rearview mirror and saw the cop for the first time. Busted. He'd get off the road. In a minute. Teddy made up lost ground and swerved to the right of the sedan as if he was going to nick its rear bumper. He saw the peddler's right hand fly to the steering wheel. Ha haaaa! Teddy fell back in behind. Only kidding.

The motorcycle cop left his siren steady on. He pulled next to Teddy and thumbed toward the side of the road.

Teddy looked over at the cop, then back at the peddler. The cop gestured again, his jaw tight. Teddy patted the air with his hand. Okay, okay. The cop dropped behind Teddy and turned his siren off. The guy was going down voluntarily.

Teddy inched closer to the peddler, focusing on his rear bumper like a mantra.

The man's brake lights flashed red. The peddler was slowing down!

Teddy braked hard. His face flushed red. He accelerated into the American sedan's rear bumper. A love peck.

The sedan swayed with the impact.

The motorcycle cop drove next to Teddy, gesturing. Get off!

Teddy slowed a little then sped up, righteously ramming the sedan. The driver swerved into the right lane, almost hitting the cop, who swerved into the lane to the right of him. Cars made impact and scattered like a broken trail of ants. In thirty-five seconds, all four lanes of traffic were blocked.

Teddy cut across three lanes in front of the commotion and headed for an off ramp, nicking a compact car and spinning it across two lanes.

"Argghhhh!" Teddy screamed. He took his hands off the steering wheel and waved two clenched fists out the sunroof. His heart felt like it was going to burst out of his chest. Argghhhh!" He rotated his fist around his right ear, "Rwoof, rwoof, rwoof, rwoof!" He was king. King of Lane One.

He ran the red light at the bottom of the off ramp, turned left underneath the freeway, and got on the One-oh-one in the opposite direction. He saw a black-and-white on the northbound side with its lights flashing. Gooseneckers on the southbound side slowed down to look at the accident on the other side. Two cars collided in a distracted fender-bender in front of Teddy.

He pulled the Beemer onto the shoulder and headed for the next off ramp. Too much traffic. He'd take the surface streets

Twenty-Nine

Iris drove through the beach-town streets of Santa Monica with the top of the TR still down the way Jaynie had left it, the sea mist and street people that blanketed Palisades Park sobering her thoughts.

She had spotted the periwinkle blue Cadillac five signals and two turns ago. She was convinced that it was following her. The Cad reminded her of her great-aunt Iris, who had bought a new Cad every year since 1961, the new Cads painted the same blue mist and champagne frost hair-rinse colors as the heads of Aunt Iris's friends, who crowded the back seat. But it was 11:00 on Monday night, late for a cruise.

At the next stop light, Iris stared backward in the rearview mirror. The short one was driving and grim; the tall one smiled a Casanova smile, as if he'd just charmed everyone in the place, then gone home and kicked his dog.

A rush of prickly cold fear tickled Iris's spine. "Victim" rolled around in her head. She hated it. She hated it until it turned into anger. Then she wasn't afraid anymore.

She reached into her purse and pulled Steve's gun onto her lap. She twisted around and waved at the geeks, like old friends.

The small one nudged the tall one and pointed. They exchanged words and shrugged. Iris turned back around and smiled to herself. That's right. Keep them off base. Try and figure it out. Jerks.

Iris got on the Ten east where it started its transcontinental journey, at the business end of the New World. She bowed to the green-and-white Day-Glo Christopher Columbus Transcontinental Highway sign.

She cruised down the Ten's middle lane at a comfortable sixty-one. Traffic was light. The Cadillac stayed a casual distance behind her, like a friend following her home. Iris wished she hadn't had that wave of acquisitive guilt and had bought a cellular phone. She looked around for a cop and anticipated her next move.

She reached the junction with the Four-oh-five. She held steady. Then she pulled the steering wheel hard right and cut across lanes three and four with a squeal of tires.

A car behind her braked and fishtailed.

Iris jammed the accelerator down and swung up and around the banked junction, grabbing the TR's steering wheel hard in her fists. The tires complained but held the inside rail.

She came off the junction and merged into the northbound traffic with a maneuver as delicate as a sledgehammer's blow. There were angry horns. She honked and honked back until the horn fuse blew, then she shook her fist at the other drivers out of the open roof. She swerved from behind a VW beetle that spewed smoke as it trudged up the steep grade of the Sepulveda pass, pulled in front of it, swerved from behind the next car, shifting from forth to overdrive to third and back, zigzagging across the freeway as if she were tacking up the main channel of Marina del Rey.

She pulled in front of a pickup truck that was four tires wide across the back and drove there, hidden from approaching traffic. She didn't see the Cad.

A red Ferrari Testarossa appeared beside her, hovering like a humming bird. The driver's grin said, Race cutie?

Iris smiled pleasantly and shook her head. No thanks.

He gestured as if he were drinking something. C'mon cutie.

The Testarossa stood out like a beacon. Iris turned her head and ignored him. The driver persisted without patience, then disappeared the same way he'd arrived.

Damn TR. Trading it for the most plain Jane thing I can find.

Iris checked her mirrors and didn't see the Cad. She exhaled in relief, patted the TR's dash, and felt guilty for her moment of betrayal. Love the car. Gotta love the car.

Then she saw the periwinkle blue Cad speed past her on the left.

They'd missed her. They were probably on their way to Bakersfield by now.

There was a chain reaction of brake lights ahead. Traffic broke around a slow-moving car like a stream around a boulder.

The Cad was now even with Iris. The tall geek waved at her.

He rolled down his window, cupped his hands around his mouth, and yelled something. His words were lost on the wind. She cupped her hand over her ear. He leaned toward her and she leaned toward him as they rose over the pass going seventy.

"Car!" he yelled, pointing toward the rear of the TR. "Stop!" He waved his arms like railroad signals.

Iris put her hand over the stick shift and felt the TR's pulse. The six pistons of its tractor engine purred contentedly after the freeway run. Baby was solid. Cool ride. Sweet steel.

Iris gestured "okay" with a circled thumb and forefinger and pointed to the shoulder of the road. Let's rock and roll.

The Cad fell in behind her. Iris turned on her right signal indicator and crossed lane three.

A train of tailgating cars wouldn't let the Cad in. The geeks lost a beat.

The junction with the One-oh-one was coming up. A window opened in lane four. Iris closed her eyes and accelerated to freedom.

The Cad followed, nicking a minivan's rear quarter panel.

The TR held the curved junction. The Cad skated across the asphalt.

Iris looked in her rearview mirror, then ahead. She mashed her feet on the brake and clutch pedals.

The geeks slammed on their brakes.

The cars painted twin tire marks on the road. The air stank of burned rubber.

Iris winced and prayed as her brakes squealed. The TR finally stopped. The Cad whined behind her. It stopped. They were both stopped.

So was everyone else.

A news helicopter and a police helicopter tore up the air overhead.

The white lights of a Freeway Condition sign said:

TRAFFIC CONGESTED   MAJOR ACCIDENT
USE ALTERNATE ROUTES

Cars piled behind them and around both sides, pinning them in.

Iris looked in the rear view mirror at the Cad. She blew the geeks a kiss.

Traffic moved ahead four inches.

"Now what?" Sally Lamb asked.

"Let's just pop her. Freeway craziness," Jimmy Easter said.

"Now that's smart. See that helicopter up there? Besides, we're just supposed ta talk to her. Remember talking, dick head? Scare her. See where the dough is."

"I got a idea," Jimmy said.

"Oh, good."

"I'll go sit in her car. Then she can't go nowhere."

The traffic moved ahead eight inches.

"She'll scream."

"She won't. I'll show her my piece and tell her nothin's gonna happen if she cooperates."

"You gotta promise me she's not gonna get hurt."

"C'mon."

"C'mon nothin'. We're in enough trouble."

"Nice and easy. Watch."

Iris saw the tall one open the passenger door and get out of the Cad. He walked to the TR and grabbed the door handle. The drivers in the surrounding cars watched with interested disinterest.

"Hi." He cobra smiled.

Traffic moved ahead five inches.

Iris let up hard on the clutch and jerked the TR forward.

Jimmy hopped alongside, his hand caught in the door handle. He held the snake smile. "Howyadoin?"

"Don't," Iris said, "if you want to keep that."

Jimmy saw a .45 pointed at his crotch. He raised both hands in the air and showed Iris his palms. He turned and walked back to the Cad with his hands still up, opened the door, sat down, and unconsciously cupped his hands over his crotch.

"What happened?" Sally asked.

"She's fucking crazy! She pulled a gun on me," Jimmy said indignantly.

Sally looked at Jimmy's hands in his lap. "What kind of a whacko are we dealin' with?"

"I tell you one thing." Jimmy took a cigarette from a pack and put it between his lips. "I'm sick of this. We oughtta just off her and be done with it."

"How many times do I have to tell you? We're not supposed to off her. We're supposed to find out what she did with the boss's money."

Jimmy took another cigarette from the pack, rolled down the Cad's window, and threw it at the TR. "But she's pissing me off."

The cigarette landed on the TR's passenger seat. Iris picked it up. She shot a gimlet eye in the rearview mirror. She unzipped the backpack and took out a hundred-dollar bill. She wrapped it around the cigarette, twisting the ends like a Chinese firecracker, then tossed it back at the Cad. It landed on the hood.

Jimmy got out and picked it up. He unwrapped it and held the money in front of the Cad's windshield. "Fuckin' A."

Something hit the side of his head. He reached in his hair and pulled out a tiny paper airplane made out of a hundred-dollar bill. He spread it open on the Cad's hood.

Iris twisted around to face him. Jimmy looked at her slack-jawed, gingerly holding a hundred-dollar bill by the edge between the thumb and index finger of each hand.

"What the fuck?" he asked her, flipping his hands, waving the money.

Iris started laughing. "It's only money, baby." She wiped tears from her face. "Keep it. It's a gift."

Jimmy walked backward and got into the Cad.

Traffic moved ahead four inches.

"What's this supposta mean?" Jimmy fluttered the money in Sally's face. "We gotta call the boss."

"And say what? That she threw money at you?"

A big truck painted with fruits and vegetables and a supermarket chain's logo drove next to the TR and the Cad. The driver had one tanned arm leaning out the open window.

Iris tugged at the hem of her miniskirt. She threw the backpack on top of the gun.

"What's happening up ahead?" she asked the truck driver.

"Some guy flipped out and started playing bumper cars." He appraised the TR. "Great car. What year?"

"Seventy-two."

"Cherry."

"Thanks."

"Looks like the accident's not the only action on this road," he said, looking back at the Cad.

They approached an off ramp. Cars were lined up to get off. The truck partially blocked Iris from the entrance.

"I gotta lose those guys," she said. "Can you let me in so I can get off?"

"No problem."

Iris turned the steering wheel hard right. She moved forward, then threw the car in reverse and backed up to get enough room to make the turn. She drove onto the shoulder of the off ramp past the waiting cars, waving back at the truck driver.

The Cadillac moved to follow Iris. The truck driver rolled his rig forward, closing the gap. He rolled up his window, changed cassettes, turned on the air conditioner, and pretended they didn't exist. The L.A. block-out.

People honked and yelled and shook their heads and fists at Iris as she came down the shoulder. The driver of one car moved onto the shoulder to try and block her. The TR's right tires ran over the weeds and trash and tangled ice plant at the side of the road.

Iris ran a red light at the bottom of the off ramp and plotted a surface street route to McKinney Alitzer.

She hoped he was still waiting for her.

Thirty

"What are you thinking, my son?" Vito Camelletti took a cigar from his inside jacket pocket. He punched the cigarette lighter on the dash of Joe's Jag and lit the cigar. He puffed clouds of white smoke and stroked the bulb of his nose.

"Makes no difference, Pop. No difference."

Joe Campbell jammed his finger on the window switch, sliding all four windows down a few inches. He gripped the steering wheel hard with both hands and stared out the windshield.

Vito puffed the cigar.

"Everything's got an angle for you. I admire that in you, Pop. I do. You're thinking all the time."

"I made a good life for my family. All the nice schools and nice clothes and nice friends and nice this and nice that. Just don't forget that."

"No chance, Pop."

Silence hung in the air like Vito's cigar smoke. Vito stared through the windshield at the while lines rolling under the Jag.

Joe cleared his throat. "I'm not trading on Worldco anymore, Pop. It's done. I can't bring that money home and make it clean. Not after what happened to Alley. It's dirty. It makes everything dirty. I can't do it, Pop. It's over."

Vito smoked his cigar.

"If you cut me off—" Joe shrugged. "If that's how it has to be, so be it. That's my decision."

They drove in silence.

"Say something, Pop."

Vito again stroked bulb of his long nose. He puffed the cigar and exhaled a billow of smoke. The world rolled quietly under the Jag's tires.

"I won't give up my only son."

Joe clenched his jaw, trying to hide his emotions. "What does that mean?"

"You just changed your name. You didn't change your blood. Now, hurry up."

Thirty-One

Downtown was quiet. The commuters had fled at the close of happy hour.

Iris Thorne parked on the empty street in front of the McKinney Alitzer building, behind a shiny black Mercedes with tinted windows, comforted that someone else's work was running their life, too.

Lucille, the bag lady, had spread a soiled blanket underneath the portico of the building and was arranging assorted bottles of perfume on top of the blanket's thin fleece. "Hey, babe," she said to Iris, smiling with grimy teeth.

Iris unzipped the backpack, counted ten hundred-dollar bills, and handed them to her. "Enjoy."

"Whatcha expect me to do with this?"

"What do you mean? Spend it. Get off the street."

Lucille folded the money in half and handed it back to Iris. "I can't spend a hundred-dollar bill. I'll get busted. Shopkeepers will call the cops. Besides, street's my home, sugar."

Iris shoved the money into the backpack, took out her wallet, and pulled out all her cash. About forty bucks in small bills. She handed it to Lucille. A perfume sample in a small glass vial had dropped to the bottom of her purse. She handed that to Lucille, too.

"That's more like it." Lucille stashed the money somewhere inside her many layers of clothing, having the grace not to count it in front of Iris. She displayed the perfume on the blanket with the rest of her vanity items.

"Wear some on one of those big nights on the town."

"Sugar, every night's a big night on the town for me." Lucille laughed.

Iris laughed too, hard. Too hard. She felt a hysterical lightness in her head. She grabbed control and came back. There was work to do. She walked up the marble steps to the tall glass doors.

"Hey, Scarlet," Lucille said.

Iris turned.

"Remember." Lucille held up a dirty finger. "Tomorrow is another day."

Iris gave her a thumbs-up.

In the building lobby, the guard sat behind the desk reading a Hollywood trade paper. "Hey! The executive woman in a mee-nee skirt. Whoa!"

"Hi, Nicky." Iris swiveled the sign-in clipboard around and felt a nostalgic pang when she scribbled her name. Another last time. She scanned the sheet for his name. It wasn't there.

"No one else from McKinney is here?"

"No. But I stepped away for a minute. Someone could have slipped in."

She held out her hand. Nicky shook it.

"What's goin' on, baby doll?"

"Thank you. For your humor and big heart."

"Part of the service. Part of the service. This sounds final. You goin' somewhere?"

"Yeah."

"Oh, no! She's leavin' me! Be back?"

"Maybe."

"Good luck, baby doll. Remember, offer's open. House husband to the executive woman."

In the elevator, Iris took the .45 out of her backpack and stuck it into her skirt waistband against the small of her back. She pulled her T-shirt out to cover it. Just in case the geeks turned up again. The metal felt cool against her skin. She pulled at the hem of her mini and wished she'd worn something more commanding. She patted the .45 and played out several deliciously morbid office fantasies in her mind. "Like my new power suit, Drye?"

The air inside McKinney Alitzer's suite was warm and still. The air conditioner had been shut off for hours. The suite was dark except for a light shining from a corner office that illuminated a triangle of carpet outside the door and a corner of a secretary's desk. A small, metallic balloon on a stick in the secretary's pencil holder reflected a light beam back at Iris.

She walked down the corridor. A paper rustled. She spun around on some premonition. There was nothing behind her. The gun tugged at her waistband. She stepped up the pace and took quick steps toward the end of the suite, anxious for resolution, her tennis shoes silent on the thick carpet.

Tomorrow is another day.

Stan Raab was writing on a yellow legal pad.

Iris rapped on the door frame. It sounded sharp and metallic.

He jumped, startled, and looked up with bellicose eyes.

She recoiled, her fist still in the air.

"Iris." His expression turned warm, as if he'd pulled a shade over a window. "I was starting to worry about you."

He stood and extended his palm. She took it and he gripped her wrist with his other hand. It had the correct effect. She felt welcome.

"There was a big accident on the freeway," she said.

"Traffic." He shook his head. "We'd do better with horse and buggy."

They tsk-tsked about the traffic, which makes more interesting small talk than L.A.'s limited weather flavors, if there hasn't been an earthquake.

"I'm glad you called me, Iris." Stan sat down.

Iris took the cue and sat also. The upholstery of the antique chair felt rough against the backs of her bare legs. Another last time. She savored the feeling of closure.

"Stan, I apologize for calling you at home."

"You know I'm here for you."

"I know. I appreciate that. This is hard, Stan. I'll just say it. I'm resigning, effective immediately."

"Resigning?"

"I'm going to travel."

"You're resigning to travel? Have you given this enough thought? Your career..."

"Alley made me think about a lot of things. I need some time off the merry-go-round."

"Having fun is great, Iris. But you have to consider the long term."

"Stan. I can't work here anymore. Not after our conversation today."

"Put yourself in my position, Iris."

"I have. But there's a credibility issue. Mine's gone."

"My conclusions were logical. I'm not taking anything back."

"Then, there we are. Can I still count on you for a letter of recommendation?"

"That goes without saying."

"Thank you. I'll send you a formal resignation letter tomorrow. But before I leave, I want to clear the air about Alley."

She stood up and leaned over Stan's desk, unzipped the backpack, and upended it. The cash and the stock certificates tumbled out. A bundle knocked into the chained silver-ball toy. A ball broke loose and started the device's pendulum swinging and clacking.

"This was inside Alley's safe-deposit box."

Stan picked up a bundle, licked his thumb, and quickly counted the bills. "A safe-deposit box?"

"Alley gave me an envelope with the key. Told me I'd know when to open it."

"Who else knows about this?"

"No one."

He counted the bundles and arranged them into neat rows. He unfolded the EquiMex certificates and tapped the edges on his desk to straighten them. His brow was creased. He turned them, tapped, turned them, and tapped. "There's what? Two, three hundred grand here?"

"Two hundred thirty-eight thousand."

"Iris, please sit down. I can't think when you're standing up like that."

"I have to go, Stan."

"You can't dump this here and leave. You have to explain."

She sat. "I told you, Stan. It was in a safe-deposit box. Alley left the key and told me I'd know when to open it. Gave it to me a couple of weeks ago. There was the money and stock and some trinkets. I threw the trinkets into the ocean, off my friend's sailboat."

"Someone else does know."

"No, no, he didn't know what I was doing." She dragged the backpack onto her lap and started to stand. "No one knows. Okay, Stan? No one knows about the money. No one knows I'm meeting you. It's clean. It's done. It's our secret. I have to go."

He chewed his lower lip and patted the air for her to remain sitting. He again tapped and turned the stock certificates on the edge of the desk. "No one knows you're here?"

Iris got up. "Someone's waiting for me, Stan." She took a step toward the door.

His left eye started to pulse. "You didn't answer my question."

She took another step toward the door. "My friend Steve knows I'm here. He's waiting for me."

"So someone does know you're here. No matter. No one knows *I'm* here. That's the point. Just Susan." Stan tapped and turned the certificates.

Iris took another step, reaching the doorway. She slung the backpack over her shoulder. The .45 cut into her waist. She almost pulled at it, forgetting. "Stan, this is everything. I'm going now."

"Not everything, Iris. Not by a long shot."

"Stan, you always told me I was a bad liar. Look at me. I'm not lying to you."

"This is not everything. You don't realize the implications. I need everything. If not everything, I have to have a good reason. A damn good reason. Four million is missing. Four million out of ten."

Iris ran.

Stan grabbed the corner of the desk and swung around it, scattering the certificates.

Iris was already halfway down the corridor, running, the swinging backpack knocking pencil holders, photographs, papers, and plants off desks.

He was close behind her. She swept a desk lamp into him. The cord twisted around his feet. He threw himself into a headlong tackle, catching her around the ankles. He went down. She went down, crushing a pencil box from someone's desk underneath her.

She thrashed her legs, crawling on her belly, kicking madly. She reached behind her and grabbed the gun, sweeping it across the carpet in her hand. Stan tried to grab her arm. She twisted and pointed the gun at his face. He lunged and pinned her gun arm over her head. She pulled out a handful of his hair with her free hand and dug her thumb into his eye. The gun discharged into a wall. Stan pried her fingers backward until her hand was forced open. He got the gun. He held it beneath her chin.

He rolled back onto his heels. "Get up."

Iris scooted backward on the carpet, rolling over pens and pencils. She brushed them away, scattering them. She pulled a sharpened pencil from beneath her hip and jabbed it into Stan's cheek.

He dropped the gun and grabbed his face.

She got to her feet and ran. She reached the glass doors of the suite. Her mind raced. Was the elevator still there? Should she take the stairs? Lock herself in an office? She pushed the heavy doors open. The elevator. If it didn't come immediately, the stairs.

Then she saw spots before her eyes. Then darkness.

Stan touched his cheek where blood streamed from the puncture wound in his face. Blood ran down his neck and onto the collar of his pink polo shirt. He examined the revolver butt. A blond hair was stuck to it. He carefully picked it off and dropped it onto the carpet. He ran a hand through his hair as he looked down one end of the suite, then the other. He again touched his cheek, looked at the blood on his hand, then pulled the front of his shirt out and looked at the wet red on pink.

Iris moaned.

Stan looked at his watch. "Okay. All right." He shoved the gun in his waistband. He bent over Iris and grabbed her legs. Blood from his cheek dripped onto her skirt. He felt lightheaded, but got a good hold. He started to drag her to the supply room.

Thirty-Two

Iris awoke to the smell of mint.

She looked up at steel shelves lining the walls, neatly stacked with reams of paper. She was on her stomach. She had never seen the supply room from this angle before. She heard twine being pulled from a roll. Scissors snapped. Her ankles were held together. They were being bound. The twine felt coarse against her skin. Must be the jute Alley used to wrap packages. Her wrists felt like her ankles. They were tied, too.

She saw the butt of the gun protruding over the edge of Alley's desk. There was mint again. Stan leaned over her. He was chewing one of Alley's Certs.

Iris tried to sit up. Pain turned everything white. She stayed on her belly, level with dropped paper clips and rubber bands and lonely staples.

"Iris, I'm sorry if this hurts." Stan had cleaned his face and bandaged the pencil wound.

Her ears roared. "Don't act like you care about people," she yelled down a wind tunnel.

Stan sat back on his heels. "I care."

"You just care about yourself more."

"That's life, isn't it?"

"Why, Stan?"

"Because that's how it is."

"C'mon. You needed the cash that bad?"

The twine whizzed off the roll. Scissors snapped. Her legs jiggled.

"Grudge against Joe? His dad?" she asked.

"It's not what you think." Stan sat on his heels and drummed his fingers against his lips. "Please be quiet. I have to think."

"Alley caught on," she said. "You had him killed."

He pulled another length of twine from the roll and snipped.

"John Somers said he threw money around Mexico. The Mexican police were going to arrest him on his next trip down."

Stan wrapped one end of twine around his left hand, the other around his right, and pulled it—snap—taut between them. "Arrest him?"

"Untie me. I'll tell you about it."

He studied how the twine cut his hands.

"Somers knows I'm here. He's expecting me back. When I don't show up..." She rolled over on her back. She saw what he was doing.

"It's painless, Iris. Read that somewhere."

"You won't get away with it."

"I will."

She scooted backward and sat up.

He straddled her, grabbed her shoulders, and pushed her down. "I will get away with it."

She jackknifed her legs. They thumped against his back and he almost lost his balance.

He grabbed her and harshly turned her over to face the floor. "Don't look at me." He walked to Alley's desk.

She twisted around and sat up again.

He dug through Alley's desk drawer, finding and putting on a pair of white cotton, ink-stained gloves—the gloves Alley wore to change printer ribbons. He again wrapped the twine around his hands and pulled tight. Snap.

"It's about money, isn't it, Stan? You're overextended, building that house and everything, the kids and the private school tuitions, Susan's liposuction and tummy tuck. Your bonus was cut."

"Jaynie told you."

"Yeah, she told me."

"I'm going to have to talk to her about these confidentiality issues."

"She's dead, Stan. She was murdered by two geeks who probably work for Joe's dad. They thought she was me."

He gaped at her, rearing back, blinking. "What?" His gloved hands dropped by his sides. He averted his eyes, avoiding hers.

"It's getting screwed up, isn't, Stan?"

He shook his head. "Could have been unrelated."

"It wasn't, Stan."

He rewrapped the twine around his hands. "You came to the office late at night. You've done it before."

"Nothing's turned out as planned, Stan. Everything's been screwed up, right?"

"Vagrant wandered in. Attacked you. Security in this building… Could easily happen." He walked toward her.

She scooted backward.

He grabbed her shoulders.

"Your face, Stan. Explain that."

"Accident… at home. Glad you didn't scratch me. Fingernail marks would be hard to explain."

She wrenched her shoulders back and forth. He put his knee on her chest and forced her down. She gasped, the wind knocked out of her.

Stan blathered as he struggled to flip her over onto her stomach, "No one saw me. Didn't sign in. Took my wife's car. She knows I'm here. So what? She wouldn't…"

Iris desperately writhed, trying to break free. She tried to bite him. He straddled her on his knees. She pummeled his back with her bent legs. He sat on her thighs, pinning her legs and cutting off her blood flow.

"It's ugly, Stan. Can you do it?"

She kept writhing, trying to knock him off but couldn't. The twine around her wrists and ankles cut into her flesh.

"Shut up, Iris."

"You have to finish it, Stan."

"Shut up."

"It won't be easy. Do you have the guts to finish it?"

He started to make a pass over her head with the twine then stopped.

"Do you, Stan? Think about covering your tracks. Nothing can go wrong. It has to work like clockwork. Can you guarantee that, Stan? Murphy's law."

He wrapped the twine around his hands again.

She lay her cheek against the carpet, thinking she should reserve her strength. "This is not fitting for a refined man like you."

He stopped. He looked at his hands. He looked at her. He looked at the blood in her hair where he had hit her.

"Wasting time," he said.

The twine went over her head. It easily slipped around her neck. He pulled it tight.

She coughed. She twisted her body with all her might and struggled to breathe.

He pulled harder.

Then, there was no air. The carpet nap was rough against her chin. It was an ant's forest. Dust in the corners. Under the desk. Talk to Jaynie. Has to speak to the cleaning crew. Iris lay facedown in the sun. Facedown on her hill. She'd been box sliding. The dog panted nearby. She was eye level with the dirt world. It roared and clicked and whirred in her ears. A different world. She was tired. She'd nap. She let her eyelids drop. The edges turned black. But she wasn't resting. She was dying. There was the toe of a shoe. A polished oxblood loafer toe. No white light. Figures. She saw shoes.

"Stan!" The authoritative baritone resonated in the small room. "Stop."

The twine released. Iris inhaled. The air siphoned in slowly through her constricted windpipe. Her back was free. She curled up. Fetus. The black edges turned to spots. Her breathing was labored. She was sick.

"Joey, help her."

Her head was lifted. Someone wiped her mouth with a rough cotton handkerchief. Someone stroked her head. Her head was in a soft place. She looked up at Joe Campbell's face. He held her head in his hands.

"What... why...what are you guys doing here?" Stan said, angry and dizzy.

The folds in Vito Camelletti's face deepened. He looked at the gun, the ink-stained gloves, the twine, Stan's bloodstained collar, his bandaged cheek, and the magenta line circling Iris's throat. He stroked the bulb of his nose.

"This isn't what you think, Vito" Stan said.

Vito took the scissors from Alley's desk and handed them to Joe. "Cut her loose."

"It isn't how it looks," Stan said.

Iris tried to sit up. She listed to starboard.

Joe pulled her near a row of shelving and leaned her against it.

"Joey, Vito. She tried to kill me! Look." Stan peeled the bandage from his cheek. "She shot at me. I had to fight her for that gun. She had it stuck in her skirt." He stepped toward Alley's desk.

Joe snatched the gun.

Vito silently watched.

"He's lying," Iris croaked.

"Bullshit!" Stan yelled.

There were fast, muffled footsteps on the thick carpet outside the door.

Sally Lamb peeked his head inside the supply room. "Aww, man... Jimmy, look who's here."

Jimmy Easter sauntered into the room and gave Iris an antagonistic once-over. He took the toothpick he was chewing out of his mouth, pointed it at Iris, and laughed. "Lucky it wasn't me. I would have finished it."

"Mr. Money," Iris said.

"You got your triple-X underwear on under that, Nasty?" Jimmy asked.

"Nasty?" Iris said. "It's spelled N-A-S-T-Y, idiot."

"I told you, Jimmy," Sally said. "Just like I told you about that other chick." Sally reached into his back pocket, took out a snapshot, and compared the photo with Iris. "Here, see. It's easy close up."

Joe stepped over Iris and grabbed the photo. "Where did you get this?"

Sally shrugged and glanced sheepishly at Vito.

Joe wheeled around and pointed the gun at his father. "From you?"

"I had to find out about my money, Joey."

"Who gave you this snapshot, Dad?"

Stan chewed his lower lip. He forehead was damp. "Joey…"

Joe spun and aimed the gun at Stan. "You! Why?"

"To divert attention from himself," Iris said.

"She's a liar," Stan blurted. "She has a quarter million of Vito's money. Go look at my desk, Vito."

Vito jerked his head toward the end of the suite. Sally and Jimmy headed off down the hall.

"I was just trying to do right by you, Joey," Stan said. "You and your family. I just wanted to help." He reached his hand toward Joe's shoulder.

Joe stepped back, avoiding Stan's touch. "Do right by my family? All they do is wrong."

"Joey," Vito said. "Give me the gun. Relax."

"Iris tried to kill me, Joey." Stan raised his hands. "You have to believe me."

"She was tied up," Joe said.

Sally ran back into the supply room holding the blotter from Stan's desk between his hands, the money piled high on top of it. The crepe sole of his shoe caught on the thick carpet. The bundles flew across the floor.

Stan picked one up and waved it like a street-corner evangelist with a Bible. "Look! Alley gave this to her. Vito, it's your money."

"Stan had Alley bring it up from Mexico," Iris said. "Probably wired it there from the Caribbean. After he was finished with Alley, he had him killed."

"Alley was killed by a street gang,"

Stan said, "The police—"

"Stop it." Joe dropped his hand with the gun to his side and raised his eyes to the ceiling.

Iris continued. "Stan set up EquiMex, transferred money from Worldco into it, and put Alley's name on everything."

"You saw how she was with Alley," Stan pleaded. "She was sleeping with him."

"Stop it," Joe said again. He lowered his eyes to look at Stan and slowly aimed the gun at him. "You were the only one I told about Worldco."

"Joey," Vito said. "C'mere. Give me the gun."

"Alley found out!" Stan wailed. "He snooped around. Iris put him up to it."

"Stan took the Worldco documentation from his own filing cabinet," Iris said. "He set you up, Joe. He used you like he used everyone else."

"We were friends," Joe said. "I trusted you. It meant nothing to you."

Stan dropped to his knees. "Joey, Joey. I'm sorry. I have most of the money. I'll give it back. We'll be square. Joey, Vito." Tears and mucus streamed down his face.

Vito stepped over Iris and reached for Joe's hand. He stopped in midstep. "What are you saying, Stan?"

"It was working great, but Alley told Iris and gave her four million." Stan rolled back on his heels and looked up at Joe. "Until Alley screwed up, it was going beautifully. The money went to EquiMex, then to a bank in Mexico City, then Alley brought it up—in a gym bag, can you believe it?" He wiped his face with both hands. "After the last of it came up, Alley was killed, just like the plan." He turned to Iris. "It was best. You could see at the funeral, his suffering was over."

"He wasn't suffering, you narrow-minded, bigoted son of a bitch." Iris raged at him. "He respected you. He obeyed people in authority, and you took advantage of it."

"But he didn't obey me at the end. I went to the safe-deposit box—a different box than the one Alley sent you to, Iris—where Alley was supposed to have dropped the money, but it wasn't there, and it was too late to stop his… disposal."

Iris said, "Then the cops got wise and you decided to offer me up. Now Jaynie's dead because of it."

"Jaynie's dead?" Joe asked.

Jimmy and Sally nervously shifted their feet.

"Vito," Jimmy said. "It just kinda happened. We saw we got the wrong girl. She was freaking out and… I don't know… I guess I…" He shrugged.

"Jaynie's dead, Alley's dead, because of you, Stan," Joe said.

"Joey, give me the gun," Vito said.

John Somers pivoted around the doorway, where he had been listening, into the room, holding his gun out front. "Nobody move. Drop the gun, Joe."

"Joey, give me the gun," Vito said.

Joe held the gun loosely in both hands in front of him, pointed toward the ground.

Somers took a step toward Joe. "Just bend down slowly, and put the gun on the ground in front of you."

Vito said, "Joey, give me the gun. This is business. Family business."

"That's right!" Stan said. "It was just business, Joey. Just family business."

"It's my business." Joe raised the gun and shot Stan in the chest.

Iris screamed.

The geeks went for their weapons.

"Oh shit!" Somers screamed. "Freeze! Freeze! Show me your hands. Up against those cabinets."

Sally and Jimmy turned to the wall and put their hands against the stacks of paper.

"Oh, Joey," Vito said.

Joe put the gun on Alley's desk. Somers grabbed it. Joe leaned against a wall of shelving, folded his arms across his chest, and watched Stan bleed. Then Joe collapsed, dropping beside the desk and putting his head in his hands.

Blood oozed brilliantly across the champagne carpet.

Stan's breathing grew rough. He blew blood bubbles. He babbled. "Told them to close the door. I love them anyway, my boys, my Susan... tell my boys... the best laid plans... cramming tonight... see you later... after midnight... I'll plan to... my plan..."

Then Stan stopped talking.

Vito patted Joe's hair. Joe circled his arms around his father's legs and stared off, his expression stony.

"That's all she wrote," Sally said.

"Beginner's luck," Jimmy said.

Somers gestured to Joe. "Get him up."

"You're safe, officer," Vito said.

Somers looked into Vito's eyes and slid his gun inside his holster. He picked up the phone on Alley's desk and punched in 911. "Get everyone down here." He knelt beside Iris. Her knees were pulled up to her chin and she was rocking on the floor. Somers looked at her neck and let air out through pursed lips.

"You'll be okay," he softly told her.

Joe got to his feet. He raked his hands through his hair and tucked in his shirt. He was ready.

"You saw it was self-defense, officer," Vito said. "We came in and Stan was strangling Miss Thorne. He threatened us with that gun. My son struggled with him. It's a shame."

Thirty-Three

Iris sat at Jaynie's desk with Jaynie's plush Garfield cat in her lap. It held a little flag that said: IS IT FRIDAY YET? All the fluorescent lights in the suite were on. Outside Jaynie's office, Iris heard the steady baritone murmur of men's voices.

The police measured, photographed, and collected. A busy beehive.

Someone set Iris's backpack in front of her on the desk.

Iris looked at her tank top. It was covered with blood and vomit. She wanted to change. The only thing she could find to put on was the blue shop coat Alley wore to keep from getting dirty when he did the mail. The thought didn't appeal to her.

She thought about the deaths. The course of lives were changed. She didn't know the significance for her. For Somers, all it meant was more work, she guessed. More work.

The paramedics had checked her out and left. They'd wanted to take her to the emergency room. She'd refused.

"... turned himself in an hour ago, looking like someone stole his puppy." Paul Lewin was outside the door. "He walked the last two blocks. His Beemer finally died. The piece that Easter used to kill Jaynie is in the lab."

John Somers was with him. "Strange. The mob doesn't go for offing women."

"Looks like the geeks acted on their own. They were after Iris, got Jaynie instead, and that psycho, Easter, went off on her."

"Trace the weapon back to the big man?"

"Camelletti? Forget it. It's one more time he'll come out smelling like a rose. What about this self-defense thing?"

Somers shrugged. "Iris was on the floor. Stan was standing in front of her, so she didn't see anything. Plus she was out of it, barely conscious. There was a struggle for the gun."

"And Camelletti says that you didn't get there until it was all over." Lewin studied him.

"That's right."

The detectives stared at each other.

"Trial's over," Lewin said.

"But we're back where we started, Shamus. We still don't know who killed Alley."

"What brought you down to McKinney?"

"Susan Raab. I called Raab's house and she said her husband went to the office. And sushi."

"Sushi?" Lewin said.

"I never liked the stuff to begin with."

Lewin looked at Somers quizzically.

"I'll tell you about it later. Raab jabbered nonsense the whole time he was bleeding to death. Something about plans."

"Plans?"

Iris rasped, "A yuppie's death rattle."

Somers poked his head inside the door. He smiled. "I didn't know you were there. How are you doing?"

She nodded. "Okay. Throat hurts."

Lewin poked his head inside the office and nodded curtly. "Ms. Thorne."

She mimicked the nod. "Detective."

"I'm gonna check on things over there," Lewin said. "They're probably taking pictures of their shoes." He walked away with heavy footsteps.

"I hate people who walk heavy like that. It's so"—Iris shrugged—"intrusive."

Somers laughed. "I'll run you to the hospital."

"Can't I go home?"

"Sorry."

"Thanks for tracking me down."

"Just doing my job, ma'am."

"Wanna buy some stock?"

"Yeah." Somers laughed. "Maybe I do. I'll be back in five minutes."

Iris tried to stand, to see how she felt. She rolled Jaynie's desk chair back. It hit the draped wall behind her. There was a soft paper crunch. Iris leaned on the edge of the desk to steady herself as she slowly got to her feet. She was dizzy. She walked behind the chair, pulled back the drapes, and saw a large manila envelope propped against the wall. She leaned over. Blood throbbed in her head. She stood straight until her head cleared, then held on to the chair as she leaned over to grab the envelope by the corner. Her name was written on it in Alley's handwriting. She touched the heavy, round script and thought of Alley's Certs that Stan had taken. Her eyes filled with indignant tears.

She pulled open the glued flap. Neat stacks of hundred-dollar bills were crammed inside. She took one out and fanned it with her thumb. About two hundred bills and about twenty stacks.

"Ready?" Somers stuck his head in the door.

Iris slammed the flap closed. "Yeah... just one second."

She zipped the envelope inside her backpack. She went to the door. Jaynie's suit jacket hung behind the door on a hook. She put it on and buttoned it to cover her gore-stained clothes. She turned off the light and locked the door.

Thirty-Four

"Hello Mr. Byrne. You don't know me and I realize this call is an intrusion on your busy day, but you're a person with substantial net worth and business acumen and a person like you is busier making money than investing it. My business acumen is turning money into more money. I understand. No problem. I'll call you next week. How about Thursday at two o'clock? Friday at two o'clock…"

"Same to you, Mr. Byrne," Iris said to no one.

She swiveled her chair to look at the skyline and unconsciously smoothed the neck of the sleeveless silk turtleneck she'd bought in twelve colors to hide the red mark that seemed to never fade.

She studied the upholstery of the twin chairs facing her desk and the wallpaper and thought that she would change the color of the contrasting wall after all. Fortunately, Joe Campbell had good taste. She was mostly happy with how he'd decorated his office.

"You got flow-wers," a secretary sang. She carried in a dozen white roses in a tall vase.

"Wow." Iris picked up a large rubber dildo that she used as a paperweight and moved it and a stack of papers to the credenza behind her.

"Why don't you get rid of that thing?" the secretary asked.

"Tried. They multiply around here like bunnies. I'm having this one bronzed."

Iris saw Billy Drye and some of the Boys' Club loitering outside her office, preparing their report on her flowers for the troops. Iris pulled a small envelope off a long plastic fork in the middle of the bouquet. She took out the card. Multicolored heart-, star-, and crescent-shaped confetti flew across her desk.

Holding the card in front of her, she said in a loud voice, "Thanks for last night."

A whoop went up outside her office door. Billy Drye peeked inside her office door, grinning broadly.

Iris smiled crookedly at him.

The boys walked away, laughing. That Iris.

Iris read the card to herself:

Roses are red.
Violets are blue.
Try dinner again?
Call me if you'd like to.
John

Iris took out his business card. She knew where it was.

"I would," she said into the telephone.

"I'd wanted to ask you sooner, but I thought I'd let the dust settle first. No South Pacific?"

"There's enough adventure around here."

"Steve must be lonely."

"He won't be for long. I moved into Joe Campbell's old office. It's a step up."

"Congratulations."

"Thanks. Although my detractors are calling it my A.D.D. strategy—Advancement by Death and Disgrace—forgetting I was the largest producer after Joe. We have a new manager. He's really smart and low-key. What else? The SEC is investigating us. They've hired replacements for Jaynie and Alley. And Teddy's in jail."

"He'll be out in six months. Sounds like the place is different."

"It is. I talked to Joe Campbell. He went to Europe after the hearing but he's back now, as Joe Camelletti."

"What's he doing with himself?"

"Nothing right now. He banned from the industry for life. I don't know what his plans are."

"We found Alley's murderer."

"You did?"

"Actually, Lewin did. He stuck to the case like glue and it finally broke. Raab hired a homeboy from another neighborhood to kill Alley. The homie had a friend drive him from the scene in a black hearse.

"Alley decided to play Robin Hood after he withdrew the last of the Worldco cash from the Mexico City bank. Raab never got that last delivery. Alley dropped a shopping bag with about three million in cash on the doorstep of a school for handicapped children in Mexico City. They kept it without spending it, then felt guilty and told the police. Then there's the two hundred thirty-eight thousand from the safe-deposit box. Raab's estate had cash and receipts for about six million. That's about eight hundred grand that hasn't turned up. You were right about Alley. You stuck with him."

"Yeah. My mother's still on Valium. John, there's something I have to tell you. The night Stan died, I found a manila envelope that Alley had left for me. It had four hundred thousand dollars in it. I want to turn it in."

"Keep it."

"What?"

"Keep it. The case is closed. It probably wouldn't make it past the clerk in the Evidence Department."

"It's in a safe-deposit box. I'll just leave it there."

"I didn't hear a thing. Dinner Saturday? I'll cook."

"Will your daughter be joining us?"

"She'll be with her mother."

"I see."

They completed arrangements and Iris hung up. She swiveled her chair to face the brown skyline. It was October. No matter. It was hot and smoggy. The Garfield cat from Jaynie's office and the Smurf figure with the briefcase from Alley's desk were on the credenza. Iris turned them around so they could share the view with her. She looked west, over the buildings of downtown, then east, toward the hills of East L.A. where she'd come from. She again faced her desk and punched in the next number on her prospect list. Her goal was twenty-five cold calls before noon.

She picked up her BUDGETS ARE FOR WIMPS mug. Wet confetti from the card floated on the surface of the coffee.

"Hello, Ms. Morgan. You don't know me and I'm probably an intrusion on your time right now..."

BONUS: EXCERPT FROM

SLOW SQUEEZE

The second Iris Thorne mystery

Chapter One

It was Easter Sunday. Barbie Stringfellow was lying on her back in bed, propped up against fluffy goose down pillows, wearing a negligee of many yards of fabric, some sheer and some slippery satin, all purple. Barbie was not a slender woman. Her breasts and thighs tested the fabrics. Her pose seemed casual and relaxed, in spite of her dishabille. She had a pleasantly surprised look on her face, the look of someone who had won five dollars in the lottery or who had been tapped on the shoulder by a friend at the supermarket.

The morning light filtered between the wood shutters. A moment before there had been silence, but all at once the birds came alive and started chirping merrily. Outside the bungalow, the air was fresh. A rainstorm had moved down the coast during the night, raising the scent of the pine, eucalyptus and cypress trees and of the musty soft soil underneath the fallen pine cones, seed pods, leaves, and needles.

Barbie's red Mercedes convertible was parked beside the cabin. The rag top had been left down during the night. The white leather interior of the car was now wet and covered with leaves and needles. Curious squirrels had gathered their courage and were exploring the car's interior, periodically lifting their heads and sniffing the air.

The ocean had been stirred up by the storm, and it pounded the cliffs bordering the Central California coast town of Las Pumas. Barbie was in the Central Coast's best hotel, the Mariah Lodge, and in the lodge's best bungalow, the one called the Cabin in the Woods, nestled in the forest with a garden fronting a cliff.

At the base of the cliff in a sandy alcove out of reach of the waves, a flock of sea gulls had lighted. Several gulls were fighting over something that lay in the sand. Something fleshy. Another gull flew up to the group, landed, then circled around the others, intimidating them until they scattered. This gull grabbed the prize in its beak and ascended the cliff. One of the gulls that had been chased away rallied. The two gulls struggled in midair. The object was dropped in the fracas and fell against the side of the cliff. They tried to retrieve it, skimming close to the cliff, but it was lost. They flew away, side by side across the ocean, and were soon joined by the others.

Inside the cabin, Barbie's expensive clothes had been carelessly tossed around the room as if there were plenty more where they had come from. A purple silk blouse lay across the back of a rough-hewn wooden chair, which had snagged it. Designer jeans were in a twisted heap on the floor. Leather cowboy boots were near the fireplace, where the fire was now dead. A full-length red fox coat was spread across the bed, near Barbie's feet, like a faithful dog.

A platter of untouched fruit and cheese withered on a wheeled table near the door. The table also held a bottle of bourbon and another of soda water. An almost empty bottle of flat champagne rested in a silver bucket full of melted ice next to two cut crystal champagne flutes. The rim of each flute had a lipstick imprint, one hot pink, the other red.

Barbie still lay in her negligee on top of a patchwork quilt that covered the bed. The quilt was handmade, sewn in the broken star pattern with scraps of red, blue, and green fabric.

The Mariah Lodge spared no expense in decorating its cabins in rustic Americana.

Dark purple and red bruises circled Barbie's neck. Her hand was lying palm up next to her on the comforter, the fingers curled inward in repose. Blood had pooled beneath her hand in an irregular circle. There was a stump of red flesh and white bone where the little finger of her left hand had been.

A key jiggled in the lock and the bungalow door was pushed open. Police Chief Charles Greenwood stepped inside, his cowboy boots on the hardwood floor conspicuously announcing his arrival. He rolled a milk chocolate Easter egg around his mouth, lodging it against his cheek, where it made a small protuberance. The rich color of the chocolate matched the color of his skin. He walked heavily to the bed. A maid peeked behind him through the doorway.

Barbie didn't stir. A dead woman wouldn't.

ABOUT THE AUTHOR

Dianne Emley is a *Los Angeles Times* bestselling author and has received critical acclaim for her books which include the Detective Nan Vining thrillers: *The First Cut, Cut to the Quick, The Deepest Cut,* and *Love Kills* and the Iris Thorne mysteries: *Cold Call, Slow Squeeze, Fast Friends, Foolproof* and *Pushover.* Her books have been translated into six languages. A Los Angeles native, she's never lived more than ten minutes away except for the year she lived in Southern France. She now lives in a hundred-year-old house near L.A. with her husband Charlie. Learn more at: www.DianneEmley.com